The great house stood overlooking the English coast and bordered the Loving Sands, a beautiful strip of beach that became a deadly trap for any victim caught there at high tide. When Margaret Walters comes to serve as housekeeper to her wealthy cousin and his two daughters, she never suspects the danger that eventually envelops her, her two young charges, and the man she once had loved.

The broken engagement she had mourned for ten long years had left her with an awful secret she vowed to keep forever. When circumstances forced her to go into service on the Walters estate, Margaret suddenly was swept into a terrible series of events which led her to the hidden Bluebeard Room. The mystery in that room, bound up with the horrifying legend which promised death to anyone who dared open the door, nearly drove her mad.

Loving Sands Deadly Sands

Charlotte Keppel

DELACORTE PRESS / NEW YORK

Manufactured in the United States of America

First printing

Designed by Karen Gurwitz

Library of Congress Cataloging in Publication Data

Keppel, Charlotte.
Loving sands, deadly sands.

I. Title.
PZ4.K392Lo   [PR6061.E]   813'.5'4   74-13801
ISBN 0-440-05085-5

Loving Sands
Deadly Sands

Chapter One

The Frenchman, who was to be the tutor up
at the Hall, and the new housekeeper, who was a poor
relation, arrived at the village of Adeney Cross at
almost the same moment.

The village, in this winter of 1798, already knew
about the French, and what it did not know it was
prepared to invent. The Hall and the Walters family
were always news, even in these days of war, with
Bonaparte ready to pounce and the locals patrolling
the coast, on the lookout for invading ships. The

beacons were there, ready to be lit, and two newly
painted signposts were directed toward the Loving
Sands, presumably in some kind of desperate hope
that marauding Frenchmen would immediately rush
there, to be swallowed up and drowned in the sands'
treacherous depths. This was Mr. Ted Clay's idea. Mr.
Clay was the landlord of the Loving Sands Inn. He
was a large, amiable, and stupid man who equated all
Frenchmen with poisonous snakes, and held the view
that they should all be killed off, whether it was
peace or war.

"They've no call to have a French tutor. What do
those silly girls want to learn French for?" demanded
Mr. Clay night after night to the villagers drinking
there. "It's bad enough having all those *parlez-vous*
prisoners by the sands. Why, last year the devils got to
Fishguard, didn't they? It'll be us any moment now.
Besides, the fellow's bound to be a spy. What would
he be doing here if he wasn't? Why isn't he fighting
the bloody war? You mark my words, he's come here
for some diabolical purpose. I'll lay ten to one we'll
be invaded before Christmas, and that's not even two
months away."

The customers enthusiastically agreed with him,
and ordered another pint of beer. And certainly
Adeney Cross, facing the French coast and not so
many miles from Calais, was in a dangerous position.
One morning the villagers might wake up and find
the sluggish November sea, which swooped so greedily
over the Loving Sands, displaying another Armada.
But the Walters family had lived at the Hall for five
generations, Colonel Walters was as much part of the
scenery as the sands themselves, and it was difficult to
believe that the family would invite into their home a

gentleman who might betray them and the whole
country.

Thomas Lee, who worked up at the Hall, doing
odd jobs in the kitchen and garden, remarked, "The
Frenchy's a parole prisoner from Elchester."

He spoke in a bragging, authoritative voice. He
dared do this only when he was away from home, as
everyone knew, for his mother was a tiny little virago
who ruled her seven grown-up children with a vicious
tongue and a talent for throwing kitchen utensils at
their heads. Her roost of five large sons, all twice her
size, and two embittered daughters had never dared to
marry. It was said that if they ever presumed to disobey her, she was quite capable of thrashing them
with her broom, backing them into a corner as if they
were rats. Thomas asserted himself only when she was
not there, and now, full of beer, he was enjoying
himself.

But Mr. Clay only answered somberly, "They're the
worst of all." And then, having expressed himself so
firmly on a matter of which he knew nothing whatsoever—for, indeed, he had only the vaguest idea of
what a parole prisoner was—he abandoned the subject and fell again to serving beer, which he did very
well. The activity distracted him from thoughts of
spies and invasions.

The French gentleman was at this moment toiling
up the sea front toward the Hall. His first name was
Philippe, and, being now landless, he chose to call
himself Monsieur Sansterre. It was not, of course, his
real name. His real name was blazoned in the pages of
French history books, sometimes gallantly, sometimes
ingloriously. His ancestors had put kings on the

throne and knocked them off again; they had flirted
with queens and princesses; they had lost their heads
on various conveniently sited blocks; and they had
earned both honor and dishonor throughout six centuries. The Frenchman had once been a Marquis,
until the citizens had decided to put *ci-devant* before
the title (canceling out the very notion of nobility).
Then he began to see that he might well become a
Marquis without a head, for those were the days when
the guillotine held court, and all his friends and relatives were tumbreling toward it. And, being a devious,
if angry, man, he slipped out of Paris and went down
south to Provence, where he had been born, and where
there was still a family mansion. There, amidst the
vineyards and sweet-smelling fields, he put on a
peasant's smock, reacquired the Provençal accent,
which he had never entirely forgotten, and lived
quietly and secretly in the cottage of a man who had
once been his tenant. Like the English Charles II on
the run, a century back, he was unusually dark and
tall. In addition, the family features, with the long
aquiline nose, dark eyes, and black hair, were unmistakable. Everyone knew who he was. Those features
had reappeared in generation after generation, in
both the legitimate issue and the by-blows. It sometimes happened that a visitor who knew nothing of
the history would begin to believe that he was suffering from delusions, when at each corner of the village
he encountered men six feet three inches tall with
identical features. But this was an advantage for the
quiet Monsieur Sansterre, for he now looked exactly
like many others in the town, and no one except the
local people would know if he was the original or
the copy. Not that anyone would betray him. The

men around him called him simply Philippe, and any over-zealous citizen wishing to bring one more marquis to the block would have quietly disappeared, never to be seen again.

When the Terror was over, the Frenchman did not return to Paris, nor did he resume his title. There was little left for him to go back to. Most of his friends were dead, his family had been murdered, his home had been destroyed, and the young woman he had once believed he would marry had left him, presumably to marry someone else. If Monsieur Sansterre wept over her or reviled her or planned some kind of vengeance, nobody knew about it, for he never referred to the matter again. When France went to war, he joined the army as an officer, and even there it might be said that his luck lasted, for he was taken prisoner in Ireland, at Ballinasloe, transported down to England, and there stationed in the parole town of Elchester, a few miles from Adeney Cross.

For most men—and the Frenchman was still reasonably young, being thirty-five—it would have been a dreary and tedious existence. A shilling a day provided nothing but the barest necessities; his lodgings consisted of two almost empty rooms; and his compatriots were not particularly congenial. But the life he had led in Provence had made him quiet and retiring and self-contained; the young ladies of the town, at first excited by his height, his swarthy complexion, and the intent, dark eyes, soon dismissed him as a dead bore. He did not pay them the extravagant compliments they expected, he did not seem to care for dancing, and half the time he was to be found with his long nose in a book. They were not to know that the Frenchman had had a surfeit of light, gay

ladies, that their bright chatter bored him, and that
he was so desperately homesick for his village in
Provence that Elchester, a small, provincial town with
little of interest in it, merely drove him further into
himself. He would retire to his small, wretched rooms,
where he could at least read in peace, for, apart from
one family signet ring and some clothing, books were
the only things he had with him.

Ironically, it was his distaste for Elchester's not very
dazzling social life that was responsible for his new
post at the Hall.

When Colonel Walters, after a certain amount of
family persuasion, at last made up his mind to educate
his two young daughters, he applied to the prisoners'
agent in Elchester Garrison, and, being as he was,
laid down the law with his usual lack of finesse.

"I'm sick of those two girls doing nothing," he said,
"and the Hall's falling to pieces. They are just running wild, and what with the war and all . . . Flora
seems to think that just because she's marrying young
Lewis Moore, she can moon about all day in her
room, changing her dresses, and I am really beginning to believe Albertine is gone in the wits. She lives
some extraordinary life of her own, and nobody ever
sees her. I know she don't walk very well, and I dare
say I'm saddled with her as an old maid, but surely
she could be more obliging, take some interest now
and then. Why my wife couldn't produce sons, I'll
never know. Girls are the most tiresome creatures, and
if you shout at them they only burst into tears. I am
damned if I'll go on putting up with all their chitter-
ing and chattering! Besides, these tea parties every
Sunday for the young officers aren't at all the thing.
They need a chaperone."

The Major, whom he was bombarding with this information, knew the Colonel well enough, and had sometimes attended the parties referred to. Colonel Walters was making them sound like Roman orgies, but in fact they were harmless and boring—the kind of entertainment conducted by most families in the district. The mamas claimed they were befriending the officers, but in fact they were seeking husbands for their daughters.

Flora, aged twenty-four, had now found her husband. The Colonel tended to speak of his daughters as if they were withered old spinsters, but Flora was a raging beauty, while Albertine, two years younger, was a strange little mouse of a creature, as dark as her sister was fair, with huge eyes and one dragging foot that made her limp slightly in a fashion that was not entirely unattractive. As children, Bertie had been the wild one, but now, eclipsed by her sister's beauty, it seemed as if she had deliberately retreated into the shadows. The Major had met her only half a dozen times, but often wondered about her. It sometimes struck him, as he once told his wife, that she remained far more constantly in his thoughts than the magnificent Miss Flora, with her yellow-gold hair and beautiful rose-petal English complexion. It was odd that the tiny younger sister, so demure and soft-voiced and insignificant, should make so forceful an impression. Of course, one had to admit that Flora, despite her beauty, was a ninny, with no sense and less conversation.

The Colonel was still talking in that over-loud parade-ground voice of his. "They don't even look after the house properly," he said. "I'm having to get myself a housekeeper. It's bloody ridiculous. I just do

not know what girls are coming to nowadays. You'd
think they'd take a pride in keeping their own home
shipshape. I always thought women enjoyed that kind
of thing. I sometimes think my poor wife must be
turning in her grave."

The Major was letting most of this pass over his
head. He was a busy man. He made the right assent-
ing noises from time to time, saw that his visitor's
wineglass was kept filled. Meanwhile, his eyes wandered to the pile of correspondence before him, and
his mind formulated appropriate phrases on how to
tell a young wife that she was now, alas, a young
widow, and how to compose a disciplinary letter to a
French officer who had entangled himself disastrously
with one of the young girls from the town.

An explosive remark from the Colonel—did the
man never modulate his voice?—jostled him back to
the occasion, and he wondered what the devil the old
man was talking about now.

"Poor as a church mouse," declaimed the Colonel.
He was never one for the original turn of phrase.
"Still," he added, "it's an act of charity to take her in.
I can only hope she's a lady. Not that she'll be dining with the family, of course. Still, one likes to keep
up the tone . . . I suppose you consider me a damned
fool to do this, but she has no money and no family,
and I was always cursed with too kind a heart, can't
help it, it's like a disease."

The Major was baffled, for the last he remembered
of the conversation seemed to concern the girls'
education. He said, clearing his throat, "So this is
the governess, is it?"

"Dammit, man, you're not listening!" cried the
Colonel, outraged. "You're providing׳ the French

tutor. I've already told you. This woman, Margaret, will be the housekeeper. Only remembered about her the other day. Some family correspondence . . . Don't suppose the woman can even read. I believe there was some damn silly affair, years back. She's quite long in the tooth now, of course, too old for that kind of nonsense, just another old maid. I've never even seen her. Only hope she won't disgrace us."

The Major at last managed to sort it out, and a few patient questions made the matter clear. Miss Margaret Walters, a remote cousin of the family, and apparently quite elderly, was to take up the post of housekeeper at the Hall, where she would certainly be worked to death for the minimum of payment. In the meantime, the Colonel had decided that his daughters should learn French, and proposed that his friend should find for him some French parole officer—"not one of those loose-living types, must be a decent kind of fellow"—also to live in the Hall, give daily lessons, and—the Major had known the Colonel for some time—do a variety of odd jobs with no fee except board and lodging.

The Major, like Ted Clay at the inn, had to find it a trifle strange that the Colonel should choose a time when there was a war to the death with the French to give his daughters French lessons. He could understand only too well the choice of an elderly poor relation for housekeeper, and was in no way impressed by the remarks about the Colonel's kind heart. He had from time to time dined, unwillingly, at the Hall, and afterward he and his wife had had to stop at a local inn for a restoring glass of wine. The meal was always excruciatingly bad: served late and poorly by one of the local girls, usually cold, and mainly uneat-

able. The Hall itself was a vast, dark, cold place, built
on by various generations of Walters, with an eleventh-
century section that was in ruins, and a more modern
part that was dirty, dusty, and shabby. The house
looked generally uncared-for, and this was quite
unnecessary, for the Colonel, as everyone knew, was a
wealthy man. But then, it was perfectly true that
neither of the two girls was in the least interested in
domesticity. Miss Flora, apart from her beauty and
her obvious adoration for her young captain, Lewis
Moore, now on duty at the Cross Prison, was incapable of sewing on a button. No doubt, if a button
came off she would simply buy herself a new gown.
As for Miss Albertine, with her huge dark eyes and
her limp, it was as her father said. She seemed to live
in her own world, and her main interest lay in the
prison, where she and her sister went regularly every
Sunday to buy the articles made from bones and straw
by the yellow-suited prisoners, who held a kind of
market there on weekends.

The Major promised, a trifle reluctantly, to look
out for a suitable French officer to act as tutor. But,
as the Colonel was leaving, he could not stop himself from asking, "But why, sir, do you want your girls
to learn French?" And then, with a faint twisted smile,
he added, "Are you so certain we'll be defeated?"

This was unfortunate, as the Colonel possessed no
sense of humor. And it was not so amusing, either, for
England was now threatened by the French, Spanish,
and Dutch fleets. There had been severe mutinies at
Spithead and the Nore, and Austria had capitulated
to Bonaparte. The Colonel went a bright red with
outrage and horror and he made it plain that this
suggestion was blasphemy to him.

Then he said, with some reluctance, "It was Bert—
Albertine's idea."

"What the devil for?"

"Oh, how should I know? You know what girls are.
She was quite persistent too, the silly minx. Had to
learn French, you know. Thought one of the prisoners
could teach her, but I soon put a stop to that; not
going to have her wandering about the Cross. But
it's not such a bad idea, it'll keep the pair of them out
of mischief. Why not? I dare say the fellow can make
himself useful. The garden's grown wild, it's almost
like a jungle."

The Major sighed, mainly from exasperation. Prisoners of war could hardly object to any work given
them, but it would be difficult to explain to an officer
on parole that he was expected to do such menial
jobs as gardening and—if he knew the Colonel—a
great deal more. It probably had nothing to do with
Miss Albertine at all: The Colonel just wanted cheap
labor. Certainly, he had never seen a garden run so
wild as the one at the Hall—it really was a disgrace.

When the Colonel had departed, the Major reflected on whom he could possibly choose.

He dismissed most of the names that came to his
mind immediately. This one was too handsome—not
at all the thing with two impressionable young girls
around—and that one too undependable. Besides,
many of them would refuse to perform the duties that
would obviously be required. Others he preferred to
keep far from the Cross Prison. There had been several escapes lately, with men sneaking off to the cartel
ports and managing to return to France.

He did not think of Monsieur Sansterre until the
next day, then wrote to ask him to call.

At their interview, the Frenchman listened in silence. He was, the Major thought, an odd-looking fellow, and such a height—it must have been difficult for him to escape from Paris. In his own way, he was attractive, even good-looking, but not in a fashion likely to appeal to two young and foolish girls. He sat there, his head bowed so that it was impossible to read the expression in those deep-set dark eyes. He had never been the least trouble. There was, so far as the Major knew—and it was his business to know—no attachment. He spent most of his time in his rooms, which were cheap lodgings at the far end of Elchester. He seldom accepted invitations. If he drank, he drank in privacy, and a shilling a day scarcely permitted over-indulgence. He always kept to the curfew hours. He spoke excellent English, though with a strong accent. The Major knew his real name, of course, although little of his past history, but he understood there was some rumor of a broken engagement. Certainly, the Frenchman was an oddity, even an eccentric; he was possibly the kind of man who would accept the Colonel's offer just out of curiosity. For Monsieur Sansterre was an inquisitive man. The Major had been aware of this instantly, or perhaps he had assumed this from the other man's long nose and the occasional sharp glances from those dark eyes. Moreover, he did not seem to be the kind of person on whom one could easily impose. If Monsieur Sansterre tidied up the garden, it would be because he chose to do so; if he were told to do something absurd, like cleaning the silver, and refused, nothing on earth would make him change his mind.

The Major, who by virtue of his position dealt a great deal with people, was understandably anxious to

find out how the Frenchman and the Walters family
would get on.

He said casually to the Frenchman, who sat before
him, "Well? How do you feel about it, sir? There is
no compulsion on you to accept." He added, with
some emphasis, "I should not be surprised if they try
to overwork you."

"No," said the Frenchman. He did not say this
aggressively. He merely uttered the word with a calm
finality.

"They'll do their damnedest!"

Monsieur Sansterre, who had once been a Marquis
and now preferred his anonymity, raised his eyes.
They really were quite remarkable, those eyes. They
were the eyes of a man who, when he said no, meant
no. He did not repeat the word.

"Well," said the Major again, a little disconcerted.
He wondered if he was doing right. Could this
strange fellow possibly be a spy? There were dozens of
potential spies in Elchester, though most of them
were so obvious and harmless that they were hardly
worth troubling about. But there had never been the
faintest rumor about Monsieur Sansterre, and if he
were a spy, he would undoubtedly be a dangerous
one. However, no doubt Captain Ross, who held
the equivalent of the Major's position in Adeney Cross,
would sort him out easily enough. He went on,
rather hurriedly, "Perhaps the whole idea is a foolish
one. I doubt you'll get much in the way of payment.
I gather they are also taking on a housekeeper, and
about time, too. But you might find it all very tedious.
The two young daughters—oh, they are nice enough
girls, but not much brain between them. I think
perhaps . . ."

The Frenchman rose to his feet. He was shabby, as
all the prisoners were, but impeccably neat. "I believe," he said in his slightly formal English, "that I
will accept the post." For the first time, he smiled, and
the Major saw that in his younger and more carefree
days, before the Revolution had knocked the world
out from under him, he must have had considerable
charm. Perhaps with two silly young girls . . . The
Frenchman went on speaking. "It will occupy my
mind," he said. "It may prevent me from remembering. When does this Colonel—Colonel . . ."

"Walters. W-a-l-t-e-r-s."

"Thank you. When does Colonel Walters wish me
to come?"

"Oh, as soon as possible, I gather. But—"

"Then I will immediately pack my things. Where
does this Colonel live?"

"In Adeney Cross. It is almost walking distance
from here, though, I dare say, a conveyance could be
arranged."

"Is that not where they have these dangerous
sands?"

"The Loving Sands. Yes indeed. You do not walk
on them, sir. They are killers. But I trust you are
sure that you wish to take this post. If anything
goes wrong . . ."

"Nothing will go wrong. Why should it?"

And why should it, indeed? A French parole officer,
down on his luck, obviously with some dreadful past
history, tutoring two silly girls in Adeney Cross, one
of them engaged to be married and the other a strange
little creature, odder than himself. It was all a trifle
foolish, but it would give the poor devil something to
do, and it was better than sitting alone in his rooms

all day. The Major could not understand why he felt so disturbed about it, but he sat down to write a brief confirmatory note to Colonel Walters, and then forgot the matter. His life was a busy one, and there were many other things on his mind.

And the Frenchman went back to his two depressing rooms. He stood for a while by the window before packing his few possessions. There was little, this bleak November morning, to comfort either eye or heart. He stared out at the small streets of Elchester, with small people bustling down them. Some of them were his own compatriots, with whom he no longer had much in common; most were the local citizens, whom he had never met. The people of Elchester were, on the whole, kind to the French parole prisoners; so far there had only been one tentative invasion, and that many miles away, so they had never thought of them as enemies. Their daughters enjoyed meeting these dashing young men with their pretty accent, who were so much more romantic than the English. The whole situation created a kind of drama that enriched their lives and added a delightful spice of danger. The French officers were invited everywhere; the curfew was seldom observed. Sometimes they were wild, occasionally quarrelsome, and often drunk; romances sprang up like pebbles on the beach. Occasionally there were marriages; mostly there were not. The new Elchester generation might perhaps prevent any future wars, for England and France were becoming remarkably intertwined in this small town.

Nobody now invited the Frenchman, apart from the deaf old lady who had presented him with a muffler. She was a formidable woman of an immense age, and every week she invited one dozen—no more and no less—parole officers to tea. There were no other women present, and the occasion was strictly formal. Indeed, it resembled a royal invitation, and no one ever refused. The guests were awed, bored, and a little derisive, but the Frenchman liked the old woman. She was very deaf, and this factor restricted conversation. She spoke impeccable French, however, and he wondered sometimes if there had been a romance many decades ago which now prompted this strange hospitality to Frenchmen. This was his first acquaintance with an English tea party, drinking tea out of the most beautiful china cups and eating little cakes while the lady discoursed on France as she had seen it as a girl, holding forth in the loud, toneless voice of the very deaf. The occasions could hardly be termed lively, but as the hostess reminded the Frenchman of his own grandmother, he grew fond of her and once he threatened to knock down a colleague who had jested openly about her. Last Christmas she had presented them all with a small gift of her own making —his was a blue muffler, which so far he had never worn. He saw that she had taken a fancy to him, and she told him once, "If you ever need any help, you have only to call. I know we are enemies, but I have a great love for your country as it used to be, and you will always be welcome here."

This had touched him very much, and he had kissed her hand, seeing, to his pleasure, that the delicate gesture made her flush up to her eyes. And now he wrote her a little note of farewell, explaining the circumstances and promising to call if ever he had the opportunity.

But she was the only one he would miss. At the beginning he had received invitations like everyone else, and he had, of course, accepted, for there was nothing else to do. But he had been bored at these affairs, and now he preferred to stay at home. Yet he was beginning to see that one could not entirely absent oneself from humanity and life. It was as if he had lost the power to be friendly, as if everybody and everything had grown tedious to him, as if he could do nothing now but criticize. Once he had loved people, enjoyed their company, laughed and chatted, been entertained. He saw now, with a sudden, bitter clarity, that this could not continue—this was death. Even an eccentric colonel and two foolish girls—he did not care over-much for the English misses, who tended to giggle and so often were lacking in wit and charm—might be better than these two desolate rooms. A terrible loneliness of spirit suddenly overcame him. It was almost as if he were dying, as if the living warmth and understanding and gaiety that had once been his was leaving him for ever. Even if he could return to his beloved Provence, he would still be alone, and now, deep in the secret recesses of his heart, he knew that it was not safe to be alone any longer.

So it would be the colonel and the two silly girls.

Not that all girls were silly, nor did they all giggle, nor did they all lack wit and charm. There had been a girl once, a very young and very pretty girl, with all the charm in the world, and a great deal beside, whose father taught the daughters of wealthy families, and whom one day he had met in the house of a friend. In those days he was still a Marquis and she was nobody, but it had not seemed to him important. He was twenty-five, she was eighteen, and he had fallen headlong into a wild, romantic love that rendered such things as class and position and money completely inessential.

However, there was no point in remembering such absurdities, and the Frenchman, his face grim and a little pale, set to collecting the few shirts and articles of clothing that, apart from a dozen books, were now his only possessions. He packed them very neatly in his small valise. Only, the thoughts would not leave him, however much he wished to push them away, and he packed with his belongings the memory of a beautiful face. It had seemed so innocent then, and her voice—a soft, lying voice—covered up a penchant for cruelty that seemed unbelievable in a creature so lovely and so young. And the memories lay folded between the shirts, all so excellently mended and darned, but one could not mend a memory. By God, it was time he moved away from himself and learned to forget.

There was no one to say good-bye to except his landlady, who, from the very beginning, had intimated that there was no need for him to lie in his bed alone, and he could have a well-cooked meal and sit by a warm fire besides. The Frenchman had from time to time accepted the offer. Now, in this strange state in which he felt so withdrawn from his fellow human beings, and seemed to live in a permanent dusk with the light about to fade, it seemed cold and unnatural that he should sleep with a woman for whom he had no feeling, of either affection or dislike, and whom he would have forgotten by tomorrow.

She was older than he. There had been a husband lost from a fishing boat one stormy night. She was good-natured, vulgar, and handsome in a countrified way. He had nothing in common with her. And this, as he went toward the kitchen to say good-bye to

her, shocked him too, though if he had stayed the
same relationship between them would have continued.

She already knew he was going. She was crying. He
could not imagine why, for he had given her nothing
but the physical solace that they both needed. Still,
he was exasperated, and touched, to see her standing
there, the tears streaming down her red-cheeked face.
Finally, she flung her apron up to hide her emotion.

He said, knowing that he was lying, knowing that
she knew he was lying, "Don't cry. I'll be back to see
you. This village is not far away."

But she only cried harder, even when he kissed her,
and when he slid into her hand a little box of sweetmeats that had taken his last money from him, she
became almost hysterical.

He wanted to shout at her, *You know nothing
about me. You cannot possibly be in love with me.
We have never even talked.* But it would have been
no use, and it was plain that nothing would check
her tears, so he gave it up, said good-bye again, and
walked out of the kitchen and out of the house. He
hoped there would soon be a new and obliging
tenant. He forgot about her as he climbed up the hill
that led to Adeney Cross.

But, though he could not know it, she stopped
crying almost immediately. Only, he was so tall and
romantic and sad with those enormous dark eyes, and,
of course, he came from a class miles above her. The
lack of human warmth and contact seemed to her,
insofar as she considered it, perfectly natural. She sat
down cosily by the fire and ate her sweetmeats. She
would have to see about a new tenant, perhaps another of those *parlez-vous* prisoners.

And the Frenchman was now well on his way to
Adeney Cross—a five-mile walk.

The two Walters girls were in no way enchanted by
Papa's new plans for a housekeeper, though the idea
of a tutor was not so displeasing.

Flora and Albertine had never got on very well,
even when children, but the emergency had brought
them together temporarily. As the Frenchman and the
poor relation were making their ways to the Hall, they
were sitting in Albertine's room, eating sweetmeats
and talking with unusual friendliness.

Albertine was not pleased by the arrival of a tutor.
"It is preposterous," she said, selecting a large piece
of marchpane. She looked more put-out than Flora
could remember seeing her, for, unlike her sister, she
was usually quiet, dreaming, as if entirely preoccupied
with nonexistent affairs. She was curled up on her bed,
and the pointed, secretive face was scowling with
temper, the dark hair falling over her cheeks. "It is
almost," she said, "as if he were coming here to spy
on us. After all, we are no longer little girls. We don't
need a tutor. You'll grow fat and blowsy if you eat so
much."

"You're eating more than I am," said Flora, and
this was true, but then, Bertie would always remain
skinny, and she recognized in herself a marked
tendency to put on weight. She took another sweet,
defiantly, adding, "It was you who suggested the
tutor, anyway. It was!" she insisted. "It was, Bertie. I
heard you. 'I want to take French lessons.' That's what
you said. I thought it was ridiculous at the time.
You're always doing this kind of thing, and then you
blame everyone else. It's all your fault."

Albertine shot her a menacing look. She had nothing of her sister's flashing beauty—indeed, her temper made her ugly—but at times, as the Major had remarked, there was a strange, unusual charm to that small face with its magnificent eyes, which drew the young subalterns almost unwillingly to her side. Soon, however, she would grow spiteful and make some barbed remark to drive them away. Flora, in one of the rare moments when she considered anyone other than herself, thought this might be because of her sister's lame foot, and because she could not dance very well. From time to time there would be a kind of flame in this little changeling sister; it was a pity she had such a wicked tongue.

Albertine said in her high, prim little voice, "You quite misunderstood. But then, you always misunderstand everything." She raised her eyes to Flora's face. "I dare say you were dreaming of Lewis. You probably weren't even listening. But I'll tell you what I did say. I said I would like to take French lessons from one of the prisoners at the Cross. I've always wanted to go right into the prison. You've never been there either. You've only seen the barracks, where your precious Lewis lives. It would have been so amusing. I can't think why Papa wouldn't let me."

"Well, I can," declared Flora, astonished and disapproving. "It must be a horrid place. I don't even like the barracks, but they are at least clean. Some of the prisoners are like wild animals. Lewis says so. Those terrible *Romains*, those gambling gangsters who gamble everything away, even the clothes they have on—"

"Do they go naked?"

"Oh, how should I know! Really, Bertie! But I do

know they frighten all the other prisoners. Lewis is always having to put them in the Black Hole. They would probably attack you. I don't know what they might do to you. Oh, you're out of your mind. You could never go into the prison, even if Lewis were there to protect you."

"Lewis, Lewis, Lewis!" mimicked Albertine in a fluting voice; her dark eyes were dancing with malice.

"Besides," said Flora, ignoring this, for she knew that Bertie and her darling Lewis did not get on at all well together, "the prison is dark and cold, and it —it smells. It's different just being in the courtyard, buying those things made out of the bones left from their dinner, but then there are plenty of other people around, and it's safe, and sometimes it's quite amusing. But to go inside . . . You don't really mean it, you know. You just said it to be tiresome and upset Papa. And it's really too bad of you, because now we've got to have this horrid tutor, and I don't suppose he's even handsome. Papa would never let us have a handsome tutor. And I don't want to learn French. It's a silly language, and it's too absurd that we have to try to speak it when that horrid Boney is making war on us and killing off all our young men."

"I have every intention of learning French and speaking it like a Frenchwoman," said Albertine. "After all, I have a French name. And I adore Bonaparte. He put down an insurrection, and he defeats everyone, and he's so romantic-looking, with all that dark hair and those beautiful eyes. He'll end by ruling the whole world. I don't know why we don't give in now—fighting him is just a waste of time."

Flora had heard this too many times to make much protest. But she frowned at this unpatriotic little sister, who had apparently seceded to the enemy. She did not answer, but instead, looked down at the diamond engagement ring on her left hand, and touched the stones with a kind of loving bewilderment, for she could never entirely believe in her own good fortune. Like Albertine, she resented the unexpected intrusion of these two strangers, but, after all, it was not important, for soon she would be married and away. Every day she uttered a prayer of thanksgiving that Lewis was on duty at the Cross Prison and not fighting the French abroad, where he might so easily be killed. To the world she normally presented a charming and gentle appearance, but she was in her own way a passionate girl, prone to wild tears and wild laughter, and always, since her childhood, concentrating a passionate adoration on one person. Once, for a brief period, she had adored her father, but the Colonel, going about his own life, had been simply unaware of it. Flora, at first bitterly hurt and angry, now almost ignored him. Despite her beauty, she was not a coquette; she placidly accepted the masculine admiration lavished upon her golden hair and soft complexion, but her whole ambition was now centered on the thought of being married to Lewis, having a home of her own and at least six children. And, thinking of this, as, indeed, she did all the time, she looked away, her face blurred and a little vacant. She did not even notice the sharp, spiteful glance that Albertine was bestowing on her.

Albertine remarked, after a pause, "Is not this Margaret Walters somehow connected with the French side of the family?"

Flora was not interested. There was not really a French side of the family at all. Albertine was simply making this up. Bertie was always exaggerating—

indeed, she often told lies, though it was hard to say whether she believed her own lies or not. She had always had a dramatic nature. Flora had said to her once, "You should have been on the boards," and at this Albertine's face lit up; she pirouetted around, despite the dragging foot, and cried out in such ecstasy that Flora was quite alarmed. However, it was true that there was some remote relative who had married a French girl and gone to live in Paris, though it was unlikely that this Margaret had anything to do with him. As for Albertine's name, it had been bestowed on her simply because the late Mrs. Walters, who, like Flora, was a trifle simple, had met the appellation in a romantic novel.

"She will be old and beastly," announced Albertine in a melodramatic voice, and at this the two girls became friendly again, for both at once visualized some monstrous dragon of a housekeeper who would order them around, spy on them, report all their doings to Papa, and turn their lovely, untidy house into something like the Cross Prison.

"If we are naughty," said Flora, "she will have us put in the Black Hole."

Then they both began to giggle, and Albertine, now abandoned to drama, added, in a grand, tragic voice, "She'll beat us with her broomstick. She'll put us on bread and water. She'll shout at us. Oh, Flora, she'll persecute us and make our life a misery."

Flora, as the elder sister, felt she should not really be encouraging this, but she was too intrigued to protest much. But when Albertine suddenly reached under the bed and pulled out a half-full bottle of wine, she was compelled to exclaim, "Oh, Bertie, no!"

"How missish you are, sister dear," Albertine said

calmly. She proceeded to pour some of the wine into a glass that stood on the washstand. To do this she had to cross the room, and the limp at once became very evident. Flora was sorry for Albertine, as she always was, yet sometimes, in a rare moment of perception, she thought that her sister often exaggerated the limp, much as a dog might display a wounded paw for sympathy. It was, after all, quite appealing, for she was such a tiny little thing, and it often brought young officers leaping forward protectively to fetch and carry for her. In another age Albertine might have spent her life reclining languidly on a chaise longue—even now, when she did not want to do something, she would fall back in her chair and complain pathetically of exhaustion.

Flora demanded, "Where did you get that wine from?" She took a tentative sip, then giggled weakly. God knows what the dragon-housekeeper would think of this debauchery—young girls drinking wine in their bedroom!

"From the cellar," returned Albertine. "Where else, pray?" There was an oddly reflective and satisfied look on her face, as if all this amused her very much.

"Do you mean to say you actually went down into the cellar—oh, Bertie, you can't drink from the bottle!"

"There is only one glass," said Albertine, who now had the neck of the bottle to her lips. Flora could see the liquid traveling down her throat, and as she swallowed she rolled her eyes. "I like wine," she said. "And Papa is so mean. He'll only allow us one glass at dinner. It's not as if we're poor. Besides," she added, "what is there for me to do but drink? I am not engaged to a handsome captain, like you. I am plain and small, and my foot hurts me. Aren't you sorry for me, Flora?"

Flora did not answer this. There was an odd malice to Albertine's words that made the color come to her cheeks, though Flora could not see any cause for mockery. She sipped at her wine. She wondered then whether this might not be the first bottle to be hidden under Bertie's bed. However, there was no point in lecturing her, for she always went her own way, and if it pleased her to remove bottles from the cellar, there was no stopping her.

She said at last, "Margaret will not approve."

"Oh, Margaret," said Albertine, "drinks like a fish. She's never quite sober."

"Bertie, you must not say such things!"

"But I know it. And I know she looks like a witch, too. She has a beard, and her nose and chin meet—so —and when she's done beating us and locking us in our rooms, she'll go to her own room and drink and drink and drink until she's completely foxed."

"Bertie, you really—"

"And then she'll sing terrible, vulgar songs, and swear just like Captain Ross."

This was too much for the girls, who burst into peals of laughter, and for a moment the wicked, witchlike Margaret was forgotten.

Captain Ross, in charge of the prison garrison, was an old crony of their father's, and neither sister could abide him, for he was elderly, Scottish, and disagreeable, and he had only one arm. He always arrived on Sundays and ignored the girls, shutting himself up with Colonel Walters in the library and never making the faintest attempt to be civil. It was true that, although he drank a prodigious amount of wine, he

always remained sober. He tended to exclaim, "Damn
my soul," and "In Christ's name," which was very
blasphemous of him, and quite unsuitable, as Albertine once remarked, for the tender ears of such young
and innocent misses as themselves.

Presently the two girls had finished the half bottle
between them, which left Flora a little tipsy, though
Albertine seemed unaffected.

Flora said, "What shall we do with the bottle?"

"I'll show you," said Albertine. She rose from the
bed and walked across to the window, which she
opened, then flung the bottle out. They could hear
the small crash as it landed in the garden beneath.

Flora was shocked. This was too bad of Albertine,
it was quite unladylike. She said, a little bemusedly,
"The maids will see it."

"They are hidden in the long grass. No one cuts
the grass. It don't matter," said Albertine, with the
utmost calm.

Flora did not fully take in the plural pronoun. But
Albertine's next remark made her open her blue eyes
very wide.

"I think," said Albertine, with a wicked twist to
her mouth, "that we are not going to let ourselves be
bullied by that Margaret." The great eyes glinted. "I
think she may not be with us very long."

"What do you mean?" asked Flora uneasily. Despite
all this play-acting, she was a good-natured girl who
was fully prepared to be agreeable to the new housekeeper. There was sometimes an odd streak of cruelty
in Albertine that frightened her. To the rest of the
world Bertie was usually a little mouse who said
Yes, Papa and *No, Papa,* who crept self-effacingly
around the house, and who made big eyes at the

young subalterns who flirted with her. It was Flora
with her handsome looks who attracted most of the
attention; Bertie was simply the younger sister.

Yet sometimes odd things happened, of which the
Colonel and the subalterns knew nothing.

Such as bottles of wine in the bedroom; a housemaid who had interfered too much for her own good,
who had been frightened into hysterics, who had run
back to the village and never reappeared; a butler
who had once presumed to report a fifteen-year-old
girl to her father, who a few days later had grown
pale and silent, then, like the housemaid, left the Hall
for good . . .

Flora was incapable of analyzing these events, but
she had to see that after they occurred Albertine
looked like the proverbial cat with cream. Flora knew
better than most that, despite her sister's meek appearance, she could not endure being crossed and was
vindictive in paying back grudges. Therefore, Flora
did not like this last, threatening remark, for, after
all, there was no reason to assume that Margaret
would be anything but a pleasant old woman who
simply went about her duties and never interfered
with the family.

"There are ways," said Albertine, now curled up
again on the bed. "Oh, there are ways."

"I think you are being rather silly," said Flora in
her most elderly-sister manner. She was growing a little bored with the conversation, and perhaps afraid as
well. Nowadays they were both old enough to behave
in a civilized manner, but Flora clearly remembered
occasions during her childhood where little Bertie—
very beguiling as a baby—got into mischief and
earned Flora the whippings. Flora was too old now to

be disciplined, and, moreover, she led an independent life, but she still did not trust her little sister. She sometimes wondered if Albertine would ever marry and, if she did, what kind of man it would be who could possibly love her.

As she banished these thoughts from her mind, she remembered that Lewis would look in today, as he always did when the guard changed at the prison, and she began to think happily of doing her hair and changing into a fresh gown. The Colonel had retreated into himself since his wife's death, and saw little of his children. Indeed, he had never been anything of a family man, and considered that, in letting them have their own way and giving them a generous allowance, he had done his duty. Flora was not in the habit of brooding on such things, but she was an affectionate and demonstrative girl, and she could not call up one occasion in the past when her father had taken her on his knee or inquired about what she had been doing, or, indeed, shown the slightest interest in her affairs. Even when she had told him about Lewis, his main reaction had been one of relief that soon she would be off his hands. The girls had had a strange, cold upbringing, without love; the only advantage was that both of them had had far more freedom than was normally permitted, and unlimited amounts of money to spend. Flora, who adored luxury, indulged herself in new dresses and jewelry and was always visiting her dressmaker. And now it was comforting to think that there was a choice of at least three new gowns, and it was comforting too to know that Lewis and Albertine cordially disliked each other, so that the question of rivalry with her sister never had arisen.

She opened her mouth to say that she must go and change, but Albertine was speaking again. She could be extraordinarily talkative at times, while at others there was not a word to be had out of her.

She now said, in a pensive manner, "Of course, there is always the Bluebeard Room."

"Now really, Bertie, I don't know what's the matter with you today," said Flora, pausing on her way to the door. But she giggled a little as she spoke, catching her lower lip in her teeth.

"Poor Margaret might find herself locked in there," said Albertine.

"There is no key," said Flora quickly. "No one can open the door. The bolt is completely rusted."

"There might be a key," said Albertine. "You never know, Flora dear. Things have a habit of turning up, especially when one needs them."

Flora, torn between amusement and apprehension, said, "And what are you planning to do, pray? Imprison the poor soul there?"

"Why not? Nobody would ever find her again, not for years and years. Nobody ever goes to that part of the Hall. And then one day," said Albertine, in a tense, dramatic voice, "someone will manage to open the door and find a skeleton in rags, lying on the floor, pressed against the door, fingerbones broken where she has struggled to claw her way out—"

"Bertie! Will you be quiet at once!" Flora had grown quite pale while listening to this, and, indeed, there was a strange, savage delight on her sister's face that terrified her.

Albertine shrugged. "Oh, very well," she said. She added crossly, "I was only funning, you know. You are so stupid, you always take everything so seriously.

You have no sense of humor." But perhaps Flora's
pallor amused her, for suddenly she declaimed in
French—surprisingly good French for one who
wanted a tutor—"*Et alors, madame? Vous êtes entrée
dans le cabinet. Eh bien, madame, vous y entrerez, et
irez prendre place auprès des dames que vous y avez
vues. Il faut mourir, madame, et tout à l'heure.*"

This was too much for Flora, who fled, banging the
door behind her. She heard Albertine burst into a
great peal of laughter, and the thought crossed her
mind that this little sister was at times a wicked and
dangerous girl. She seemed to take a twisted pleasure
in other people's pain. But, of course, the Bluebeard
Room—which had nothing to do with Bluebeard
whatsoever—was part of the family history, and many
a time a younger Flora had shuddered her way into
bed, thinking of the terrible things that must have
happened there.

The Bluebeard Room lay in the eleventh-century
section of the Hall, which nobody now used, and
which for many generations had been left to rot in its
own dark, dank cold. It lay at the bottom of the
garden, past the kitchens and the high wall at one
side, overlooking the Loving Sands and the prison.
There were stories of ghosts, but there were no
ghosts; there never had been any ghosts. It was only
the children's imagination that had peopled it with
headless nuns and (this, naturally, was Albertine)
shrieking skeletons. There was little left of the
original keep, simply three chambers, which according
to legend were dungeons but which had been nothing
of the kind, two without roof or doors and one, the
celebrated Bluebeard Room, which remained intact,
with a great iron-bolted door, which, it was true, was

thick with rust and impossible to open. The rest of
the keep faded into decorative ruins—a wall here, a
doorless entrance there, and a few of the narrow slits
through which arrows had once been aimed at oncom-
ing foes. The grass grew green through the ruins, and
on a sunny day it was pleasant, lazy, and amusing, fine
for small children to play in, and safe too, for the
wall overlooking the sands was far too steep for them
to climb, and there was no gate. To reach the prison,
one had to walk out of the front entrance of the
Hall and make a roundabout tour by the sea wall.
Only at night, when the sun went down, did the ruins
grow somber, and even now, at the age of twenty-four,
Flora did not like to pass that way after dark.

It was Albertine who, some five years ago, had
heard the shocking story of Bluebeard from one of
the prisoners, the tale of the man who murdered his
wives and shut their headless bodies up in a locked
room. It had, inevitably, greatly appealed to her. She
had asked the man to speak the terrible words in
French, and then had learned them by heart, even
teaching them to Flora, who was no good at languages
but repeated them parrot-fashion. For a while she and
Flora had mouthed them at intervals, often at innocent visitors, who naturally were startled. What really
lay behind the door, nobody knew, and certainly there
was nothing, but, of course, there was always a faint
possibility of the headless corpses and the bloodied
key that could not be wiped clean.

Once the Colonel, hearing their fantasy and exasperated by what he regarded as childish hysteria, had
threatened to have the door knocked down, but this
had provoked such shrieks of terror that he had
abandoned the project. In any case, it would have

been almost impossible to do, for the walls of the ruins were as thick as they were wide, so the Bluebeard Room still stood there, sealed and sinister. Flora decided it really was quite horrid of Bertie to talk so of shutting up a poor old woman who had done nobody any harm, and who would spend her time cooking and tidying up the Hall.

But soon, slipping into an enchanting new gown of deep crimson wool—the weather was bitterly cold, with a nor'-easter blowing across the Loving Sands, and the Hall was never properly heated—Flora forgot about both the tutor and the housekeeper. As she tied up her yellow hair, wishing she had a neat little maid to help her, she dreamed of Lewis, who shortly, at low tide, would be making his way across the sands to have a few precious moments with her. Sometimes she thought with terror that he might be caught when the tide swept in and made the sands so deadly, but he, like all the garrison, knew when it was safe to cross. There was also a kind of safety belt before the prison, where the ground remained firm; the quicksands, or whatever they were, suddenly ended, as if a line had been drawn across.

And as Flora brushed her shining hair, and dreamed and sighed, Miss Margaret Walters, who had descended from the stage a mile outside Adeney Cross, walked toward the Hall, carrying a portmanteau that seemed to grow heavier with every step.

Chapter Two

Miss Margaret Walters was neither old nor a witch. She had no beard, her nose and chin did not meet, and she did not wear the air of one accustomed to beating young girls. At this moment she was simply an extremely exhausted and unhappy young woman of twenty-eight. She had once been a beauty; even now she was a good-looking girl. The fine bones still upheld a handsome face, the skin was pale but clear, and the eyes, which were hazel-brown, were as lovely as they had always been, even if now they were more

deep-set and shadowed. The brown hair was bound
back tightly under an unbecoming bonnet. But mis-
fortune, loneliness, and insufficient food had destroyed
a great deal of her youth; she had grown thin, there
were hollows where there should have been roundness, and sorrow and discontent had etched deep lines
round what should have been a generous mouth disposed to laughter.

There was no laughter in her now. There had
been little laughter for the past ten years. She was
cold and tired, her head was aching, and it seemed to
her extremely uncivil that the Colonel had not sent
his carriage to meet her. It was true that he could
not know the exact time of her arrival, but there was
only one stage a month to such an outlying place as
Adeney Cross, and one would have expected his
daughters—had he not said there were two of them?
—to remind him of the housekeeper's arrival. Perhaps a mere servant did not warrant such attention.
Perhaps they had forgotten all about her, an insignificant creature, a poor relation. Miss Walters, who did
not entirely lack a sense of humor, even at this moment of exhaustion, smiled wryly at her own self-
pity, and struggled to convince herself that she should
be thankful to have found any kind of post where she
would at least have food and a roof over her head.
The world was not kind to unmarried women of a
certain age; one had to accept being a governess or a
companion. Margaret was not of the most patient
disposition; she could not see herself pandering to the
whims of some cantankerous old lady, nor did she
fancy teaching reading and sums to spoiled, unwilling
children. It was not that she disliked children. Indeed,
she loved them very much, and sometimes her own

childless state grieved her so deeply that the sense of humor left her altogether. But other people's children would, she believed, be too much of a reminder of all that had happened, so when the Colonel's letter miraculously arrived, she accepted his offer almost without hesitation.

She had few illusions left. Henry, the cheap philanderer who had been part of her ruin, those last days in France, had long ago destroyed such foolishness. She did not for one moment think the Colonel was offering her the position from the kindness of his heart. She suspected he hardly knew who she was—he seemed in some odd way to be confusing her with her dead mother, addressing her as if she were an old woman. But certainly he regarded her as an unimportant poor relation, and it was true that she was not only poor but remote in terms of family connections—she had never managed to work out the ramifications. He simply wanted someone to work for him, for as little money as possible. There would be no little friendly chats with the daughters (one, she remembered now, was called Albertine—what an extraordinary name!), only a great deal of hard work, much fetching and carrying, endless cooking, and no doubt sewing and washing for the young misses. That, after all, was what poor relations were for, and their great advantage was that they did not have to be paid much money. Ten pounds a year, the Colonel had said, of course, with full board. He had found out her whereabouts by the purest chance. Some old family correspondence had turned up while he was clearing out his desk, and it had apparently struck him that she might be the housekeeper he was looking for. It seemed to Margaret a little strange that he could not find someone

locally—what sort of house did he keep?—but his
letter arrived when she was so near rock bottom that
she was virtually drowned: Papa was dead, Henry
nothing but a bitter memory, and other memories
that she struggled to push down into the very depths
of her mind were still eating at her. The bills that
could not be paid were constantly arriving, there was
no alternative now but to sell the little house, and
the future before her was horrifying: Nothing but
some wretched employment, or shabby lodgings and a
kind of genteel poverty that appalled her.

Margaret had been a spirited if silly girl; the silli-
ness had been knocked out of her, but the spirit remained. This post at least promised her some inde-
pendence, if only behind a kitchen door, and she
would be with civilized people.

And so she continued on her way to the Hall, walking now by the sea wall. The arm that carried the
portmanteau seemed to be nearly breaking. She suddenly felt she could endure it no longer. She sat down
on the wall, dropped the portmanteau at her feet, and
pulled off the hideous bonnet, which had always been
a little tight for her and which was undoubtedly
causing her headache. She had already inquired as to
the whereabouts of the Hall, and she could see it
dimly in the distance, at the top of a steep hill.
Adeney Cross seemed full of hills. It did not look an
inviting building, but then, on this gray November
afternoon nothing really looked its best. *I certainly
do not*, thought Margaret as her hair blew untidily
about her face, and she cast a disparaging glance
down at her cheap gray woollen dress, which had
done duty for nearly five years, and had never been in
the height of fashion.

Once she had loved clothes. Once she had dressed prettily and fashionably, with ornaments at her throat, on her wrists and fingers. Once . . . but that was a long time ago; that was in the past. There was no point whatsoever in being sorry for herself, and, after all, it had been entirely her own fault. Margaret was sorry for herself; the tears stung her eyes, and she was forced to sniff and fumble for her handkerchief. It was, of course, mainly fatigue. She had traveled all the night, down from York, and had changed stage three times. She had had no money to buy herself a hot meal, and had been forced to make do with the small parcel of food she had brought from home. As she was still young and had a healthy appetite, this was in no way sufficient. Indeed, she had grown so hungry and depressed that at one posting station she had spent almost the last of her money on a glass of hot punch. This had warmed and encouraged her, but then there was a gentleman who, seeing a young woman on her own, tried to engage her in conversation. He sat himself down beside her, a red-faced fellow with a leering eye, and he looked at her in such a way that her hand itched to slap him. She was forced to leave her cosy seat by the parlor fire and wait once more in the cold, uncomfortable coach.

Margaret found her thoughts still centered on food and warmth. I hope, she told herself, there is some kind of meal waiting for me that I do not have to cook, and a good hot fire. Then, having blown her nose and shaken the tears back, she continued to stare out at sea, deriving an odd comfort from the bitter wind and gray water.

She knew enough about the village to make out the Cross Prison, overlooking the Loving Sands and at

the side of the Hall. It was an ironic name for sands
with so evil a reputation. She had spent her very last
coins on a bowl of soup at the local inn after arriving at last at Adeney Cross, and there, blurred by
fatigue, she had listened to the local chat and gossip,
some of which she found disturbing, though she was
almost too tired to care.

But a great deal was said about the Loving Sands,
of which the inhabitants were both proud and terrified.

"You don't walk alone on those sands, ma'am," the
landlord—it was Mr. Ted Clay—told her, and Margaret, being of a contradictory disposition, decided to
do so at the earliest opportunity, though she would
make sure it was during low tide. However, when she
heard a little more, she was no longer so sure. It
seemed that the sea swept across in a matter of half an
hour and that, owing to some strange, unexplained
formation, the unhappy traveler would be instantly
sucked under, so violently and swiftly that there was
not the remotest chance of escape. Strangely, there
were a few, isolated patches which remained safe,
even when the tide was coming in, but one could discover them only by pure chance, for there was nothing
to make them seem any different from the expanse
around them. There was the tale of a man who found
one of these oases and had to stand there, shaking
with terror, until the tide went out, not daring to
move one step. When at last he was safe, he collapsed
in a dead faint, and afterward was so afflicted with
rheumatics in the joints that he was a sick man to
the end of his days. But he at least saved his life,
and many were not so lucky. A number of children
had been caught and killed, and several of the

unhappy prisoners had died in an attempt to escape. Only when the tide was low was it safe to cross the sands; the moment the sea started coming in, one had to run "like hell," said Mr. Clay, and he looked as if he meant it.

Margaret surveyed the sands with a kind of fascinated fear, then turned her gaze to the Cross Prison, which distressed her even more, for she had a horror of being enclosed in a confined space; her heart grieved for the unhappy men shut up there, whose only fault was that they had been fighting on the enemy side.

Everyone in the village seemed to know she was working at the Hall. Through her weary, dust-rimmed eyes she could not avoid seeing the measuring, inquisitive glances that passed between the inn-keeper and his customers. She longed to ask them questions, but felt that it was not proper in the circumstances to do so, so she simply looked down as she drank her soup, and listened, hoping for information.

They did not say much, but there was an under-current to their words. She received the impression that there was a strange wildness in the family, especially with regard to the younger daughter, Albertine. "A strange young lady," one of the men said, and was instantly hushed by his companions. As for Miss Flora, it seemed she was engaged to a young captain from the prison garrison, and this too, as it was mentioned, provoked sly glances, and Margaret was sure she saw one of the men tap his elbow in a meaningful fashion. However, Miss Flora apparently was a "nice young lady," if a little silly and childlike, though this information also was checked by the landlord's wife. "You'll have plenty of work to do, ma'am," she told Margaret. "Those two girls haven't been brought up to do a hand's turn."

This was only to be expected, however, and Margaret could remember the days when she too hardly did "a hand's turn," so she was not surprised or dismayed to hear this.

As she was preparing to continue her journey, she heard a mention of a French tutor who was either coming or had just arrived. "One of those frog prisoners-of-war," said Mr. Clay; then he burst into a long tirade against the French, which nobody listened to, apparently having heard it many times before.

But he seemed a kindly man, and his wife insisted on giving Margaret a glass of wine. When she said that she had no money to pay for it, the woman tut-tutted and told her not to mind. As Margaret, a little refreshed, was making for the door, she added, "You look tired, ma'am."

"I am a little. I have been traveling down from York."

"Don't you let them overwork you, now!"

"Oh, I can look after myself," Margaret said, with a cheerfulness she did not feel. She thanked Mrs. Clay for her kindness and set off on the long trudge to the Hall.

She thought now, in this moment of weakness and fatigue, that she could not look after herself at all, that she would give anything in the world to have someone to care for her and protect her. Perhaps all women, however strong-minded, felt that way. But, after all, she had done better than might have been expected from a spoiled, pretty girl who was accustomed to having her own way. She had nursed Papa through that sad, exhausting last illness, and she had done it single-handed. She had seen to all his affairs after he died, she had managed to sell the house, and now she had even found herself a job. She had survived her broken love affair, she had even survived Henry—not totally, perhaps, but more or less so: hearts did not break as easily as the poets said, and pride and self-esteem could in the end be a little restored.

And yet, all she wanted to do at this moment was cry, as if she were some silly miss fresh from a seminary, and the wretched tears were springing out again, and she was cold and tired and miserable, and really, she just could not bear it. The best thing—indeed, the only thing—was to walk out on the Loving Sands and end it all.

It was at this dramatic moment, in a state quite unusual in Miss Walters, who was on the whole a sane and sensible young woman, that she heard footsteps approaching. This acted more quickly on her than a bottle of wine, for she could not bear to be seen in such absurd disarray. Instantly she wiped away the tears, straightened her back, then turned her head with an attempt at cold dignity, as if somehow the newcomer were responsible for this imbecile display.

In that moment of shock, as they looked at each other, she went scarlet and he pale. Her hands released the bonnet, which was instantly caught up in the wind and went sailing out across the sands.

For a while neither of them could utter a word.

Then he said—what words to speak at such a meeting—"I fear you have lost your bonnet."

They both turned to look at it, and their gaze was concentrated on this small, shabby gray thing, whirled in circles by the wind, which suddenly dipped onto the sands. It might have been the most important thing in the world. It might have been of unimaginable significance. They stared at its passages as if they dared not look away, their eyes lifting and sinking with its flight, following every convolution with passionate absorption. And as they watched, something horrible occurred. The little bonnet, made by a local milliner, now in its third year, due for no worse fate than to be handed down and finally dumped on a rubbish heap, fell like a wounded bird onto the Loving Sands. And it was as if a gaping mouth opened beneath it, for the sands gave a kind of shudder, and the little bonnet was instantly absorbed. It vanished completely from sight.

Margaret exclaimed, "Oh dear God!" Her hands moved up to her breast, as if somehow she had watched the death of a beloved friend. She had never cared for the bonnet, even in its heyday, but to see it disappear as if into the jaws of a savage beast was shocking, and made her instantly recant her foolish vow to walk on these diabolical sands and put an end to her existence.

The Frenchman said, in a dry, taut voice, "They say this happens when the tide comes in. These sands are very dangerous. You should never walk there alone, even if the sea seems miles away."

Then at last they turned and looked at each other fully, in silence.

After a while she spoke. She said, her voice small and trembling, "Well, Philippe. I never thought I would see you again, certainly not in such a place as this."

He answered, "I have prayed to God that I might never meet you again."

And again they were silent, thinking of the dreadful circumstances of their last meeting. She looked down at her lap, the hair half hiding her face, while he watched her almost with savagery, biting his lower lip and scowling, his hands twisting together.

"I suppose you live here," he said finally. "Are you married?"

"No," she said. "And I do not live here. I have just arrived."

She looked up at him, her eyes moving across his face, then down. She saw how much older he had grown, and a shadow of pain crossed her face, for that was how he must see her too. It did not matter, it should not matter, but oh God, it did matter, she wanted him to see her young again, and beautiful, and elegantly dressed. And here she was, in her gray gown and drab cloak, her hair, to which she instinctively lifted her hand, whirled into wild tangles by the wind. Then she was ashamed of this preposterous vanity. What the devil did it matter how she looked? He could only despise her now as he had done then, it would hardly make any difference to him if she was in rags. But she had to look at him again, noting the face that had grown gaunter and more lined, the streaks of gray in his hair, the wary, watchful lines about his mouth, the thinness of his body aggravated by that enormous height. And as she looked, it was as if the face shivered like the sands before her eyes, so that briefly she saw again the eager, violent young man who had been so much in love with her that he was prepared to go against his family, his upbringing, and the tradition of his friends to marry her, a nobody, a little English miss whom his world despised.

Margaret flushed scarlet, furious at her own stupidity for thinking back and wanting to recapture the past. She tried for the dozenth time to brush the hair out of her eyes. The sea was now receding across the Loving Sands. This was the period of comparative safety, and Captain Lewis Moore was at this very moment walking quickly across, on his way to call upon his fiancée, Miss Flora Walters. They both could see him in the distance, a tall young man in full uniform, his sword at his side. But neither really saw him at all, for both were suddenly consumed with a helpless anger, anger at this waste of emotion, anger at this brutally cruel coincidence that had brought them together again, anger at the hopelessness of making any kind of human contact.

The Frenchman looked at her, long and hard. "I see no point in mentioning our past relationship again. It was a long time ago. It is best forgotten by both of us."

"I am not excusing my behavior, but your own was not so exemplary!"

He gave her a look of such fury that she instinctively backed away. He said, "No. I recognize that. It was unpardonable. But two unpardonable things do not make the situation more excusable. If that is all we have in common, the sooner we part, the better."

And he moved a little, as if to walk on, but he did not do so.

She said, in a bitter whisper, almost as if she were the young Margaret again, "Oh, you could never begin to understand all that has happened to me. Could you not try to? I suppose you will laugh, but though this meeting is dreadful for both of us, I have always dreamed that one day I might see you again, and talk things over—"

"Talk things over!"

"Yes. Yes. Couldn't we do so? And then you can go, and tomorrow we'll forget all about each other. Only, oh, don't let us be enemies any more, Philippe. It does neither of us any good. Please let us at least say good-bye as friends. I have wanted to do so for many years."

He came closer to her, towering over her. He said, in a voice she had never heard from him, "I think it is certainly time we understood each other. I agree that this meeting is unfortunate . . ."

The extraordinary word brought a wan smile to her lips. She said, "Yes, it is indeed."

"It—it's unbelievable. But it does not warrant all this sentimentality. We can never say good-bye as friends. There is no friendship between us, there never can be. After what has happened! Do you imagine," he said, in a quick, cold, clipped voice, "that I will ever forgive you? If so, you are mistaken. I will never forgive you as long as I live. We are enemies and we will always remain so. Only a lunatic could think otherwise. You made a fool of me. You made me a laughingstock. And, yes! You made me behave atrociously. I will apologize for that, if you wish, though I cannot think it makes much difference."

She disconcerted him by saying quietly, "It makes all the difference. I think it is yourself you cannot forgive, Philippe, not me."

She thought for one moment he was going to hit her. But he checked himself, saying, in a choked voice, "Perhaps there is some truth in that. If you like, we have both humiliated each other. And you think that makes for friendship! That is the one thing friendship cannot endure. And now you say such foolishness. Asking me to say good-bye as if we were friends! But of course, this is typical of you—indeed,

of all women. I see that you have not really changed
at all. You obviously imagine that you only have to
shed a few tears, play the little woman, and at once
we are reconciled. There is no reconciliation, never
will be. Only a fool could expect it." He added, with
deliberate brutality, "We are not young any more,
Margaret. A great deal has happened in ten years. You
tell me you are not married . . ."

"No," said Margaret. She had grown very white,
but the eyes she raised to his were dry. For that
moment she did indeed look old—older than her
years. Her face was drawn and still.

He said savagely, "Did he leave you, then, that
Henry? He takes your reputation from you, he takes
you from me, then he leaves you. What kind of man
is that?"

"Like other men," said Margaret, and saw him
flush. She slipped off the wall and rose to her feet.
She felt as if she had been beaten. She was sick and
cold with despair and anger, but she had never lacked
spirit, and that last remark had fallen from her lips
before she had realized what she was saying. But now
the fury died within her, and she could not pursue
her triumph, for, after all, it no longer mattered. The
Frenchman might be brutal and unforgiving, but he
had once loved her, and she him; there was little point
in their savaging each other. She turned away from
him, leaning her hands on the wall. The Loving
Sands looked peaceful and white, for all the sea was
coming in; it was hard to believe in their danger.

She said quietly, "You have the right to know about
it, if it interests you. We went away together—you
know that. It was an incredible folly. But we were
only together for one night, and, if it pleases you,

that night was the most appalling one of my life.
After what happened between us . . . But I did not
wish to mention that again, I'm sorry. There was
never any love between me and Henry. He thought I
was rich. That is all. I don't mind saying it now. He
thought I came from your society, that I was a silly
girl, ripe for the picking. In the morning he simply
went out and never came back." She suddenly smiled,
turning her face to the Frenchman. It was a bitter,
ironic smile, which shocked him, despite his anger.
"Do you know, Philippe, I wept the whole night and
spoke of nothing but you. Poor Henry. You cannot
blame him for running away. I have never seen or
heard of him since. And I . . . I went home to Papa.
What else was there for me to do, except perhaps
become a whore? I don't think that would have suited
me, do you, Philippe?"

This he did not answer, and she smiled again.

"Perhaps you do," she said. "Thank you for being
gentleman enough not to say so. It might have happened, if my darling Papa had not been so generous
and forgiving. And . . ." She was standing now, with
her back to the wall, and the next words seemed jolted
out of her: "Oh, you shall know the worst, Philippe. I
never meant to tell you this, but now it don't matter,
you shall hear it. Why not, if it gives you pleasure?
I will make my confession. You have no need to shrive
me. You can say to yourself at nights, *This is what
happens to women who insult me.* There was a baby."

His face changed. He stared at her, disconcerted,
then briefly ashamed.

"The baby died after two months," said Margaret
calmly. She paused, as if she would add to this, then
seemed to change her mind. She went on, "It was

fortunate, perhaps. I don't know. I shall never cease
to regret it, and I think of it very often, wondering
what would have happened if the baby had lived. It
still makes me cry. We are foolish, aren't we? Especially as it was such a long time ago, and, as you have
said, I am no longer young, not as our world knows
youth."

She broke off. A rebellious urge came upon her to
cry out, *But I am still young—twenty-eight is still
young. I am not yet an old woman, why do you try to
make me one?* But, after all, in these marrying days
anyone over twenty-five was regarded as being on the
shelf. As Margaret saw it, she had lost her looks, she
had no money, and even if there were some elderly
suitor, he would certainly run like the wind if he
knew of her past. There had been a couple of offers,
but there had always been some old woman to tell
the story, and, naturally, the suitors had disappeared
at once.

She went on, "My father was so good to me. You
cannot believe how good he was. Most men would
have disowned me and thrown me out. After all, I
had left him, as I left you, and he lost all his work
because of me. The Comtesse refused to employ him
any more, and of course everyone else followed her
example. I suppose I had offended against your society, Philippe, and my poor Papa had to pay for it.
We came back to England, and there I was, pregnant
with my baby, and nobody would speak to me, and we
had no money. He had to take a horrid job in a
school. I think he was a saint. Do you know, he never
once reproached me." She added, after a pause, "He
is dead. He died a year ago. I suppose I am fortunate
that anyone at all wishes to employ me. I may have

made a fool of you, Philippe, and I would never deny
that I behaved shamefully, but even you can see that
I have not had much happiness since I left you. At
least I now have work, which is why I am in this village. I hope it is hard work, really hard work. It is
the only thing left to me, and I never was a lazy
person."

She became aware that his expression had changed,
that he was looking at her in the strangest way. He
made no comment on her story. Indeed, for a minute
he made no comment at all. Then he said, in a suppressed voice, "This work you speak of—are you
working here, in Adeney Cross?"

She was surprised that he should show so much
interest, for her work could hardly concern him one
way or another. She answered, "Why, yes. I have just
told you so. I have been offered the post of housekeeper. Up at the Hall. That building on top of the
hill, by the prison. Colonel Walters is a distant cousin
of mine, and he wrote to me. I imagine he knows
nothing about me, and I hope it will remain that way.
I think perhaps I should go now. They will be expecting me. So I will say good-bye to you, Philippe. I
suppose you will regard it as impertinent if I say once
again that I would like to part friends."

The tears, confound them, were coming to her eyes
again, so she did not see the look compounded of a
disbelieving horror and something that was almost a
dreadful humor crossing his face. She whispered in a
choked voice, ashamed of herself, yet unable to stop,
for the tears were now openly trickling down, "Don't
leave me with this ugly memory. I know I deserve
nothing from you, and I am not asking you to forgive
me, but it is just that I cannot bear to part in anger
like this. Will you not at least shake hands with me?"

He answered, in a brisk, unemotional voice, "Why, certainly, ma'am, if you wish it." To her utter amazement, he then extended his hand, shook hers briskly, then said, "I think I had better help you with the portmanteau. The hill looks steep, and I can see you are fatigued."

She protested weakly, wondering if she were going out of her mind, for this simply did not follow on what had occurred.

"Why, no," she told him, "I am quite rested now. There is no reason for you to go out of your way."

He was looking at her, his mouth stretched in an angry smile. He said, "I would not have believed it possible. The fates are certainly taking the oddest hand in our lives, Margaret. So you must be the new housekeeper."

"But I told you . . ." Then, suddenly, the memory of the talk she had had at the inn came to her mind. Her hand shot to her mouth, as if she were a child caught out in wrongdoing. She whispered, "Oh *no!*"

"And I," said the Frenchman, "am the new tutor." He seemed to have recovered from both his rage and his emotion. The look he was bestowing on her was not kind, but it was a little bewildered, as if he derived some bizarre amusement from this impossible situation. "It seems," he said, "that we are not to be free of each other for some time yet. We shall be working side by side, Margaret. We shall doubtless be eating together at some menial table. We shall see each other every minute of the day. I shall have the pleasure of tidying my room at your orders, and you will doubtless enjoy the spectacle of me instructing the young ladies in my language. Your portmanteau, if you please."

She whispered, "You enjoy tormenting me."

He said coldly, "Don't be silly. This is an impossible situation, but we have to make the best of it." Then he repeated, "Your portmanteau."

"I am not coming."

"Of course you are."

"I cannot!"

"I think," said the Frenchman, "you have no choice."

She gave him a look of helpless, despairing rage, for what he said was only too true. Of course, she could walk away this very minute. There was nothing tangible to stop her. The Colonel would be astonished and furious—he would then have to find himself another housekeeper. But he would doubtless regard this as the kind of thing foolish, unmarried women did. After the first outburst, he would forget all about her, not even inquire if anything had happened to her, or if she had perhaps decided to take a little promenade on the Loving Sands.

But she had no money at all, and no roof over her head. The landlord's wife had been kind to her, but there was a world of difference between offering an exhausted stranger a free glass of wine and meeting that same stranger a few hours later, homeless and penniless, asking for work. The only choice, if there was a choice, was something that she had already contemplated, but that now made her shudder.

Her eyes moved again to the Loving Sands. They looked cold and desolate. Her strong, young body flinched at the sight of them. She knew now that she only had to wait till the tide started coming in, and set foot upon them; that would be the end of Miss Margaret Walters, who had hopelessly disgraced herself, and who now faced a future that was no future at all.

She demanded suddenly, "What happens to the poor people who are drowned there? Do they just disappear, or do their bodies turn up later?"

The Frenchman was taken aback by this question. Margaret still had the power to disconcert him. He looked at her, the portmanteau already in his free hand. However, he knew all about the sands, for Elchester, like Adeney Cross, was proud of their notoriety. He said curtly, "The bodies certainly turn up, but it might be here or several miles away. The times vary. It could be tomorrow. It could be months. No one knows with the Loving Sands. The bodies are sucked under, then float up again when the tide is full. Are you thinking of your bonnet? It will doubtless arrive in Elchester harbor a few weeks from now. Do you wish to claim it? I fancy it will no longer look fashionable."

"It never did," said Margaret. Once again she pushed ineffectually at the tangled hair. There was nothing to be done with it until she could sit down and brush it out. It really did not matter. Nothing mattered. She said, with a sigh, "Shall we go?"

"By all means. I am glad you are so sensible."

The two of them set off up the hill, the Frenchman carrying a bag in either hand, while Margaret walked at his side, clutching a shabby reticule and two small parcels, which contained the only valuables she possessed in the world. There were a few books, Papa's fob watch (she refused to pawn it), Mama's wedding ring, a cheap pair of candlesticks that she kept as a reminder of home, and one small thing that the Frenchman would never know about: an initialed silk handkerchief, the kind that was once fashionable to wear attached to the wrist.

They walked in silence, except that once Margaret,

aware of a surging hysteria, stopped to exclaim in a loud voice, "This is perfectly ridiculous!" He did not answer, and they walked on. Occasionally she glanced at him sideways. His profile, that well-remembered profile, with the long nose and high cheekbones, was stony, without expression. She perceived that though he was impeccably neat in his attire, there was a darn on the elbow of his jacket, the shirt was frayed at the wrists, and the buttons did not exactly match. *He too,* she thought, *has no choice,* and this made her want to cry again, though God knows why she should waste tears on a gentleman who not only despised her but seemed determined to be as unfriendly as possible.

They walked in silence until the Hall at last came into view. Margaret asked him, "What is your—what do you call yourself now?"

He answered curtly, without turning his head, "Monsieur Sansterre."

"But that's not a name!"

"It is my name." Then he looked at her, as he set the cases down. They were at the front door. "The world calls me Frenchy."

"Oh no!"

"I have no doubt the young ladies will address me in that fashion. Perhaps you would care to do so yourself."

She made no protest, only sighed. She gave him a hopeless look, put her hands up once again to her appalling hair—what a way in which to greet an employer!—then, as the bell sounded, they stood side by side, waiting for the door to open.

As it happened, the entire household was assembled, including Captain Ross, who, as Margaret and the

Frenchman waited, was drinking his usual amount of wine and arguing fiercely with the Colonel.

They were old friends. The loud, harsh words that passed between them signified nothing more than the great friendly clout that young gentlemen sometimes accord each other. The Colonel said from time to time that it was a relief to be able to raise his voice without being accused of brutality. Sometimes he shouted at his daughters, and when he did so, Flora burst instantly into tears, while Bertie, always the more subtle of the two, huddled away from him in a terrified manner, wearing her hurt-mouse look, eyes wide with reproach, as if he were raising his crop to her.

"Sometimes," the Colonel frequently remarked, "I really find women impossible. I only hope this Margaret will run the house decently for me, and keep those two girls out of my way."

And it was true that he was awkward and unhappy in female company, and completely devoid of the graces and small elegances that women were supposed to demand. The only females he was at home with were of the lower sort whom he had encountered in his campaign days, and he had married more from convention than anything else. The late Mrs. Walters had been an amiable and silly woman, with considerable beauty—it was from her that Flora got her looks, and perhaps her lack of intelligence also—but her husband was secretly relieved when she died. He could never forgive her for saddling him with two daughters instead of the potential young officers who would have been more welcome to him. "You can't horsewhip a girl," he said sometimes, as if this were the most natural thing in the world, and when guests to whom this remark was addressed looked surprised, he added, "I can't understand why women are so different from men." He could never summon up the faintest interest in either girl, but he was kind to them, as he was kind to his dogs. He never raised a finger to them, even when they drove him to distraction, and he looked forward with ardent anticipation to the day when Flora left him for her handsome captain, and prayed that Albertine, despite the dragging foot, might also find herself a husband.

He looked now at Captain Ross, making the cross, down-drawn face that in the old days had made his regiment tremble.

Captain Ross was a Scot from Edinburgh who had come down south during the war. He was violently against his countrymen who had tried to put Charles Stuart back on the English throne, and his attitude upset the romantic Flora. He was lacking one arm, which he had lost in a deer-shoot, through someone firing in the wrong direction. As Albertine, who detested him, once remarked, he could not even do the proper thing and lose it in the war: He had to have it shot off in a silly accident. He was a tall, portly man of fifty-odd, with grizzled hair, and very sharp if small gray eyes, set slightly crookedly in his pugilist's face. He lived in a small cottage at the back of the prison, and was the official agent for the prisoners of war. Every day he spent some eight or nine hours with them, sorting out their grievances, disciplining the recalcitrant, and dealing with the tricky matter of supplies. He and the Colonel were now on their second bottle of wine, and their voices carried from the library to Flora and Lewis, in the adjoining room.

"Papa sounds very cross," whispered Flora. She

thought how handsome Lewis was, and how strong; she wished that the days would fly by so that they could get married and be together for ever and ever.

She was not an observant girl, seeing everything through her romantic imagination, otherwise, she might have perceived that her betrothed had been drinking heavily. There was a heavy aura of wine about him; his features were blurred and his speech thick. This was happening more and more frequently, as his fellow officers could have told her, but Flora, if she noticed it at all, put it down to exhaustion and overwork, even perhaps an intense desire for herself. But she had to see that the handsome face, which was very handsome indeed, if rather lacking in intelligence, did not smile as tenderly as usual, and that the hand over hers was almost reluctant, as if his mind was elsewhere. And at once she grew angry, pettish, and her normally soft speaking voice rose in a thin whine.

"Oh, Lewis," she said, like a child. "Lewis! You're not paying attention to one word I've said. It's too bad, really it is. After all, I only see you for a few minutes, and you don't even listen."

He only said, "It's a damnable thing."

Flora decided that she must ask him what was the matter—after all, she would soon be a soldier's wife, and she must show him how grown-up and sensible she was. She said coaxingly, in her normal sweet voice, "Oh dearest, what is it?"

But her mouth drooped sulkily all the same, for they were not supposed to be alone without Bertie as a chaperone, and Bertie had been bribed by a box of sweetmeats to leave them alone. And here was Lewis wasting these precious minutes by being tiresome . . .

He must have grown aware of this himself. He

leaned forward and kissed her on the cheek. The
hand holding hers tightened. He said, a little thickly,
"Oh, my darling, forgive me. Only, we are having a
very difficult time just now, and I sometimes think
that Ross blames me. It's all these rumors of invasion,
and then five men escaping—"

"Five!"

"Yes, unfortunately. I dare say that's what the Captain's bawling about. And it was my watch, too."

"Nobody could possibly blame you," said the
besotted Flora.

He gave her a wry look. "Oh, yes, they could,"
he said, "they could indeed. We cannot find out how
they escaped. There must be some underground tunnel, leading onto the sands."

"But they'd all be killed."

"I wish they had been," returned Lewis, with a
directness that made Flora shoot him a startled
glance. "It would settle the whole matter, and nobody
could blame me. But Captain Ross is convinced
there's someone in Adeney Cross who's on their side,
so that they crossed the sands at the right moment.
God knows where they are now—making their way
to one of the cartel ports, I dare say. And now it looks
as if we might be invaded any moment . . ." Then he
seemed to realize what he was saying, for he flung an
arm about Flora's waist, crying out, "But I do not
mean to alarm you, my darling girl. I don't know why
I am talking like this. I should be shot for frighten-
ing you. There are always rumors in wartime, they
don't mean a thing, and here I am babbling like
some old woman."

It might be thought that Lewis, despite his good
looks, knew little of women. Indeed, like his future

father-in-law, his acquaintance was limited to those of
the baser sort in dockside establishments and a few
minor flirtations with officers' daughters in Elchester.
Despite the handsome appearance, he possessed few
of the social graces, and it was fortunate for him that
the Colonel's daughter was so easily captivated. He
should have realized that Flora was not alarmed at all
—indeed, her cheeks were aflame with excitement. She
whispered, "Do you really think there will be an
invasion?"

He did not answer this, much to her surprise. The
handsome face grew heavy, a little secretive. He only
said, "Where is little Bertie?"

Flora had been enjoying herself, and this absurd
question roused her temper again. She cried out,
"Oh, how should I know? It don't matter, surely.
Why do you ask? I suppose you like her better than
me."

"Flora . . ."

"I know she's not so pretty, but I dare say you feel
sorry for her. Well, you need not, I can tell you that.
She is quite capable of looking after herself, and
sometimes I think she pretends with that lame foot of
hers, just to get sympathy. I've watched her when
she don't know it. She is very artful. But, of course,
if you want her, I'll go and get her for you."

She said all this with some malice as well as temper,
for Bertie and Lewis made no secret of their dislike
for each other. Bertie loved to tease him, which Lewis
bitterly resented, and after five minutes of each other's
company they tended to snarl and snap like a couple
of terriers.

But Lewis did not answer as she had expected. He
only said, in a dull voice, "She is usually with us. I

only wondered. There is no need to shout at me,
Flora. It is a perfectly natural question."

Flora began to cry. "If you don't want me, I'll go
away."

Then he came to his senses and laughed at her for
being such a silly goose, and the next few minutes
were all that anyone could desire, with such embraces
and *tendresses* as convention permitted, and no more
talk of escapes or invasion.

In the living room, meanwhile, Captain Ross had
been holding forth on this very subject, though with
a great deal more vigor. He said now, in his Scots-
accented voice, "Have you gone daft, man, to engage
a French tutor at such a time?"

The Colonel was growing tired of this particular
criticism, especially as the more practical side of his
mind could not help but agree with it. Naturally, he
was at once put on the defensive. "Adam," he said
(for he and the Captain addressed each other by
their first names), "will you be so good as to mind
your own business. And let me refill your glass."

"It is my business," said Captain Ross, with obvious truth. He mechanically held out his glass. "Do
you not realize, John, that five more prisoners have
escaped?" He leaned forward as he spoke. His voice
roughened. He was much addicted to the wine, as the
Walters girls had often remarked, but it never seemed
to affect him, however much he drank. Perhaps the
Scottish whisky had seasoned him to this effeminate
brew that the Southrons preferred. He went on, "It's
not as if it was just this one instance. There have been
seven previous escapes, and it is only too plain that it's
organized from within, and damn well organized,
too. The Cross Prison has always been regarded as

one of maximum security. We believed that the sands
would insure that. But there is someone here who
knows all about the sands, who knows the exact times
when it is safe to cross them, someone, moreover—I
trust you are listening, John?"

"I am listening," said the Colonel sourly.

"Someone who is arranging these escapes and, if I
am not mistaken, someone who is banking on an
invasion that they hope will not be too far in the
future. In addition, these men are all fully armed."

"Good God! How do you know that?"

"Because we caught one of them."

"Then surely you could get information . . ."

"No. That was seen to, too. The man was dying
when we found him. He had been shot, and not by us.
These people, whoever they are—and I fancy there is
more than one—are both cunning and ruthless. I
dare say they imagined the sands would get him, and
that would have been that. But the man managed to
struggle to the safety belt. He was not quite dead
when we found him. We could not get much from
him, he was too far gone, but we gathered that somewhere in Adeney Cross there is a cache of arms, and,
as well as a contact inside the prison, some local person who is probably the main organizer. And this is
the moment for you to bring into your home, which
is next door to the prison, a French parole officer! I
think you are clean out of your wits. If I didn't
know you, I'd begin to look on you with the utmost
suspicion."

The Colonel saw the enormity of all this very well,
and his immediate reaction was to grow cross and
sulky. He said, in a furious mumble, "Well, damn it, I
was not to know. And the girls insisted. Well, I'll

send him away. I'll tell him we no longer require his
services. He can go back to Elchester. The Major
will deal with him there."

"How long has he been in Elchester?"

"Oh, how should I know? Some time, I dare say.
You'd best ask the Major. It was he who recom-
mended him."

"Some time," repeated Captain Ross, and fell into
a brood over his glass of wine, which he revolved
slowly in the fingers of his one hand.

"He's due today," said the Colonel. "I'll throw him
out. It's easy. The girls will have to do without him.
Don't know what they want to learn French for, anyway. Preposterous language. Don't understand a word
of it, myself."

Captain Ross, who spoke the language fluently,
looked at him for a second. Then he said, "No. Let
the fellow stay. If he is the one responsible, I'd as lief
have him under my eyes. Only, I want to see him,
as soon as possible. He'll not be the only one. I regret
to say this, John, but the main person responsible is
probably someone we all know very well. Damn my
soul, it's abominable! But you English were always a
traitorous race. That Polish fellow would never have
got across the border if it had not been for the
collaboration of your own people."

The Colonel, after a long acquaintance with his
friend, knew that the Polish fellow was the man the
English called Bonnie Prince Charlie. Captain Ross
could never be brought to believe that the Prince
was a Scot, despite the royal Stuart blood, since his
mother was a Polish princess. He prepared to answer,
in a bellow of rage, but at this moment, with unin-
tentional drama, one of the Hall's servants—they

changed so rapidly that no one really got to know them—knocked on the door to say that there was a lady and gentleman to see the Colonel.

And at the same time, Flora, who had heard the bell, came into the hall, Lewis at her side, while Albertine, also aware of the arrival, limped down the stairs, her face expectant, inquisitive, a faint smile on her lips.

Chapter Three

Margaret and the Frenchman had a clear view of the whole Walters family as they stepped into the hallway.

They saw the pretty girl with the magnificent golden hair, who was so evidently in love with the young man at her side. They grew aware of the odd, intent little creature, who must be the other sister, and who watched them over the banisters. They walked toward the two gentlemen at the library door, not yet knowing which was their employer. They looked at the elderly man with the white moustache, who seemed to have been quarreling with the other gentleman beside him, who was portly, one-armed, and wore the face of a fairground boxer.

And Colonel Walters and Captan Ross found the couple strange. There was the youngish woman with traces of a great beauty in her exhausted face, and extraordinarily tangled hair, which fell about her cheeks. As for the tall gentleman at her side, he was as neat as she was untidy, he was apparently carrying her portmanteau as well as his own, and he seemed to be neither protective nor friendly to the young lady beside him.

The Colonel came up to them. He was a little disconcerted by their arriving together. In any case, he was never good at any kind of domestic situation, which, with some reason, he felt should be handled by his elder daughter—after all, this was not his milieu; he was most at home on the parade ground.

It was natural, as in all emergencies, that he should raise his voice in a bellow, while Captain Ross, after looking intently at the young woman, moved his gaze to the Frenchman, surveying him minutely from head to foot.

The Colonel roared out, "Well, well, well!" Then, looking at Margaret with some disapproval—damn it, the woman was quite young—"I believe, ma'am, you must be my cousin."

She was by now so tired that she was not sure whether to burst into tears or fall to the ground. But she managed to do neither, and she raised her head proudly as she acknowledged the greeting. Then, as if resolved to establish from the very beginning the correct relationship between them, she folded her hands before her and waited, as if to learn her duties.

The Colonel said again, "Well!" Then, cursing Flora for her inadequacy, he said in a rush, "I dare say you wish to go to your room. I believe there is a meal waiting for you in the kitchen. As for your duties, ma'am, I think they are self-evident. This is a big house, and there is a great deal to keep clean." He glanced back into the library, and Margaret followed his gaze. "I should wish you to pay special attention to this room, which is my sanctum. The books require continual dusting, and I have a great many valuable things, which I hope you will treat with the utmost care. This, for instance . . ." He picked up, as he spoke, a case of dueling pistols, in which he took great pride. "And, of course, those ornaments on the mantelpiece."

He stopped. It never entered his head to inquire if the new housekeeper had had a good journey or whether she was tired. He seemed to think he had done his duty, and he did not consider that this was, after all, a distant relative, and that he could make her more welcome. He turned toward the Frenchman, who throughout had remained silent, with the two portmanteaux now on the floor, one on each side of him.

The Frenchman had been studying both gentlemen. He saw immediately that the Colonel, despite his bellow and rough speech, was a good-natured-enough person, though obviously something of a fool; this was an army type he had met innumerable times, both here and at home. But the other gentleman, he was interested to note, neither liked nor trusted him. Such suspicion on first sight was a little strange. As for the

two daughters, who were to be his pupils, he preferred
to suspend judgment; there would be plenty of time
to know them better. Even as he thought this, his
dark eyes met Albertine's. For a second his brows
met. The other young lady seemed very much the
traditional English miss, with her fair hair and delicate complexion, but this one, who looked at him so
intently, almost fiercely, was like a changeling, with a
bold, provocative look to her that went oddly with her
tiny stature and way of standing behind everyone
else.

The Colonel said, "So you are the Frenchy."

He was not an ill-intentioned man, and he would
not normally have been so rude, but he had been
drinking a great deal of wine, the conversation with
Adam Ross had disturbed him, and the word came
out before he could check it. Captain Ross merely
grinned, as if this amused him, but Flora's kind heart
was upset by this unfortunate word, and for once she
rose to her responsibilities, exclaiming reproachfully,
"Papa!" as she came to the Frenchman's side.

She said, in a mechanical way, like a well-
brought-up child, "We are very pleased to see you, sir.
We are the pupils you have to teach French to. I am
Miss Flora, and this is my younger sister, Albertine."

Then she remembered Margaret and turned to her,
and a look of the utmost astonishment came over her
face.

She had pretended to be amused by Albertine's
description of the horrid old woman who would so
ill-use and frighten them, but instinctively had
begun to believe her, and now she fully expected to
see some ill-favored old crone, whose face would be
dark with malice, who would plainly make all their

lives a misery. The first sight of this impoverished and distant cousin was almost a shock to her, for this was a young woman, not much older than herself, who had once, it was easy to see, been quite a beauty, might indeed become so again if she had enough sleep and enough to eat. Her first reaction was one of jealousy, for though she loved Lewis most passionately, some deep feminine instinct, which never rose to the surface, warned her that he was not entirely to be trusted. This woman would be around and Lewis would meet her, perhaps in the passage when he arrived. There was a quality to Margaret, despite her woefully battered appearance, that Flora, in her primitive way, recognized as attractive and charming: This was someone a man might want to cherish and protect.

However, fortunately for Margaret, Albertine's reaction was so impertinent and disagreeable that Flora's suspicions turned to pity. The younger girl had so far said nothing, but, when she had studied Margaret, a look of anger and resentment crossed her face. Perhaps she too believed in the witch she had invented; perhaps she was disappointed that her lies had not proved to be the truth. She said, in her clear, high voice, "We had not expected you so soon. How is it you did not come by the back door? This entrance is reserved for our guests."

Margaret looked at her, then answered quietly, "I'm so sorry. I did not realize there was another entrance."

"Of course there is," said Albertine. "Did you expect us to live in a hovel?"

But this was too much for Flora, who, although foolish, was a well-bred girl. She did not give Margaret a chance to reply, only came up to her and, after the faintest of hesitations, leaned forward to kiss her cheek.

Ignoring her sister, she said, "You are very welcome, Cousin Margaret," and paid attention to neither Albertine's exclamation of derision nor her father's look of affront: *It is all very well for Flora to be civil, and there is no need for Bertie to be so damned rude, but, confound it, this woman is the poorest of relations, and has been engaged as housekeeper—not as friend of the family.*

The Frenchman silently noted all this drama. He was, as the Major had remarked, an inquisitive man. Albertine was beginning to interest him extremely. He had not thought that anyone could be so antagonistic, for it was surely perfectly normal to receive a cousin, however distant, with some show of warmth. This outburst of spite and rudeness from the younger sister astonished him. He saw that Miss Albertine, becoming suddenly aware that he was observing her, instantly masked her features; then she turned upon him a look that he, who believed he had lost all vanity, had to see was both inviting and provocative. Impassively, he met those large, wanton, dark eyes. He found her almost plain, with a great wide, greedy mouth, and a side tooth that protruded slightly. He saw that she was a little lame, but there was a boldness to her, a boldness he had met before in women of a very different class. To some she might be very attractive. But after that one glance, which was almost a crossing of swords, he looked away, wishing that this pantomime was done, for he was tired too, and his arms ached from carrying the two bags up the hill.

Margaret was moved nearly to tears by Flora's unexpected kindness. She had never been one for weeping. She had wept most bitterly over the baby, and she had wept for her father, but she had believed the tears were dried up, that nothing could affect her any more. And now, on this one day, she was dripping water like a fountain. She was disgusted with herself, especially as Philippe was no doubt watching her and despising her weakness. But she was too exhausted to be able to control herself, and could not reply, for her lips were trembling too badly. She could only take Flora's hand and incline her head. Then the other young lady, whose impertinence she found easier to take than this gentleness, spoke in her high, genteel voice.

"Really, Papa," said Albertine, "I am sure these two persons wish to retire to their rooms and make themselves a supper. It is too ridiculous the way we are all standing around, simply because the housekeeper and tutor have arrived together. And you know how exhausting it is for me to stand so much." And she sighed deeply and shifted her weight, as if the dragging foot were paining her. It was all the purest affectation, as Flora knew very well, for Albertine, despite her frail appearance, was a good deal tougher than most, and could often continue when her elder sister longed to retire.

The Colonel, however, was in hearty agreement with her, but before he could say so, Captain Ross spoke.

"I should like," he said in that lordly way of his that sometimes irritated the two girls, for he sounded as if the Hall were his private property, "I should like to have a word with you when you have eaten— what is your name, sir?"

"Philippe Sansterre," answered the Frenchman.

"What!" exclaimed Captain Ross, genuinely startled, then, quite indignantly, "Are you presuming to make fun of me?"

"But that is my name," said the Frenchman calmly. He raised his eyes to meet those of the Captain. He said, without a smile, "They usually call me Frenchy, as you, sir"—he bowed to the Colonel—"have already decided to do. It serves. I am, after all, a Frenchman."

Captain Ross was thinking, *This is a fine fellow to bring into the house, what bloody impudence!* But he had a considerable sense of humor, and the impudence did not entirely displease him: He in the Frenchman's place might possibly have behaved in the same way. He bestowed a grim smile on the new arrival. He said abruptly, "Well, we'll sort out what we are going to call you, sir, in due course. It don't matter. But I should still like to have a word with you. You and the young lady get yourselves a bite to eat, then you will come back here to the library."

The Frenchman bowed again. Then Flora, unsure of herself, being unused to taking the initiative, said, a little timidly, "I'll show you the way to your rooms."

Throughout all this, Captain Lewis Moore had not uttered one word. He was never a talkative man, and all the wine he had consumed was fuddling his wits. Besides, he was secretly afraid of Captain Ross, and seldom spoke in his presence. He should have been very put out, for his times with his betrothed were limited, and certainly he agreed entirely with Albertine that these two creatures, who were, after all, no better than servants, should have been sent to the kitchens straight away. Flora had no need to be jealous, for Margaret was not the type of female that appealed to him: She looked intelligent, which he detested, and he found her haggard and her clothes appalling. But he was not really concerned with Margaret, or even Flora; he was concentrating on the Frenchman, whom he instantly disliked and mistrusted. He decided that this damned foreigner must be put in his place at once, standing there looking so superior, as if he owned the whole village of Adeney Cross.

The damned foreigner had already remarked that Captain Moore was drunk, but this was a normal state of affairs with young officers, and there was something else that interested him far more. As Miss Flora sailed from the room, with Margaret and himself following, he saw the strange look that flickered between this very English Englishman and the little limping sister. It was an unmistakable look, the kind that is exchanged only between two people with a long and intimate knowledge of each other.

And the ring was on Miss Flora's finger.

He said under his breath to Margaret, "Do you not find this a very interesting household?"

She did not answer, because, though she agreed with him, she was overcome with apprehension at all that lay ahead of her. But she was thankful that the ordeal of arrival was over, and at least one member of the family had been friendly and kind. She was noticing, as Flora conducted them down the long corridors toward a steep stone staircase that led to the kitchens and the servants' quarters, that it was high time the Walters found themselves a housekeeper. There seemed to be a number of rooms that were not used at all, but apart from them, the house was in a most deplorable condition. The carpets were torn and

dirty, the stone flags had not seen water apparently
for years, and the whole place stank of dust and decay.
There were certainly mice, if not worse. This was
incomprehensible to her, for she had noticed that
both girls were dressed in the most expensive clothes,
and the Colonel's library held some magnificent
furniture and a great deal of silver, as well as excellent paintings and books. There could be no lack of
money, only a complete lack of care, and her eyes
moved to the handsome Miss Flora in bewilderment:
How could the young lady let everything fall to
pieces when there must be plenty of servants and she
had only to give the orders?

Flora was quite unaware of this criticism, but then,
unlike Albertine, she was not observant. Her mind
was mainly on herself and Lewis; if she had suspected
Margaret's thoughts, she would have instantly flown
into a self-defensive temper. It simply did not matter
to her that the house was dirty, and if sometimes she
grew cross at the poor, usually cold food that was
served to them at mealtimes, it never struck her that
she might do something about it.

She remarked, "This is a very old house. I hope the
work will not be too difficult for you, but there are
plenty of maids. Not," she added, unaware of Margaret's astonished look, "that I know any of them, but
then, Mrs. Beeston—she's the cook—sees to that, and
I am so busy, and one has so little time. I expect you
will find them good girls. They all come from the village. They don't sleep here, except for Mrs. Beeston,
and she has a cottage in the garden. Look out for
those steps, please. I fell myself once in the dark. I
dare say you are too fatigued to see everything
tonight, but through the kitchens is the oldest part of

the Hall. They say it was built in the eleventh century. There is not much left of it, it's mostly ruins.
There is one room left standing, but it can't be
opened, so we've never been inside. My sister calls it
the Bluebeard Room, which is rather horrid. It is a
story, you know, for children, but I think it must
frighten them, I would never tell my children such a
nasty story."

The Frenchman said, "By Monsieur Perrault."

Up till then Flora had scarcely noticed him. In any
case, her vision was bemused by Lewis; she was only
just aware that other men existed. She turned her
head to look at him. She could not see him very
clearly, for the lighting was as economical as the
cleaning: These long corridors were scarcely lit. Margaret, disliking the shadows, swore to herself that she
would soon have lamps everywhere. She did not care
for the thought of walking here alone at night, nor had
she enjoyed the description of the Bluebeard Room.
She remembered the story, which her father had
sometimes recounted to his young pupils.

Flora thought she did not care much for the tutor.
He, like Margaret, did not match the picture in her
imagination. She had already made an image of him
in her mind: He would be like a stage Frenchman,
a comic, foppish creature with a tendency to caper;
he would make wild gestures all the time, and
speak in so foreign a voice that they would all laugh
at him. But there was nothing comic about this for-
midably tall gentleman, and she knew she would
never dare make fun of him. He would probably be a
very severe teacher—he might even be able to keep
Albertine in order. She answered him nervously, having no idea what he was talking about.

She said, "Oh, I don't know, I'm sure. It is just a tale, after all." Then she said, in a shy voice, "Do we really call you Frenchy?"

"Why not?" he said, smiling. "It is a good-enough name."

"You'll not think it rude?" persisted Flora.

"I am sure you could not be rude to anyone, mademoiselle," he answered, and at this Flora, who adored being flattered, changed her mind and decided she was going to like him enormously. She said, "I think I am going to enjoy my lessons," then, "The kitchens are down there. But first I will show you your rooms, which are right at the top of the stairs."

Margaret saw that she would spend her days running up and down stairs. This back stairway, obviously intended for the servants, was uncarpeted, steep, and slippery. But she and the Frenchman followed Flora, and presently they came to a small, dark hallway, with a slit of a window at the end, and two attic rooms.

"One of these used to belong to Mrs. Beeston," said Flora, "but she prefers the tied cottage. It's hers as long as she works on the estate, you see." She added, with the alarming candor that seemed to be part of her childish nature, "She is not a very good cook. I do hope you can cook, Margaret. I love food, and what we get is so horrid."

"I'll do my best for you," returned Margaret, then opened the door of what was apparently to be her new home.

Flora said uneasily, "It is a trifle small. Perhaps . . . I am sure we could make it more comfortable."

It was indeed a trifle small, and Margaret's depressed heart was in no way raised by the sight of it.

It seemed to her little better than a box; one could almost compare it with a coffin. There was an iron bedstead, as yet with no linen on it, a small cupboard, and a dressing table. There was no means of heating, and no lighting except for a tallow candle in a broken cup. There were not even curtains at the window. The prisoners across the way surely had better accommodations.

Flora was eyeing her so guiltily, however, that she had to smile, feeling as if she were with some discouraged child. She said, "Oh, in a little while I shall have it so cosy that you will envy me."

But as this silly and willing young lady conducted the Frenchman to his room, no doubt a box also, Margaret sat down on the bed, which creaked dismally beneath her, and for a moment covered her face with her hands.

The tiny room enclosed her. Once, as a child of eight, she had been shut in a cupboard by mistake. It had only been for a few minutes, but a screaming panic had possessed her. She had beaten on the door with her fists, and when her mother rescued her she came down with such a high fever that they had to summon a physician. Since then she had been unable to endure confined spaces. Removing her hands from her face, she surveyed with dismay the four walls, which seemed to lean in upon her.

She opened the window, which looked down on the garden. The rush of cold air restored her, but did nothing to heighten her spirits, and she looked down into the dark and wished to God she were back home, even if it meant poverty, loneliness, and nothing to eat.

It was a long way from the young girl who had

believed herself in love and who had smashed that
love as effectively as if she had taken a hammer to it.
It was a long way from a young man who had so
adored her, and who now looked at her with hate and
contempt. In that depleted moment, alone in this
cold, ugly, unwelcoming room, Margaret was aware of
that strange transition from love to no-love, and, in
defiance of everything that had happened, she could
only feel bewildered and appalled by so complete a
reversal.

In that moment of non-time she was back again in
that over-ornate drawing room—the French left no
surface without marquetry or ornament—waiting for
the arrival of her father's pupils.

He made his bow to her. She had never seen him
before. She was eighteen, very pretty and perfectly
aware of it. There had always been plenty of young
men, both here and at home. She saw the instant
admiration in his eyes, and was delighted, for he was
so prodigiously handsome—she had never seen so tall
a man, and such great, dark eyes . . . It was obvious
that, in addition to his looks, he was both wealthy
and well-bred, the kind of gentleman she seldom met
socially, and she rose at once to the challenge,
excited, not yet in love, determined to make the best
impression.

*I was the silliest girl. I was not even a nice girl. I
was quite a horrid girl.*

He said, "I have not, I believe, had the pleasure of
seeing you before."

She hesitated. She spoke French very well; Papa
had seen to that. She had, of course, an English
accent, but then, the Parisians seemed to find that
charming, even complimented her upon it. This

gentleman perhaps thought her one of the Comtesse's young relatives. If he knew she was simply the daughter of the family's English tutor, he might at once dismiss her from his mind, for the French aristocracy lived in a world of its own, and danced its protocol as formally as a minuet. But, after all, she had no choice, and though she was silly, she still possessed a certain amount of practical common sense.

She answered composedly, "My father teaches English here to the young ladies. Madame la Comtesse has asked him to escort them to the Opéra, to meet their parents. I am here to fetch them."

She saw the guard come down over his face. He looked at her, then away. She knew that he was prepared to say good-bye very courteously and leave her. She was only too aware, as she had always been, that to be pretty was not enough. For the most part, gentlemen did not court tutors' daughters: They simply, if given the chance, seduced them. She did not know, of course, that he was a Marquis of the *ancien régime*, but he was plainly a gentleman, and she had no right to be surprised if this were the end of their brief acquaintance.

Then he said, "Do you come here every day?"

"Oh no. My father does, of course. I am usually at home."

"Where is your home?"

She told him, after another hesitation. It was a quiet *quartier* of Paris, not rich, but good enough in a modest, decent way. It did not shame her. She was quite a little snob in those days; if she had lived in a poorer district, she would not have told him. But then, of course, she did not know the Frenchman at all. Afterward, she suspected that he understood her far better than she had realized. It was to his credit, and not to hers, that he did not despise her.

He said, "I should like to have your father's permission to call on you."

She could hardly believe it, for what he was saying was *I do not intend to seduce you, I am prepared to come as a suitor.* Though this was not yet entirely true. He had not fallen in love, he was simply charmed by this shy little English miss, with her delicate, unrouged complexion, the soft curling hair, unpowdered, and the delightful accent she tried so hard to overcome.

And so it started. And so it started . . .

Margaret at twenty-eight looked back on Margaret at eighteen and marveled at the wanton stupidity of what she had done. Never for one moment, of course, had she ever loved Henry, who was nothing better than a cheap adventurer, who believed her to be wealthy, thought she could give him the entrée to a society that was as alien to her as to him. After the quarrel she had turned to him because he was there —the Henrys of this world are always there—and there was the shock of it all, the wine she was not yet used to, and the dangerous sympathy that Henry knew so well how to extend. She had been a stupid bitch of a girl to behave so outrageously in the first place, provoking so unnecessary and vulgar a scene, and by this time she was pretty well out of her mind, hysterical and frantic, so she let Henry take her to his rooms—so desperate that she hardly realized what she was doing.

Henry must have been a disillusioned man, with a weeping girl on his hands who screamed and sobbed at him, imploring a sympathy that was not in his nature to give. He must have been thankful to be rid of her.

And then, of course, it was too late. She thought now that perhaps it had not been too late at all. If she had only come back to Philippe . . . If nothing else, it might have saved Papa his job. It might even have saved something of her reputation.

But in the morning she ran back home—what a terrible, bedraggled sight she must have been—and then the whole scandal blew, the Marquis jilted by the tutor's little daughter, the lover she had apparently taken out of revenge, and how everyone must have laughed; no one could have talked of anything else for at least three days.

Oh, poor Philippe—no wonder he had been so angry with her. No wonder now that he looked on her with cold contempt. It was as if the gentleman who said *There is no friendship between us* slid over the shadow of a stranger who said *Je t'aime*. It was cruelly unbearable: Never mind how much she deserved it, she found she could not endure it.

At that moment she was on the point of leaping to her feet and running down the stairs, going to God knows what, anywhere to get away from such an intolerable reminder.

But when Flora returned, with the Frenchman behind her, Margaret simply said calmly that she would like to see the kitchens, and would much appreciate something to eat. For, after all, one thing she had learned during these weary years was that there was no point in creating a drama, one had to go on living. She came down the stairs, with barely a glance at Philippe. No doubt his room was equally appalling, but he would never mention it to her, and

these things mattered less to the gentlemen. She did
not think any more about running away, and, indeed,
such behavior did not lie in her nature. The kitchens,
she saw, were as bad as she had expected—rambling,
dirty, and untidy—but Mrs. Beeston, even if she could
not cook, seemed an amiable creature: fat, rosy-
cheeked, and stupid, with the inevitable cat that
followed always at her feet, and sometimes sat on her
shoulder while she was cooking.

The two of them presently sat down at a wooden
table, to eat a substantial rabbit stew, which was
reasonably cooked and probably far better than the
more sophisticated meals served in the dining room.

When Mrs. Beeston, wearing a conspiratorial air,
brought them two tankards of hot, spiced ale, Margaret began to feel that this might not be so unendurable after all. But she barely glanced at the Frenchman, and the two of them had exchanged only
monosyllables during the meal.

"You always ask me for anything you want,
ma'am," said Mrs. Beeston cheerfully. "We always gets
what we wants here, there are no questions asked,
nor should there be. It's Thomas as caught this rabbit.
They don't like such stuff upstairs, they're set on
these foreign fal-lals, can't understand it myself, but
down belowstairs we has good, wholesome food, and,
if you'll pardon me saying so, ma'am, you look as if
you could do with it. And the gentleman here don't
look over-nourished either."

Margaret saw that with a little tact and flattery it
would be easy to take over the cooking of those foreign fal-lals. It seemed to her that Mrs. Beeston would
mind nothing, provided it did not involve her in
any extra work. She drank down the ale, which she

found warming and delicious, while her eyes roamed over the kitchen. She saw that the range was surprisingly polished and gave out a magnificent heat, while the larder, when she went to investigate it, proved to be well-stocked, probably with a great deal that was never seen upstairs. There would obviously be a great deal of diplomacy involved, and she had not yet seen the rest of the staff, who had returned to the village for the night, but she was sure that, with any luck, she could depend on Mrs. Beeston for an ally.

Then, after the Frenchman had left the kitchen to see Colonel Walters and Captain Ross, Margaret carried sheets and blankets upstairs, together with a warming pan that Mrs. Beeston insisted on giving her, and went to her room.

She made up her bed and set out her few belongings. But, despite her exhaustion, she did not immediately undress, and instead went over to the uncurtained window and gazed down at the old ruins at the far end of the garden.

It was bitter cold, and the wind was still high. There was a sliver of moon. She opened the window wide, despite the cold, and rested her elbows on the sill, her eyes moving over the wild garden—*My God, do they do nothing in this house, it is like a jungle*— the bare, leafless trees, and the ruins black against the sky. Margaret could smell the sea, and this made her think again of the Loving Sands and her foolish bonnet, which, poor bit of cloth and ribbon, had met such a horrid fate. Her eyes shifted to the ruins. That one over there must be the Bluebeard Room, for it was the only section that was in any way habitable. The rest was simply walls and archways and jagged pieces of broken stone. There was nothing particularly

sinister about the outside of the room, but it frightened her—perhaps it was Miss Flora's exaggerated
account of it. She could not help thinking of Perrault's story, and somehow it no longer seemed a fantasy. She could see the poor, foolish young wife who
disobeyed her husband, who found the terrible headless corpses of her predecessors and then was unable
to wash the blood off the key.

How terrified she must have been as she waited
there, her sister at her side, for the arrival of her
brothers, who would rescue her.

Sister Anne, sister Anne, is there anyone coming?

Then Margaret, immersed in her own fantasy, gave
a faint cry, for there was someone coming, a shadow
that moved behind the trees. She stared, wild-eyed, her
heart pounding, as if somehow she were the guilty
wife, as if this might be her brothers, her only hope of
salvation. But then the moon went in, the dark storm
clouds raced across it so that her vision was blotted
out. When the silver light filtered through again,
there was no one there. The garden was bare and
deserted. The only sound was that of the wind sigh-
ing through the trees. Then, in spite of her fright
sleep descended on her, and at last she climbed into
bed and fell fathoms deep into slumber.

The Frenchman was unable to sleep. Like Margaret, he spent a while looking out of the window,
and, like her, he perceived the movement down below.
It interested him, but did not serve to take his mind
off that appalling meeting by the sea wall, which had
affected him far more deeply than he cared to admit
to himself, and certainly far more than Margaret
realized.

It was damnable, unspeakable. Why, in the name of God, should he come to this out-of-the-way little village to run into the young woman who had caused him an agony and humiliation that he hoped to forget? He knew now that he had never forgotten, though she had changed greatly, lost all the soft roundness, the charming pink and white coloring that was so very English. At his first sight of her, he believed her to have aged in appearance by double the actual years—it was only when she talked and wept and grew angry that, dismayingly, she seemed the same. He did not love her any more. He thought he hated her. Or perhaps that was too strong, too emotional, and, after all, he was no longer a green boy. She was not worth the hating; he simply despised her, and despised himself for having been such a fool and behaved so badly. What had she ever been, after all? A little provincial English miss, the daughter of a tutor who earned his money giving English lessons to the young man's friends. She had some education, for her father had seen to that, and considerable surface breeding, enough—or so he thought—not to disgrace or shame him. It had proved surface indeed. She had also a soft, low, pretty voice, and this she still had; it was one reason why he had preferred to keep his eyes on her, for otherwise he might have imagined she was the same young girl he had loved so passionately.

He thought, *Why am I here?* For he was not as badly placed as Margaret—he could go back to Elchester when he chose, this very minute if he so desired. The Major would certainly not be pleased; he was, it seemed, a personal friend of the stupid Colonel Walters, and this sudden return might put him in an embarrassing social situation. This did not trouble

the Frenchman; the English were, after all, his
enemies, although he never had felt any particular
hate for them. And he had, after all, a perfectly
reasonable excuse. On his return to the library, he
had been informed curtly that his duties would not
simply be comprised of the two hours a day of
French lessons. He would also have to escort the
young ladies to the Cross Prison, where, like half the
inhabitants of Adeney Cross, they performed a weekly
charity by buying from the prisoners' market. It
seemed an odd amusement to the Frenchman, rather
like watching animals behind bars, and he knew he
would detest this particular excursion. But apparently
Miss Albertine was most charitable (although it was
difficult for him to imagine that this might be in her
nature), and often went on her own to bring little
comforts to the poor men enclosed there. However,
this was by no means all required of him. There
would be various duties about the Hall (and in this
the Major had been correct), for he was expected not
only to rearrange the books in the library, which was
reasonable, but to tidy up the garden, which certainly
was not.

The Frenchman remembered that, while impassively listening to the Colonel recount his duties, he
had grown aware that Captain Ross's eyes had been
fixed upon him. It was as if both men were expecting
him to throw a theatrical rage and walk out of the
house. He suspected that they might be relieved if he
did so, and this served to confirm his decision to
stay. He should, of course, have refused. He was an
officer and a parole prisoner; no one in the world had
the right to use him as a servant, and it was incredible
that these two men, both officers and gentlemen,

should even suggest it. But his curiosity was now
aroused, and so he quietly agreed. As he met Captain
Ross's gaze of complete astonishment, he derived a
certain malicious pleasure from his decision.

He glanced once more at Captain Ross as he left
the room. He did not find him a prepossessing man,
with his grim, almost brutal, face, and the empty
sleeve tucked into his pocket. But the look that came
from him was one of assessment, as if he did not
understand. It was suspicious, a little incredulous, as
if he could not make up his mind.

He remembered this look again as he moved away
from the window. Perhaps the Captain suspected him
of being a spy. He decided at this point that he could
not go to bed yet. He would only lie awake, thinking of Margaret and the old days. He would only be
asking again, *Why am I here?* And this last was a
question he did not wish to answer; he did not consider himself a self-deceiving man, but there was
some truth deep down that he could not disinter, like
the secret of the Bluebeard Room.

And with this he decided to take a little walk in
the garden and inspect these mysterious ruins. The
English were mad on ruins. He understood that most
decent English homes were haunted, that it was
fashionable to possess a headless specter or two, a nun
walled up, or some skeletal apparition to choke the
life out of unwelcome guests. In France ghosts were
not so encouraged, though in his father's mansion,
now burned out and destroyed, there had been some
tale of a white lady. The Frenchman had never seen
the white lady, and did not believe in her existence.
He was not afraid of ghosts. He had discovered a long
time ago that living men were far more terrifying: He

had seen the fishwives marching down from Les
Halles, the mob storming the Bastille, the *tricoteuses*
at the foot of the guillotine. A white lady after that
would be a refuge.

Before he set out, he fastened about his throat the
blue muffler given him by the old lady at Elchester. It
was the first time he had worn it. The occasion seemed
appropriate: It had been cold enough during the day,
and now it was fiercely so. The hour was midnight.
He could hear the chiming of a church clock somewhere in the village. This, then, was the hour of
ghosts. Perhaps the shadow he had seen was some
dread apparition from the Walters' past. He grinned a
little at the thought, then noiselessly shut his door
behind him and stepped out into the corridor.

He paused for a second, staring at the door of
Margaret's room. He had no wish to see her or speak
to her, but once again the impossibility of it all overcame him, the inconceivable irony. He had seen her
for the last time ten years ago, he believed, and a more
appalling parting could not be imagined—even now
the recollection of it seared him. After that there was
the scandal, the humiliation, and then France was
overturned, so that such personal things hardly mattered. And here he was, ten years later, in England,
an enemy prisoner, and across a narrow corridor from
his own room lay this young woman, whose acquaintance with him had been such that he had never fallen
in love again.

He came quietly and quickly down the stairs. Despite his height, he was not a heavy man, and he had
learned some time ago to move without noise. Indeed,
he owed his life to this ability, for he had slipped
out of his house, dressed like a Paris workman, and

into the streets, so unobtrusively that no one noticed him.

The Hall was silent, empty, and very cold. Presumably, the young ladies would be fast asleep, Miss Flora no doubt dreaming of her dull, drunken English captain and Miss Albertine . . . Well, he had no idea what Miss Albertine would be dreaming of, but perhaps the two dreams coincided more than the elder sister knew. How strange they should both be enamored of such a very uninteresting and boorish young man. But then, Henry had never seemed to him the kind of person one would look at twice.

The Frenchman looked once into the library. He had already remarked the fine collection of books. He was certain that the Colonel never so much as turned a page, but perhaps the collection had been made by some more literate ancestor. The arranging and cataloguing of these books would be a pleasure, and nobody would notice if he sometimes removed a volume for his private reading.

He went down the kitchen stairs, through the kitchens, and out by the back door, which was unbolted. He noticed, as Margaret had, the squalor and untidiness around him, and suspected that the servants were due for a shock, for he did not believe Margaret would leave things in such a state. The washing-up had not been done; the debris from the dinner was not yet removed. But the range still glowed, and he paused to warm his hands at it.

He crossed the garden to the eleventh-century ruins at the back. He could see Mrs. Beeston's small cottage, the windows dark. No ghosts barred his way, no groaning sounded in his ears, though an owl hooted suddenly, and this, to his irritation, made him jump. Perhaps his disbelief in ghosts was not as deep-rooted as he chose to imagine. But mainly his thoughts were concentrated on the quite extraordinary state of the garden; like Captain Ross, he could not imagine how the Colonel could have let it become such a jungle. The grass could not have been cut for years: It came wetly above his knees, and within it grew a tangle of weeds, thistles, and nettles. If it really was his duty to subdue this wilderness, he might consider himself in the rank of a galley slave.

The whole scene presented an ideal setting for the ghost-lover—the long, tangled grass, the barren trees, the clouds scudding across the sky, the thin, pale moon, and the Loving Sands, down below the side wall. In his ears sounded the wind; in his nostrils was the smell of the sea. And at the end was the old part of the Hall, blackened ruins rising like broken teeth against the sky.

The Frenchman went eagerly toward them. They seemed to match his temper—they were stark and lonely and grim. As he strode on, he tripped against something in the grass, and nearly measured his length in this jungle. He stooped down to see what it was. For an alarmed moment he thought it might be some kind of trap. The Walters family, with their complete disregard for the more comfortable amenities of civilization, seemed very much the kind to put some hideous gin down to catch thieves and marauders by the heels.

However, nothing bit into his ankle, and his fingers closed around something cold and smooth and hard.

It was an empty wine bottle.

There was nothing remarkable in this—not even in the fact that it was a French wine. The English might be at war with France, but they had no quarrel with the beautiful products of its grapes. It had always struck him as ironic that even now, in the few English households he had visited, French wine was still served. But nonetheless it was a trifle odd that people should sling wine bottles into the Hall garden, and even as the Frenchman considered this he encountered yet another. It must be one of the servants. He wondered how many more bottles would turn up when the garden was tidied, and the thought of this entertained him, so that he vowed to cut the grass as soon as possible.

He was now close to the ruins. He saw at once the room described as Bluebeard's.

It did not strike him as alarming. It was a ruin and it was formidable, like all buildings of so far-off a century. The wind and rain had tempered the heavy stone so that it was a dull and slimy black. There was a heavy door, which accounted for the family legend. The room stood almost alone, with only the ruined wall running beside it, and it was completely intact, down to the bolted door. Enemies must have blasted this fortress—how strange that this one section should be left standing.

He peered down at it, rubbing his hand against the surface, then tried to shift the vast bolt. But it was completely rusted and would not budge an inch, partly cemented by the thick lichen and moss that overgrew it.

Et alors, madame, the villain in the Perrault story had said. *Vous êtes entrée dans le cabinet* . . .

Served her right, the poor, silly creature, curious like all women, waiting excitedly until her husband was out of the way, then running to disobey him and unlock the door. But it must have been an appalling moment when he demanded the key and saw the blood on it, the blood that nothing could remove.

The Frenchman was not, after all, a frightened girl,
but it was an ugly story, a strange tale with which to
regale one's children before they went to sleep. He
tried the bolt again, but it still did not move. He
doubted that anyone had moved it for centuries; that
door could only be blasted open. The girls had no
reason to be afraid—however inquisitive they were,
they could never get in. Yet it was strange that such a
legend should have sprung up, and he promised himself a closer look at the room in the morning. No one
could reproach him for spying, since he had a perfect
excuse as the new gardener.

It was too cold to stay here. He turned and then, to
his startled shame, he gave a gasp and swore, step-
ping backward quickly and once again nearly losing
his balance over that confounded bottle.

The little ghost was for a second more alarmed
than himself. It was Miss Albertine, clad in a long
gray cloak, her dark hair blowing in the wind. She
flung her hands to her breast in a melodramatic
fashion, and stared at him. The moon briefly slid
through the clouds and illumined her face, with its
huge eyes, and the mouth a little open.

He said quickly, "My apologies, mademoiselle. I
see that, like me, you could not sleep. But I assure
you, I did not mean to frighten you."

She came up to him. He noted that she wore perfume, an overbearing one. It was odd that she should
do so for a midnight promenade. She was so close to
him that she almost touched him. She said in her
small, high, breathy voice, "Oh, you did frighten
me!"

"You frightened me too, Miss Albertine. I thought
I was meeting the ancestral ghost."

Then she smiled, looking him up and down. She

put her hand on his arm, as if to steady herself. "I am so very pleased you have come," she said.

He wondered how long she had been watching him. He said, a little warily, "I gather from your father that you are very anxious to improve your French."

"Oh yes, oh yes! My sister is not, of course, interested—*du tout, du tout.* Is that not how you say it? But then, Flora is not really interested in anything but marriage. We women are such little geese, aren't we? I dare say you despise us. But we're not all so silly."

He was beginning to find this conversation disturbing. If this had not been his employer's daughter, and this his very first evening, he would have been convinced that she was flirting with him. And certainly she was almost pressing against him, the hand on his arm holding him quite firmly. He was about to say in a stern way that she should go in, she would catch cold, when she spoke again.

"Papa thinks you are going to tidy this garden," she said.

"It certainly needs it!"

"Yes, but that is not work for you. You are a gentleman. Gentlemen don't do such things. It is very naughty of Papa even to suggest it," said Albertine. "You are not to cut this grass, Frenchy. I absolutely forbid it."

"Oh," he said, "I am not so proud, mademoiselle. And a little hard work never hurt anyone."

"It is not dignified!"

"I don't think my dignity will suffer," said the Frenchman. "And I think you should go back to your room, mademoiselle. It is far too cold to be out here. I am going back myself."

She said coaxingly, "Would you like a glass of
wine, Frenchy?"

"Mademoiselle, it is nearly one in the morning."

"Oh, but that is the best hour. If you will come in,
I'll give you a glass. I have a bottle in my room." She
added, with a coyness that took him utterly aback, for
it was vulgar and quite unexpected in a young lady
such as herself, "Of course, I am not inviting you to
my room. You must not misunderstand me. But I
always keep some wine by me, and I'll go upstairs
and fetch the bottle down. We can drink in the
library. It is very good for one, I think. It keeps off
the evening chill."

He did not answer this directly. He could only
believe her touched in the wits. No one in his own
country would ever speak in such a fashion. He said
suddenly, "And what do you do with your bottles
when you have finished with them, Miss Albertine?"

This plainly took her aback, and she moved away
a little, much to his relief. She made a fluttering gesture with her hand. She reminded him of a moth. She
said in that vague, high voice of hers, "Oh, I don't
know. What strange questions you ask. I dare say the
servants . . . After all, that is what servants are for.
But you are not a servant, monsieur, and I don't
think you should do servants' work. Now, I want you
to promise me not to cut the grass. Promise, Frenchy.
Please."

He answered sternly, deriving a certain pleasure
from the ridiculous words, "I am your father's servant, mademoiselle, and I do what he asks me to do.
And I am quite certain Colonel Walters would not
like your talking to me in such a fashion, especially at

this hour of night. You should go back to your room, and I will go back to mine."

"After we've drunk our glass of wine together!"

He only said, "Good night, Miss Albertine," and turned to go.

She burst into a little trill of laughter. "Oh, how stuffy you are! I didn't think the French were so prissy. But I still find you very attractive. I always have liked the French. It is so silly that we are at war. I hope Boney wins, then we'll all be French. I find him a most remarkable man, and so handsome with that dark hair falling over his forehead. If he had been in charge, there would never have been a Revolution. Didn't he say something about the whole Revolution being put down with a whiff of grapeshot? I would like to have a portrait of him to hang in my room, but of course Papa would be so angry. I expect you would like a portrait too, Frenchy, but you mustn't say so , must you, for if you did, I might run to Papa and say, That Frenchy is a spy, he must go at once to the Cross Prison and be thrown into the *cachot.* You see, I know some French. The English call it the Black Hole. It's a dreadful place. You wouldn't like it at all, would you, Frenchy?"

He eyed her silently. If this continued, he might find himself back at Elchester sooner than he had intended. He had not the faintest intention of seducing his employer's daughter, whom, indeed, he found singularly unattractive, but it was looking unmistakably as if his employer's daughter intended to seduce him.

She continued in the same breathy voice, "Well, they can't put me in the Black Hole. And, do you know, I'm sure Boney will win. He is doing so well, he has captured Naples, and he is bound to invade us any moment. Isn't that exciting? Oh, Frenchy, do say it's exciting. I can hardly wait for the end of the war, I think it's all so wonderful."

He refused to answer any of this, merely repeated, "Good night," and began to walk away.

She pouted. He could not see her clearly, but she spoke in a pouting voice. He suspected she was making little faces. "Oh," she said, "you're being stuffy again." Suddenly she shook her fist at him. "Now, don't you make me angry, Frenchy. If you make me angry, I shall go straight to Papa. I shall say, he is a wicked Frenchy, he tries to make love to me. And do you know what will happen then? Papa will take down his horsewhip and he'll beat you, he'll beat you to death. I shall enjoy that, and you'll never, never see France again. So you must be nice to me, Frenchy. You must do everything I say, and . . ." She paused, then said, in a soft, insinuating voice, "You'd like to escape, wouldn't you? I could help you, you know. I'd do anything for a man who was nice to me —really I would."

He swung back to her. He was so angry that he could have boxed her ears. He said savagely, "Mademoiselle, I am on parole. I have given my word not to escape. This, I imagine, means nothing to you, but it does to me. I have no intention of doing anything you ask, and I have no wish to escape. You are behaving outrageously, and you should be ashamed of yourself. If I am to stay here at all, you will please understand that I am simply the tutor, I am engaged by your father to teach you French, and that is all. If you ever speak to me in such a fashion again, it will not be you, Miss Albertine, who goes to your father. I will go, I will tell him that I cannot stay here, and I will explain why. And now I suggest you go straight back to your room, and we will both try to forget this ridiculous episode."

And as he spoke, he thought that this must be the end of it. No woman could endure being so spoken to; this little bitch would surely be banging on Papa's door with talk of rape or worse, and he would end in prison, perhaps in the celebrated *cachot*. He began once again to walk back to the house, but small hands caught at his own—they were surprisingly strong for so tiny a creature—and the next instant she positively flung herself upon him, crying out, "Oh, but you must listen, it's dreadfully important, I vow I shall not let you go until you do."

He was so taken aback that he forgot himself altogether. He gave her a push, and she fell backward onto the grass, sitting there awkwardly, half hidden, legs apart, staring up at him. Then, to his amazement, she burst out laughing, and continued to laugh, quite hysterically.

It really was too much. It would now be not only rape but assault, but he did not care—all he wanted was to put as wide a space as possible between himself and this lunatic girl, whom he found not only wild and mad but positively repulsive, for all she was young and not ill-looking.

She called after him as he walked away, "You will do as I ask in the end, Frenchy. I know you will. I hate people who cross me. But I like you all the same. I always like men who hurt me. It's so exciting. I think you are very exciting. Next time we meet, you may even want to kiss me. And perhaps I shall not let you. Won't that be amusing, Frenchy? Oh, I am so glad you've come."

Then it struck him that in the name of common
humanity he could not leave her sitting there in the
wet grass. After all, she was lame; perhaps she could
not get up. But when, very reluctantly, he turned, she
was already running toward the house. She was, he
noticed, very agile, though she moved in an odd, hopping fashion. She ran so quickly that almost instantly
she was out of sight.

He waited until she was gone, then went to his
room as fast as he could. When he reached it and sat
down on his bed, he found that his forehead was
damp with sweat. He began to laugh. He had defied
the *harengères,* he had escaped the bloody Paris mob,
and here he was, worsted—he had to admit it—by this
strange, mad little slut who was a colonel's daughter,
and had presumably been brought up to be *une fille
bien elevée.* And who threw bottles out of the window. He would at that moment have given a great
deal for the proffered glass of wine, but certainly he
was not going to pay the price exacted. If this kind of
thing continued, he would certainly lay in a bottle for
emergencies.

He flung himself back on the bed, hands beneath
his head. What the devil did she think she was doing,
behaving in so insane a fashion? Had her lameness so
affected her that she was mad for men and for
power? Then, as he lay there, a further thought came
to him. What was she doing out at that hour of night,
in her long cloak and smothered in perfume? It
seemed to him, on reflection, that she had not come
from the direction of the house, so it must have been
from some assignation. Colonel Walters plainly had
no idea what he had spawned; one day there would
be a great shock in store for him.

The Frenchman swore again, thanked God that he

had no daughters, then at last undressed himself. He had realized that he was living a non-life, abstracted from humanity, but he had never bargained on being thrown into this kind of lunacy. He resolved to keep as far away from Miss Albertine as possible. During the lessons her sister would, thank God, be there, and though Miss Flora seemed a trifle childish, she was on the whole amiable, and certainly far too obsessed with her betrothed to trouble her head with French parole officers.

And, brooding on this, he at last drifted into an uneasy sleep, where, as always, he found himself back in Provence, the one place where he had found real happiness.

Chapter Four

As morning always seems better than the night before, Margaret felt more in control of herself when she awoke. But she gave herself a severe talking-to as she dressed. She had plainly behaved like a fool. If Philippe chose to stay here, it was his business and nothing to do with her. Certainly, it would be simple enough for him to return to Elchester: As an officer on parole, he had no need to accept this situation, especially as the work involved was not suited to a gentleman. But if he stayed, it did not matter. Besides

—she put up her hair as she told herself this, pulling it tightly back so that the curls did not show—their paths would hardly cross. He would be mainly instructing the young ladies, and all good luck to him; she had learned to recognize a troublemaker when she saw one, and Miss Albertine was not going to be the easiest of pupils. But no doubt he would be able to deal with her. Poverty and loneliness taught one how easily normally charming people could become insolent and ill-bred; the Frenchman also would have acquired this knowledge. And, while he was teaching, she would be spending most of her life belowstairs, dealing with the buying of provisions and coping with the servants. She would certainly not dine with the family, and her encounters with the two young ladies—she found it hard to think of them as cousins—would concern the laundering and mending of their clothes, the tidying of their rooms, and perhaps the organizing of their parties.

And, reflecting on this, she went downstairs, a little apprehensively, wearing a neat dark-blue dress that she had made herself.

She knew immediately that she was not going to keep as remote from the family as she had hoped. She heard the angry voices before she arrived at the first landing.

She saw that the tirade came from Captain Lewis Moore, who, so red with anger that he no longer looked handsome, was shouting and waving his fists at Philippe. She was both distressed and shocked, and would have given everything to be able to run down into the kitchens, but the two men blocked her path. She shot a desperate look at the Frenchman, then saw that the humiliation was not his but that of this

horrid young man, who was behaving like a tavern
bully and using such words as she doubted Miss Flora
had ever heard from him, or, indeed, from anyone
else.

The Frenchman was listening impassively, not
answering a word. The only expression on his face
was one of ironic contempt. Margaret knew little of
what had happened during the past ten years, and,
indeed, she had never concerned herself much with
French politics. She could not know that someone
who had faced the Paris mob, had heard the fishwives
shrieking for blood, was unlikely now to be moved
by a blustering and ill-mannered young man.

Captain Moore appeared to be accusing him of
somehow misbehaving last night in the garden by the
ruins. It all sounded like nonsense, and Margaret was
so indignant that she was about to tap Lewis on the
arm and demand that he let her pass. But his next
words checked her.

"If you so much as speak to her again," he was
shouting, "I vow I'll have you flogged and hanged on
the nearest tree. To insult a young girl like that, and
one so small and defenseless . . . But it's all we expect
of you foreigners. If I had my way, you'd all be
clapped in irons. I'm going to see her father now. She
is in a terrible state. I understand you tried to kiss
her, then, because she refused, knocked her down. I
find it almost impossible to believe . . ."

He stopped, mainly for breath. The Frenchman
still said nothing. His eyes moved for a second to Margaret, who now neither dared interrupt nor move.

Lewis seemed unaware of her presence. He went on
again, a little less sure of himself, but still making
enough noise to bring the ceiling down. "Poor little

Albertine!" he exclaimed. "I cannot bring myself to understand it. Of course, you were drunk—not that that's any excuse. She said you were waving an empty wine bottle. You unmitigated bastard! I swear I'll—"

He half raised his hand. Then Margaret could endure it no longer, and sprang forward. It was perhaps the threatened blow, or perhaps the realization that this was becoming more dangerous than a quarrel, and that Philippe was not going to accept this behavior much longer. She knew well enough that if he struck Lewis, he would be instantly put in prison, and the thought of this was more than she could take. She was too upset to see that neither man was pleased by her intervention, and she stepped between them on the assumption that they could hardly knock each other down over her body.

They were both tall, and she felt as if enclosed between two trees. But she said very coldly to Lewis's shoulder (which was all that came within her line of vision), "If you are referring to last night, Captain Moore, I can assure you that you are quite mistaken."

He was outraged. That this woman, who was a mere housekeeper, should presume to interrupt him was unbelievable.

But she gave him no chance to tell her so. She went on, "I myself was with Monsieur Sansterre last night. Like him, I was too fatigued after my journey to sleep, and when I saw him from my window I decided to go down and join him, in the hope that the night air might calm me. I can assure you that your accusations are quite unfounded. I believe I did catch a glimpse of Miss Albertine, but certainly there was no conversation between us. Or, indeed, anything else."

Lewis was looking down at her as she now moved

to one side. His color had subsided. His face grew
watchful and a little pale. "And may I ask," he said,
with dignity, "what you two were doing there, in
your pursuit of the night air?"

The Frenchman began to speak, but Margaret spoke
across him, with some indignation. "We were doing
nothing to be ashamed of," she said. "Why should we
be? Is it not possible for two people to walk in the
garden without being accused of bad behavior? But if
you really wish to know, sir, I was a little curious
about what you call the Bluebeard Room. I do not
like mysteries, and I wanted to see if it was really
locked. I imagined there might be some side
entrance, but I see there is not. I thought we might
use it as a storeroom. However, it is obvious we cannot. It's a pity."

He did not answer immediately. Then he spoke,
with a cold viciousness that frightened her, and she
thought again of the innocent Miss Flora, who could
have no possible defense against his cruelty. He said,
"A fine pair we seem to be saddled with! How dare
you answer me like that, miss? To speak to me so
impudently, and meddling too, with things that are
no concern of yours whatsoever. So you're nosing
around, are you? What's it got to do with you if
rooms are locked or not? It's not part of your job.
You're here simply to clean the house, wait on us,
and do what you're damned well told. I dare say the
Colonel will be interested to hear about this. What
do you think you are? But I'll tell you what you are.
You're nothing but a poor relation and an old maid,
and my God, I'm not surprised, no man would look at
a meddlng starveling such as yourself. You'd best look
for a new job, if you can find anyone to employ you.

Go upstairs and pack your bags, the pair of you. This house will be well rid of you. And—"

He broke off, to stare incredulously at the Frenchman, who came up so close as almost to stand against him.

"That will do," said the Frenchman. "And you will never speak to Miss Walters like that again. Is that understood?" Then, as Lewis, so taken aback that for a moment he did not know what to do, began to shout again, he cut into his speech. "I am delighted you are so concerned for Miss Albertine. I am sure Miss Flora will appreciate the way in which you champion her sister."

The remark signified nothing to Margaret, but, to her astonishment, she saw Lewis grow even paler, then fall silent. He looked at the Frenchman, breathing heavily, then, without another word, swung round and strode away.

Margaret said faintly, "What is all this? What have you said to him?"

But he answered only, "I believe you were trying to protect me, Margaret. I assure you, I am quite capable of looking after myself."

Then she lost her temper, for she could never endure scenes, and this ungrateful mockery was the last straw. She forgot that they were still on the landing, that the kitchen staff would be entertained by all this brawling, a great deal of which must be carrying down to them, and that this was her first day, when it was so important to make a good impression. She snapped at him, "You were both behaving like naughty children. I have never seen such a display. And you talk of being able to look after yourself—"

She broke off. She said, in a different voice, "Did you really try to kiss Miss Albertine?"

"If you choose to believe it!"

She said, less sure of herself, "What should I believe? I cannot see why she should make up such a story—it does her no credit."

"In that case," said the Frenchman calmly, "I do not understand this remarkable attempt to absolve me. Why did you invent such a story?"

"I don't know." She was almost speaking to herself. She turned back to the staircase. "In any case, it don't matter any more. You have lost us both our jobs. I should not be surprised if that bad-mannered young man has you put in prison. You'd best get away from here as quick as possible."

"I am on parole," said the Frenchman. He did not look distressed; indeed, it was almost as if he were trying not to laugh.

"Oh," she said crossly, "are you talking of honor now? That's fine under the circumstances. However, if you'd prefer to be put in the Cross Prison . . ."

"It would be the *cachot* for me," said the Frenchman. "It is what you call the Black Hole, and is used for the more hardened prisoners. I believe even the strongest do not survive more than a day there."

Margaret raised her hands in a despairing gesture. She did not answer him. She began to climb the stairs that led to her room.

He said, "Where are you going, Margaret? The kitchens are on the floor below."

She answered, tight-lipped, "I am going to pack."

He looked at her, then away. He said at last, "I suggest you defer your packing."

"Do you really imagine that after all this the Colonel will wish to employ either of us?"

"It presents a problem," he said, with a considering air. She had stopped now, and turned to face him, her

hand on the railing. He went on, "It does indeed. A
French tutor, an officer on parole at a time when, so
they say, Bonaparte is preparing to invade us. A
French tutor who disgraces himself by attempting to
seduce the younger daughter he is engaged to teach. It
is, I suppose, a form of instruction, though I am not
certain if it is necessary."

She exclaimed in despair, "Oh, I have no idea what
you are talking about. Do you really find this so amusing? I can assure you, it is not so for me. I am penniless.
Now I do not even have a roof over my head, and
certainly there'll be no reference. After this no one
will wish to employ me, someone who is dismissed on
her very first day. What do you think will happen to
me?"

He said, "You used not to be so sorry for yourself."

"Sorry for myself!" Her voice rose and instantly
sank again, as if she were ashamed of such a display.
"Yes, Philippe. I am sorry for myself. I think I have
the right. I believed I had at last found myself some
security—not a home, no, but at least somewhere to
live, work to do, food to eat. And now I am back
where I started—indeed, I am worse off. And all you
do is to make fun of me. Oh, I have changed, I know
that, and for the worse, no doubt—I think we always
change for the worse—but you have changed too. You
would not once have taken such pleasure in my mis-
fortunes. But of course we are enemies, and I see that
you will never forgive me. I hope you are enjoying
your revenge."

He seemed quite unmoved by all this temperament.
He said only, as if it did not matter, "You seem to forget that I am as involved in drama as yourself. But I
do not believe the situation is as terrible as you

imagine. I think you will go down to the kitchens and persuade that lady, whose name I have forgotten, to cook proper meals for the family, and I in an hour's time will take my first lesson with the two young ladies."

She whispered, "Do you really imagine the Colonel . . ."

"I imagine," he replied, "that the Colonel will hear nothing at all of this episode. I don't think Captain Moore will so much as mention it again."

"But how can he not?"

He said roughly, "Oh, go down to the kitchens, where you belong. It is your job. God knows, they need someone here. I have never seen a house in such a state. I think the English live like pigs. Clean it up. Stop making such a drama. And . . ." He paused; then he said, "And stop interfering, Margaret."

"That is what I call real gratitude." But she was going, slowly and irresolutely, down the stairs again.

He repeated, "Stop interfering. Leave the Bluebeard Room alone. Remember what happened to all the ladies who unlocked the door. Leave it alone, I say. It is nothing to do with you."

She said indignantly, feeling somehow restored, "I do not like being ordered around. It is none of your business what I do. And why do you talk such nonsense? It is not Bluebeard's room. It is simply an old ruin, the remnants of a castle. If one could open the door, I imagine there would be nothing inside but dust and mold."

He only said again, "Leave it alone."

This time she did not trouble to answer him. She brushed past him and made her way down the last flight of stairs to the kitchen. He turned to watch her go. His face was wary, a little irresolute. Then he too walked away, toward the little study where the two sisters would presently join him for their first lesson.

It seemed to Margaret during the first week that the Hall resembled the Augean stables—a Herculean effort would be required to clean it. Philippe had some justification for his remark about the English living like pigs. She was not by disposition the most domestic of girls, but poverty and Papa's ill health had taught her to keep a house tidy and clean, and to cook a reasonable meal. What she had seen of the Hall that first evening had astonished her, but it was nothing to what she discovered on closer acquaintance. She could not begin to understand how well-to-do, well-bred people could possibly live in such squalor.

There were a number of servants, all of whom came from the village and returned home at nights. They seemed to have no specific duties. The entire staff changed weekly, and they spent most of their working day in Mrs. Beeston's kitchen, drinking beer and eating large meals. The meals served upstairs were deplorable—indeed, almost uneatable; by the time they reached the Colonel's table, they were stone-cold. The passages and stairways had never been cleaned, the rooms were seldom dusted, and the only presentable place was the library, where the Colonel spent most of his time, and where, it seemed, he demanded a modicum of cleanliness.

Margaret, after her first moment of shock, rallied her forces together with the strange, varying army of servants. She grew aware immediately that they all resented her. Instead of sitting around Mrs. Beeston's cosy range, they now found themselves sweeping and scrubbing and dusting, worked off their feet by this blasted foreigner, for so they termed her, coming as she did from the north. The other foreigner, the real one, they all liked, for he gave them no trouble. The young girls thought him attractive, and flirted their eyes at him, while the men, prepared to mistrust him, found him so quiet and unobtrusive that they forgot about him. It was Margaret who was the dragon, and it was Margaret who supplied the gossip at night—this slave driver who gave them no peace, who jumped on them whenever they were taking a well-earned rest, and who even stopped them taking home their tithe of food from the Walters' larder.

Margaret, if a dragon, became an exhausted one. Her unpopularity distressed her, and sometimes at night in her own little room, which she had now made more comfortable, she wept from sheer fatigue and loneliness. There was no one to talk to, and she was upset by the black looks constantly daggered at her, however much she tried to pretend they did not matter. Sometimes, despising herself, she tried to ingratiate herself with the servants, making little delicacies for the girls, joking with the men. But it was no use at all. Only Mrs. Beeston was friendly, and that was probably from pure laziness, for the old woman liked nothing better than to sit down with her glass of ale, and she would watch contentedly as Margaret prepared the midday meal. But at least she talked, which was more than anyone else did, and it was a comfort to hold a human conversation, even if it resulted in Margaret's doing all the work.

She hardly saw the Frenchman, for he had his own duties, escorting the young ladies to the Cross Prison at weekends and giving his lessons daily. They faced

each other at mealtimes, and often she looked at him
sadly. Here was someone with whom she could have
shared her difficulties, and with whom he could
have shared his own—and all that happened between
them was a cool, polite conversation.

It always seemed to follow the same pattern.

"How are the lessons going?"

"Oh, well enough. As one might expect. Miss Flora
is sweet and stupid and pays no attention to one word
I say, while Miss Albertine is sharp and quick and a
liar."

"A liar!"

"Of course."

This matter-of-fact acceptance irritated her, especially as she remembered that occasion in the garden
on the first evening. She was unwise enough to give
him a quizzical look, and this successfully stopped all
further conversation, so that the meal ended in complete silence, and then it was as if the food choked
her. She jumped up, leaving her dinner unfinished,
then tried to work off her emotion in frantic dusting
and cleaning.

Once, after an unhappy dispute with one of the
village girls, she declared, "I don't think I can endure
it here much longer."

But he replied only, "In that case, you will leave,
won't you?" He met her resentful and wretched look,
and added in a different voice, "I think it would be
good if you did leave."

She answered indignantly, "You are not driving me
out, Philippe. This is the first proper employment I
have ever had. I may not be happy here, but I dare
say that will change in time, and at least I have
somewhere to live and something to eat. I don't sup-

pose you understand what that means. You have never been really poor."

And as she said this, her mind went back to that strange world, now apparently gone for ever, where the rich were so very rich and the poor so very poor, but now it lacked reality and seemed like a dream.

Perhaps it seemed like a dream to him too, for he did not answer this at all, but only said, after a long pause, "And how do you get on with the two young ladies?"

How do I get on with the two young ladies? Margaret sighed and laughed and, having made some noncommittal reply, reflected on the reality of the situation.

At first she had not seen a great deal of them. She had expected them to appear in the kitchens, order the day's menu, and organize the cleaning, but she realized within a day that such things had never entered their heads. Flora spent most of her spare time mooning around in the little parlor near the back of the house, where the Frenchman held his lessons. Margaret often saw her there, sitting by the window and dreaming; she never seemed to read any of her father's books, nor did she so much as touch the sadly out-of-tune piano that stood against the wall. Sometimes she believed that Flora still had the mind of a child. Usually she was gentle and courteous, but occasionally she flew into a tantrum, stamping her foot and screaming. But this was very rare; mostly she seemed to live in a kind of dream, becoming animated only when the time came to meet her Lewis. Then she would dress herself up—both girls had magnificent clothes—and either wait for Lewis to come to her or walk over to the prison to meet him.

As for Albertine, Margaret saw little of her and could happily have seen even less, for her manner was dictatorial and impertinent. She seemed to enjoy ordering the new housekeeper around, and was always finding fault. "You haven't dusted this bookcase," she would declaim in her high little voice, or, "Why are you always in the passage? Are you spying on us?" Then she would complain about the lateness of the meals, or the quality of the wine, and when she saw this had no effect she would cry out, "Oh, I wish you hadn't come here. You're so dowdy and dull. Go away at once, I can't bear the sight of you."

Margaret longed to slap her, but soon found out that the only effective answer was silence; this was something Albertine could not understand, and when she received no reply to her rudeness she would limp away in a temper. But mostly she was not around. What she did with herself, Margaret could not imagine, for at times it was as if she had disappeared. Apparently she turned up for her lessons (at least, the Frenchman never said otherwise), and on Sundays, when the officers of the garrison were all invited in the late afternoon to wine and cakes, both sisters, lively and gaily dressed, played hostess, while the Colonel, bored by what he called silly chatter, stood in the far corner of the room, ignoring his guests and talking to Captain Ross. But for the most part there was no sign of Albertine, and neither her father nor her sister seemed to remark her absence.

Margaret took it upon herself to tidy the girls' rooms, though when she first saw them she almost regretted her decision. Neither had ever been instructed to put anything away—what sort of person had the late Mrs. Walters been?—and the floor was

invariably littered with discarded garments, soiled
linen, a crumpled dress, a lone glove, and ribbons and
pins. Margaret hung up the dresses, washed the dirty
things, swept up the pins, and made the beds. Next
day it would be as if she had never done anything,
and she would have to start all over again. Sometimes
she wanted to take these two spoiled misses by the
shoulders and shake some sense into them, but then
Flora would appear and be so charming that Margaret was ashamed of her ill-temper.

Flora was the only one of the family who did not
treat her as a servant—at least, most of the time. She
would say in her sweet, soft voice, "You're looking
so tired. Why don't you sit down and have a rest?"
Then, before Margaret could reply, she would begin
at once to talk of Lewis, how marvelous he was, how
incredibly handsome, how sweet-natured, how she
adored him and he adored her, what an ideal marriage theirs would be. And Margaret, dusting away,
picking up the clothes that once again lay all over the
floor, would nod and agree, remembering sadly that
Flora always ignored the captain's true nature. This
poor, foolish girl would have many shocks in store
for her. And then occasionally, her back aching from
having to stoop so much, she nearly made some scold-
ing remark, but before she could do so, Flora, amia-
bly watching her, would cry, "But I have just remembered, there is a blue dress that would suit you down
to the ground, you must have it—I am quite tired of
it." And she would run to take the dress down, and
push it into Margaret's astonished and unwilling
hands.

The dress would be a good one, of excellent material, fashionably designed, and hardly worn. It was

true that there was probably a stain down the front, and one of the frills would be torn; certainly the material would be creased and crumpled; but the gown would be infinitely better than anything Margaret possessed, or had possessed for a very long time.

And she would say gently, "Miss Flora . . ."

"Oh, call me Flora. Don't be so stuffy, Margaret. After all, we are cousins."

"I am the housekeeper here," said Margaret firmly, "and I am sure your papa would not like me to address you in such a fashion. Dear Miss Flora, I cannot possibly accept such a gift. I know the dress is a little torn, but that is easily put to rights. If you will let me mend it and press it, it will be like new." And she sighed as she spoke, for the dress was lovely, and it would be wonderful to dress up again.

Flora half-heartedly protested, for already her mind was somewhere else; she was thinking that in a few hours' time Lewis would be at her side. She did not notice Margaret folding up the dress. Next day, washed, ironed, mended, it would be hanging once more in her wardrobe, side by side with a dozen others, equally handsome and equally misused.

One day, three weeks after Margaret's arrival, Flora said suddenly, "Margaret, will you come with me to the Cross Prison this afternoon?"

Margaret, surprised, demurred, and suggested that perhaps her sister could accompany her.

"Bertie? No, no. She is always too busy. Besides, when she comes with me, it is always too boring. She has to go right into the prison, and Lewis don't like her, they always seem to quarrel."

Margaret was not entirely convinced by this remark, but she said, "Then I suggest Monsieur

Sansterre accompany you. It is part of his work here, and I dare say it gives him pleasure to meet his compatriots and to have the chance of speaking French again."

Flora stamped her foot. Like her sister, she could not abide being crossed, and Margaret had met these childish shows of temper before. She cried out again, "No, no, no! Why do you always say such silly things? I don't want Frenchy to come with me, I want you. Besides, Lewis don't like Frenchy escorting me, it makes him jealous." Then, the tantrum done, she smiled that sweet, ravishing smile that had perhaps seduced Lewis, that almost compensated for the lack of wit behind it. "He is so terribly jealous," she said. "Oh, Margaret, he is wickedly jealous. It makes me so happy when he's jealous. It shows how much he loves me."

Margaret's opinion of Lewis was by no means so romantic. But she agreed that jealousy was the surest indication of love, and wished this lovely little moron would go away and let her get on with her work in peace.

"Then of course you're coming with me," persisted Flora, and, rising to her feet in a beautiful, flowing motion, she suddenly picked up something that lay upon her dressing table and pushed it into Margaret's hand. "This is a present for you. I bought it from the prison. You must take it. If you don't, I shall never speak to you again. See, I shall wrap it up in a handkerchief, and you will put it straight into your pocket."

Margaret felt she could not go on refusing. She made a resigned gesture; then, impulsively, she kissed her young cousin on the cheek. "You should not

make me presents," she said, then, curious enough
to forget herself, "What is it? Do tell me."

"Oh no!" And Flora, delighted, laughed and
pursed up her lips, while Margaret slipped the small
package into her pocket, fingering it and wondering
what on earth it could be. It was square and hard—
perhaps an ornament in a box. She laughed too,
thanked Flora, and once more set to work, praying
that the proposed visit to the prison might be forgotten.

It was not forgotten. This seemed, indeed, to be a
day for remembering. Having tidied the girls' rooms
and seen to the various household tasks that were her
daily responsibility, Margaret prepared to take the
little pony trap down to the village of Adeney Cross
to collect the day's supplies.

She had seen from the very beginning that unless
she herself saw to the ordering, there was a fine
traffic in food and drink and everything else. Mrs.
Beeston, though amiable and quite devoid of malice
or resentment, was the laziest soul alive. Her one idea
was to sit by the stove, however warm the weather,
drink her ale, and go peacefully to sleep. Far from
grudging Margaret her authority, she was enchanted
to sit there beaming and dozing while the new housekeeper did all the work. "Bless you, my dear," she
would murmur sleepily when Margaret asked her to
do something; then she would fall back into her chair
again.

Margaret endured this as well as she could. And,
indeed, the old woman's cooking was so undependable
that it seemed best to take the matter out of her
charge. She was by now too old and too lazy to learn
better, and sometimes the sight of her dirty hands roll-

ing out the pastry—one of the few things she did well—sickened Margaret and made her long to push her away and do it herself. But one thing she could not permit, and that was the giving away of all the family supplies. When butter and cheese and eggs were wrapped up and stuffed quite openly into capacious pockets and anything left over from the dinner table simply taken home, she had to force herself to protest.

This morning she had seen Thomas Lee walking away quite unashamedly with half a venison pie, a dozen eggs, and a bottle of wine. She hesitated. She was, after all, still new to the job, she knew that the servants regarded her as a dragon, and at this moment she felt as if she did not have an ally in the world. She certainly did not have one in this daft old woman who cared only for her mug of spiced ale. She longed passionately, as she longed a dozen times a day, for someone to confide in, someone to give her help and advice. But there was no point in reporting to the Colonel, who would probably pay no attention, and as for the two girls, they were far too engrossed in their own affairs to trouble their heads about such unimportant matters. She pushed out of her mind the thought of the one person who could help her if he so chose; then, taking a deep breath and hiding her trembling hands in her apron, she approached Thomas Lee.

The Frenchman was outside in the garden. Out of the corner of her eye she could see that he was cutting the grass by the Bluebeard ruins. It was ridiculous that he should have to do such work but, if he chose to make a fool of himself, that was no more her concern than her present miseries were his. It distressed

her to see him cutting away, but it was nothing to do
with her, nothing at all, and so she cleared her throat
and addressed Thomas in a voice that was strained
and unusually high.

"Are you taking those things to the larder,
Thomas?" she said.

Mrs. Beeston closed her eyes and pretended to be
asleep. She could see out the door that there was
going to be a scene, for she was not quite as daft as
Margaret believed her to be. She did not like scenes;
they upset her digestion, and besides, she might be
expected to join in, and she really could not be bothered. She could hear the angry voices, but presently
they faded in her delicious drowsiness. And so she
slumped there, her hands folded over her belly, while
Margaret faced Thomas, who was a big man and
towered over her, the illicit articles in a wooden box
that he held across him like a shield.

He was scarlet with rage. That this pale, vinegary
bitch should dare to ask him such a question! "And
what if I am?" he said.

"Because if you are," said Margaret, raising her
chin defiantly, "I have a few things here to join them.
Perhaps you would kindly take them for me."

He too hesitated for a second. Then anger overcame
him again. He had been discussing her with two of
the girls that very morning. "Nothing's been the same
since she came," he had told them, and they had
agreed eagerly, not because they really disliked the
new housekeeper, but because it was amusing to run
her down—it gave them a bit of drama. "Right old
maid, that's what she is," Thomas had said, "and no
wonder, no man'd look at the likes of her. And what
is she? Tell me that now." And before anyone could
tell him, he had gone on: "Just a poor relation,

that's all, just someone with no money who the Colonel's doing charity to. She's supposed to clean the house, ain't she, not tell us our business. Nosing around and ferreting and spying—making mischief, that's what it is. Oh, she'll come to a bad end, I can tell you that. She won't last long here, not if the young ladies has anything to do with it. Miss Albertine don't like her, that's easy to see, and folks that Miss Albertine don't like don't stay, we all knows that."

This was all very unfair to Margaret, who was not given to nosing or spying, but the memory of this delightful conversation now gave Thomas courage. Besides, she was only a half-pint little thing, and he could have sworn she was scared stiff, for all her bold words.

He said in his burring country voice, "No, ma'am, I won't. I'm taking these things for my poor old mother, and the Colonel knows all about it, he's said to me many times, 'You take something to your poor old mother, I know she needs it, and it's a real pleasure to make the poor soul happy.' "

This was such an outrageous lie that Margaret was momentarily silenced. She knew perfectly well that the Colonel was incapable of uttering such unlikely words, and probably had no idea that Thomas had a mother at all. There certainly was a mother, as Margaret was well aware, and probably if Thomas returned at nights without enough provisions for the family dinner, he would have his head broken. The absurdity of all this restored her courage. She said sharply, "You are talking nonsense. If you think Colonel Walters wants you to rob the larder, you'd better come with me and we'll ask him about it now."

This disconcerted Thomas, who had inherited his

mother's flair for bullying but who was at heart a
coward and terrified of his employer. He went redder
than ever and began to stammer, longing all the
while to shake this damned bitch to pieces.

"Are you coming?" she said, and he could have
throttled her.

But he dared not go any further, and, casting at
her a look of pure hatred, he stalked back to throw
the things into the larder. The venison pie landed on
the floor for the rats to eat later on, and half the eggs
were broken. He then retreated to the garden to brood
on vengeance, and did not so much as return the
salutation of that confounded *parlez-vous,* who was
cutting the grass with great energy and who had
amassed a stack of bottles that were piled together at
one end. Thomas was concerned only with his own
grievances and apprehension as to what Mrs. Lee
would say, and he huddled there, muttering swear-
words and curses. When he went home much later, he
had begun to forget the whole matter, but his mother,
five feet of white fury, took one look at his empty
arms, then, seizing the rolling pin, began to belabor
his head and shoulders, smiting with a wild vigor.
Thomas, nearly a foot above her, could have broken
her in two with one twist of his powerful fingers, but
instead he stood there whimpering, shielding his face
with his hands and wailing, "No, no!" After this
beating, his rage returned, and he slunk up to the
attic room he shared with his brothers, and there
dreamed of the hideous things he would do to this
housekeeper who had so insulted him.

Margaret might have felt she had won a victory, but
she could only think that life in the Walters' house
was indeed very difficult. Instead of going into the

village, she moved, a little blindly, out of the kitchen
and stood by the back door, shivering and struggling
not to cry.

It was still bitter cold, and the wind had risen so
that her petticoats blew about her and the tightly
bound hair tugged at its pins. She was too blinded by
the tears that she was fighting to restrain to hear the
footsteps, but the Frenchman's voice brought her
whirling round, her pale cheeks suddenly red.

Fortunately, the shock stopped the tears from coming. She turned what she hoped was a cold, calm
countenance upon him, as if somehow he were responsible for her predicament.

He stood there, his hands in his pockets. She could
see that half the grass was now cut, and it must
have been warm work, for, despite the cold, there was
sweat on his forehead. The uncut section still looked
like a meadow.

He remarked in the detached, conversational manner he now always adopted with her, "This is a
strange household. There were nearly two dozen bottles in the grass. I do not know your country well,
but surely it is not normal for well-bred young women
to throw bottles out of their windows."

She answered with an indignation that surprised
herself. It was as if these days she always had to
contradict him, even if the matter neither concerned
nor interested her. She exclaimed, "You have no reason to assume that Miss Albertine—"

"Did I mention the name of Miss Albertine?" he
asked, smiling in that derisive way of his that always
infuriated her.

She flushed up. "You implied it," she said.

"It is true that her room is just above." He swiveled

around to stare upward, for this was true, and the
only other window that faced the ruins was a narrow
one in the passage. Then he said reflectively, "There
is, of course, no reason why the young lady should not
indulge her taste in wine, but there is a remarkable
number of bottles. And there is one more thing.
Would you be interested to see it, Margaret?"

"Not particularly. I'm busy." But of course this was
not true, and her curiosity was already aroused. She
said in the same breath, "What is it?"

He gave her a look. She thought for a moment that
he would refuse to let her see it. But he relented and
pulled something out of his breeches pocket. It was a
pistol.

She looked down at it with surprise. She shrugged
her shoulders, saying, "That's not very interesting, is
it? I suppose one of the servants has dropped it. People go about armed these days. I can't see why it con-
cerns us."

He said, almost contemptuously, "How unobservant you are. Or perhaps as a woman . . . Look at it
more closely."

"I don't know anything about weapons."

"It is a French army pistol. It is of the kind I had
myself."

She said, "Well, why not? There's a garrison here.
We are surrounded by soldiers. It probably belonged
to one of them."

"It is interesting, all the same," he said.

"I still don't see why it matters," she said impatiently, for this was a stupid conversation, and she
had so much on her mind. "I cannot imagine why
you find it even interesting." Then, her voice suddenly sharp, "You had best go on with your grass cut-

ting. Since you are making a servant of yourself, you should do the job properly."

He made no reply to this, only stepped back as if he were obeying her.

Then she could bear it no longer. It was as if the whole day had conspired against her, as if the long years when she had learned to cope with loneliness, poverty, and deprivation had taught her nothing. She ran after him and caught at his arm. The look he turned on her seemed to be of hatred and revulsion, but she was past caring. "Philippe," she said, the tears beginning to fall again, "Philippe, please listen to me."

He answered stonily, pulling his arm away, "I am a servant. I have work to do. So have you, surely. Why are you wasting time in gossiping with me?"

She only whispered, "Please. Please. For just one moment. Oh, Philippe, can't we be more friendly? I am so much in need of a friend. I know you want to punish me, but there is surely no reason to be quite so cruel. There is nobody here I can talk to."

He said, smiling at her, "How unfortunate you are, poor Margaret."

She backed away. She said, in a low voice, "This afternoon I have to accompany Miss Flora to the prison. It will be almost my first human contact with the outside world."

He said, "I have to do this every week, sometimes more than once. It is a kind of contact I could dispense with."

"Yes," she said sadly, "I can understand that. I shall not enjoy it much myself. Perhaps you are right. But if only I could talk things over with you. You must understand that. I didn't mean to call you a servant.

I am the servant here. The two young ladies would laugh at me if I ever asked for their advice. Colonel Walters is interested in nothing but his friends and the wine they drink together, he don't want to concern himself with the running of the house. As for poor old Mrs. Beeston, all she wants to do is eat and sleep. She wouldn't care if I died, except that it would mean extra work for her. But you and I—"

He interrupted her. She could see that he had grown very white. "You and I," he repeated. "Yes, madam, you and I. Let us have no more of this sentimental nonsense. Are you hoping to revive our love affair?"

"No! Of course not. How could I—"

"How could you, indeed! There is as yet no known method of reviving a corpse, and a stinking one at that. We have been thrown together by a damnable and disastrous coincidence. I never wanted to meet you again. I believed I had forgotten you. And now we live in the same house. I assure you, that is no doing of mine, and if there had been the smallest alternative, I would have left instanter."

"There was nothing to stop you," said Margaret. She had stopped crying. She was as pale as he. She felt raw, as if the skin were being stripped from her.

"Was there not?" He grimaced as he spoke, but his eyes did not meet hers. "What sort of life do you imagine it was for me at Elchester? Do you not believe other people have feelings? I too was alone. I had nothing to do. Anything to me is better than that. This at least has given me a chance to work, even if the work is of a menial kind. It earns me a little money; it permits me to meet people. Do you expect me to throw that up just because of you? You flatter

yourself. You are utterly unimportant to me. I cannot now see how I ever believed myself in love with
you. What were you, after all? A silly little English
miss, a tutor's daughter, with little breeding and less
wit, nothing but a pretty figure and a fine complexion. Any whore could provide as much. I don't blame
you for that. I was more stupid than you. But then I
was young too. Perhaps you did me a good turn, Margaret, when you left with your Henry. I was idiot
enough to plan to marry you—God help us both from
such a marriage. And now you propose to embroil me
again. No! We live in the same house, and it is a
pity, but there is no reason why we should meet
except at mealtimes. I want nothing more to do with
you. I would be thankful never to see you again.
Whatever love there was between us is gone, and I
believe it is so for you as much as for me, only, like
all women, especially the unmarried, you must have
your drama. It pleases your vanity to think that I
still have feeling for you. You must believe that is
not so. I feel nothing for you, not even hate. If you
are unhappy here, you must either learn to endure it
or leave. I do not wish to receive your confidences.
Now, will you please let me go on with my work? I
am sure you are very busy yourself. I hope we will
never again have such an absurd and unnecessary
conversation."

She said quietly, "I hope you feel better now,
Philippe. You have said things that should not have
been said. But, as you point out, perhaps it don't
really matter." Then, driven by something entirely
out of her control, she looked him full in the face
and said, "There is something I will tell you. I did
not mean to. Perhaps I should not. But after what

you have said . . . The baby that died. It was yours,
Philippe. It was exactly like you."

And she stepped back into the kitchen, her head
held high. Her heart was pumping against her breast
as if it could scarcely be confined, and the sweat was
trickling down her, but she merely picked up her
purse and bag and collected her shopping list before
going into the village.

The Frenchman stared after her. If she had struck
him full in the face with her fist, she could not have
overwhelmed him more. He was white and shaking.
He screwed up his eyes as if he could hardly believe
in his own existence. He did not think for one
moment that she was lying. And the image of her was
painted on his eyes. She had lost a great deal of her
looks, including the delicate coloring that had once
so charmed him. She had grown very thin, and there
was a touch of gray in the pretty brown hair. Her
eyes were hollowed as if she had done a great deal of
weeping. There was little remaining of the charming
young girl who had enticed herself so sweetly into his
heart. And the baby . . . It was not true that he had
forgotten. The dreadful evening, submerged in his
mind, roared to the surface—everything that he most
passionately wished to forget.

A little out of his mind, not knowing what he
should do or could do, he fell savagely to cutting the
grass. His blade touched yet another bottle. He broke
into a loud, wild laugh. Miss Albertine certainly had
a fine appetite for wine.

Then he could not continue working. He could
only hear the quiet, sorrowful voice that had said,
*The baby that died. It was yours . . . It was exactly
like you . . .*

And she had not told him.

He dropped the scythe and sat down on one of the ruined walls. And presently he put his head in his hands, and the years fell like the grass before him. It was as if life was returning to him, in an astonished pain that was almost unbearable.

Chapter Five

*M*argaret drove into the village. She was still
numb with what had been said to her, and savagely
ashamed of what she herself had said. She had sworn
never to mention this to Philippe. It was finished and
done with, many years ago. The baby was dead—the
baby that in the strange way of small infants was so
unmistakably like its father. And now she had said it.
It was wicked and unnecessary, and she had said it,
and it could not be unsaid. What effect it would have
on Philippe, she could not know, but the dreadful

retribution was the effect it had on her. The numbness was already vanishing, and the pain growing, threatening to overcome her. She was remembering again the agony of the baby's death, the futility of this small life that meant all the world to her and that, she had seen, could not last. It seemed to her that the core of the pain lay not so much in memory as in a strange inability to separate past and present. If only she could look back on her silly self ten years past, she might not find the present so appalling. But the silly self was at her shoulder, and the dying baby in her arms. The past shrouded her in a fog; it was as if she could no longer see her way through the blackness.

She flicked the reins against the flank of the amiable pony that was taking her to Adeney Cross—a gentle, fat creature who accepted sugar and carrots from her, and made pleasing whinnying noises when she approached him. She remembered (although she tried desperately not to), those wonderful days when Philippe had spoken to her tenderly, when his eyes had held nothing but love, when such words as had now passed between them would have been an impossible nightmare. And the speakers were the same men, she and the young Margaret the same women: Love turned to hate, gentleness to anger, a desire to kiss to a desire to kill. A sob of dismay and angry helplessness rose in her throat. The barrier between them was ten years wide, and nothing, nothing at all, could bridge it.

Then, in spite of her hatred, she remembered a time when she had very different feelings, and she knew that on her side there was no past and no present. The Marquis of ten years ago was Monsieur Sansterre now, and she loved him not only as much as she had ever done, but more. It was hopeless, it was the end. A mutual indifference might not matter, but love on one side and hatred on the other was like the war between France and England—there was no solution, only victory or defeat. For her there was no barrier any longer; for him it was permanent.

She let the reins lie slackly on her knee, and the amiable pony, glad to rest, lowered his head to nibble at the grass by the wayside. And Margaret simply sat there, staring ahead, seeing nothing at all. The only rational thing to do was to leave the Hall at once, never mind that she had neither money nor employment nor a roof over her head. And she knew she would not do so; she had no alternative but to stay in her torment. *Madam, you must die*, the wicked Bluebeard had said, and it was true, she must die, there was no escape.

Then she drove on into Adeney Cross, to have the various supplies lifted into the back of the cart.

She was glad to exchange friendly words with Mrs. Clay, who did not seem to share the local dislike of her, and she accepted an invitation to come into the inn's parlor and have a glass of wine. Mr. Clay, she knew, did not care over-much for her, but he greeted her in a friendly manner. Only, after a while he suddenly remarked, "You be careful of that Frenchy, ma'am," which jolted the blood into her cheeks. God knows, the warning was true, if impossible to obey.

She managed to say, "Why, Mr. Clay? He seems quite a harmless man."

A harmless man indeed—a fine description for Philippe! She wondered irrelevantly through the bitter pain—it was as if one's mind functioned in layers —if the two young misses, so preoccupied with their own affairs, regarded him in this light. No doubt they did. They would probably not look on a tutor as human—only, with Miss Albertine one was never sure, and certainly there had been a moment when her attitude had hardly been impersonal.

And over these thoughts she smiled at Mrs. Clay and sipped her wine, and some of Mr. Clay's words —he was a compulsive talker, and no one really listened to him—floated to the surface of her mind.

"You can never trust them *parlez-vous*," said Mr. Clay, as he said a hundred times a day. He threw back into his throat the ale that he preferred, choked into a cough, and then went on again. He was, as usual, a little drunk. He was never quite sober, but he never became disorderly, so this was accepted by everyone, including his wife and family. It was said that the last time old Clay was sober was fifteen years ago, when an abnormally high tide brought the sea roaring into the village and the shock of cold salt water triumphed briefly over the alcohol in his system. He went on now, "They say there'll be an invasion."

"Oh, I'm sure that's nonsense," said Margaret almost automatically. He said the same thing every time she met him; if it had been true, England would long since have been overrun. She added, "Nelson would never permit it."

"Oh, him!" said Mr. Clay, as he spoke of Nelson and the other defenders of his country. "He'll not have a chance, the poor bastard. Those frogs will come over in their millions. Why, I dare say their ships are waiting there even now."

Fortunately, at this moment Mrs. Clay related a tale of her grandson who had become religious and a

Nelson-worshipper at the same moment, and who now suffered from some confusion between Lord Nelson and the Lord Jesus.

"As long as he don't confuse Lady Hamilton with the Virgin Mary, that is all right," said Margaret, at which Mrs. Clay called her a naughty girl and gave her some more wine, and the subject of invasion was forgotten.

Mr. Clay was not simply talking through his hat, though he himself would have been astonished to know it. Across the sea the transport in the northwest of France was waiting hopefully; there had been one abortive invasion a year back, and there was the hope of a more successful one. There was no definite plan, the danger was slight, but two people in Adeney Cross were very much aware, a number of others were praying that it would happen, and one person was wary and suspicious.

But the bleak winter sun flickered over the village cobbles, and the villagers went about their business as usual, glancing with faint hostility at the new housekeeper who was such a right schoolmarm where Hall property was concerned. The sea crept smoothly over the Loving Sands, so treacherously innocent. It was an ordinary day, like other days, but Margaret's mind was still ten years away, and she walked back to the pony cart wondering if she would find the strength to bear the burden fallen on her.

As she climbed in, with an over-willing customer from the Loving Sands Inn giving her an unnecessary lift up, she saw that Mrs. Lee had come to the door of her cottage.

She did not greet her. She knew Mrs. Lee disliked her, but then, Mrs. Lee disliked everyone. She only thought, as she picked up the reins, how strange it was that this skinny slip of a woman, the size of a twig, should so terrorize her own family. She did not realize that the grown-up sons were so cowed that they submitted to humiliating beatings, but Mrs. Lee's reputation was known through the district, and improbable and lurid stories were related about her. No one remembered Mr. Lee, but none of the seven children had been allowed to marry. Indeed, the thought of Mrs. Lee as a mother-in-law was enough to frighten any suitor away.

Mrs. Lee looked up at this young woman high on the pony-cart seat, and Margaret bestowed on her a faint, guarded smile, thinking that she had never seen such implacable hostility in a human face. It was frankly impossible to imagine Mrs. Lee laughing, let alone performing such human functions as marrying, making love, and bearing children. The late Mr. Lee must have been as odd as herself.

As she reflected on this, a little shocked by her own inelegant thoughts, she saw Mrs. Lee shoot out a lean and filthy hand, making the two-fingered gesture of warding off the evil eye.

The shock of this shot the color from Margaret's cheeks, for no one likes to be regarded as a witch. As she urged the pony on, Mrs. Lee screeched after her, "You'll go straight to hell, that's what you'll do. Letting a poor old woman starve . . . I hopes you burn. I hopes you rot."

Some of the watching villagers laughed, and Mrs. Clay tut-tutted and went back into the inn. Margaret, driving as swiftly as the pony permitted—he was not by build or breeding fitted to be a racehorse—sighed, exasperated, and resolved to forget the episode.

What Mrs. Lee thought of her was, after all, quite immaterial, and in this one instance at least she could not imagine that this hostility was entirely personal. If Mrs. Lee had ever loved anyone, it remained an undiscovered secret.

However, as she saw that everything today was becoming exaggerated, Margaret found that her spirits were a little restored. Mrs. Lee was plainly furious because her rations had been taken from her, yet she could not be in need with seven working children who would certainly be compelled to hand over every penny, and this served her right for being so dishonest and greedy. Adeney Cross had no reputation for witch hunting; it was unlikely in the year 1798 that a pyre would be lit for a mere housekeeper.

Arriving back at the Hall, Margaret jumped out and looked around for Thomas or some other unwilling helper to lift out the supplies.

She was surprised to see Captain Ross coming toward her. She had seen little of him since her arrival, but then, he was usually closeted with the Colonel, and Margaret spent most of her life below-stairs, emerging only to make sure that the rooms were tidy and the passages kept sweet and clean.

She thought now that he was not an agreeable-looking man, with his one arm and rough, pugilist's face. But she was beginning to learn that one cannot always go by appearances, and when he spoke to her she thought that at least he had a pleasant voice, despite the strange Scots accent, and that his eyes, which were keen and observant, were not those of an evil-dispositioned man.

She wished him good morning, made a bob of a curtsey, and turned to speak to Thomas, who was coming down the garden path. Thomas, she suspected, longed to be insolent, but dared not with Captain Ross looking on. The younger man scowled at Margaret but did as she bid him, and she stood there waiting until the last package had been removed and the pony led off to his cosy, straw-lined quarters.

Captain Ross said, "Is he being impertinent to you, ma'am?"

"Oh no, not at all," answered Margaret, compelled by the absurdity of human nature to defend a young man who had grossly insulted her, and marveling secretly at her own lie, for she really had no sympathy for Thomas at all. She added, unnecessarily, "I find everyone here most agreeable."

Captain Ross eyed her as if he did not believe one word of what she was saying. She could not imagine how he knew anything of what went on in the kitchens, but she was beginning to think there was not much that escaped his attention.

He said bluntly, "If you receive any insolence, you will be good enough to let me know."

Margaret, astonished, said meekly that she would. Captain Ross was not, after all, her employer, but it was comforting to have an ally, and certainly he would be more effective than the Colonel, who would not concern himself if someone spat in her eye. However, she was growing very cold standing there, and was preparing to go when he said, "You look as if you could do with a glass of wine, ma'am."

She said weakly, "Why sir, Mrs. Clay was kind enough to offer me one in the village, and I think I must—"

"What the devil use is one glass?" demanded Captain Ross, a question which Margaret had already heard put, in varying forms, by everyone who worked in the Hall. The Captain was notorious for being a three-bottle man. Then, not waiting for a reply to what in any case was a rhetorical question, he seized her by the arm and led her into the house by the front door, and from there to the library.

The Colonel was out. He was a poor landlord, little concerned with his tenants, provided they paid their rent, but twice a week he was compelled to ride around his estates, a business that bored him and always brought him back in a bad temper. Margaret, however, felt uncomfortable in what was his private room, and saw with a faint self-mockery how easy it was to fall into the servant's way. Once she would have expected to sit down and be offered the wine; now she could only worry what would happen if the Colonel or his daughters arrived.

Captain Ross snapped at her, "Oh, for Christ's sake, lass, what the devil ails you? Sit down, in God's name. I want to talk to you. Do you imagine I can hold a conversation with you standing there like a schoolboy waiting to be whipped? Unfasten that cloak of yours and drink this wine. It'll put some color in your cheeks. You're as peaky as a new-born lamb. Don't they feed you properly? I dare say they work you off your feet. You'll have to learn to stand up for yourself, you know. Like that damned Frenchman. He'll accept nothing, confound him."

A far less observant man could hardly have missed the color that flared into Margaret's face. At that moment she did not look peaky at all. The Captain's heavy brows met.

She managed, however, to reply, in a suppressed voice, "I have nothing to complain about, Captain Ross."

"Well," he said in his ungentlemanly manner, "if you don't sit down and do as you're told, you will." Then, to her irritation, he burst out laughing and gave her a positive shove, and the next moment she found herself sitting opposite him with a brimming glass pushed into her hand.

He let the silence lie for a while. He was a restless man, and he paced up and down the room in a fashion that beat sadly on her already sharpened nerves. She sat there, the untouched glass in her hand and her eyes roved around the room, which to her was the only attractive one in the whole house, being full of books that nobody read and furniture that, although shabby and neglected, was still beautiful. She thought that the late Mrs. Walters, who had died seven years before, must have been the oddest woman to leave everything to rot—not only these fine things but her daughters, who so plainly revealed the lack of maternal care.

Captain Ross snapped at her, "Why don't you unfasten your cloak, ma'am?"

She obeyed him in silence. For the first time she smiled at him, and, to her surprise, he smiled back.

He said, "You're a good lass. I've never seen this confounded place so well kept. And the food's almost eatable."

"Thank you," said Margaret with some asperity.

"Why don't you drink your wine?"

She answered, more to her astonishment than his, "Why do you bully me like this? I am not a soldier of the line."

Then he laughed again. He had a strange, barking laugh that reminded her of the seals that congregated around the northern coasts. "No," he said, "and you are no housekeeper either. Oh, I've been observing

you, lass. You're a fine-set-up young lady, too good for
this sort of work, and you've a fine, observant pair of
eyes on you too, I dare say. Now, is that not so?"

She said primly, "I am the housekeeper, Captain
Ross, and I am not here to observe."

"Oh, oh!" he said. "Fine words, ma'am, fine words.
And I don't believe a syllable of them. It's your eyes
I'm interested in, that and something else. But we'll
come to that later. I want your help. Will you give it
me?"

She felt she should query this, beg him to explain.
But something about him, his directness and honesty,
coupled with what she now believed to be a genuine
kindness, made her answer simply, "Yes."

"That's the answer I want to hear," said Captain
Ross with great satisfaction. He came close to her,
looking down from his great height. "Now," he said,
"I'm going to talk, and you, ma'am, are going to
listen. You're a poor sort of drinker."

But she covered her glass so that he could not refill
it, and indeed, she had not tasted a sip. She looked
up at him in an expectant silence, and presently he
continued.

"There are a great many things going on here,"
said Captain Ross. "I know very little and suspect a
great deal. Maybe there'll be an invasion. But I doubt
it, I doubt it very much."

"The village talks of little else," said Margaret.

"Oh, the village! The village knows nothing about
it. If there was an invasion, they'd all be shocked out
of their skins. When the Normans really did come, we
were all unprepared. You should know, ma'am, that
in any war people always babble about invasions, for
it makes them feel important. But I am not the vil-

lage, and there are other matters that interest me far more. Did you not know that there have been twelve escapes from the Cross Prison within a matter of months? I know that more are planned. I know there is someone in the prison who is an enemy agent, and I know there is someone else outside—maybe more than one—who is helping. I know that somewhere there is a cache of arms, that there are mooring posts by the sea that no one in Adeney Cross admits to putting there, that there are sometimes signals at night that cannot be explained. When the prison was built, Miss Margaret, we thought it doubly safe, for not only is it well fashioned and well guarded, but there are the Loving Sands, and a better protection you could not find. These people, whoever they are, know the sands, and know the right time to cross them. I don't know who they are. I wish to God I did. But I'll find out. I swear to Christ, I'll find out. We're not having those damned prisoners decamping back to fight us again, and maybe bringing an invading transport with them.

"What do you know about this Monsieur Sansterre? Oh, you know something. Every time I speak his name, you go as red as a berry. Come. What do you know? Is he already your lover? They say these Frenchmen move fast."

Margaret leaped to her feet. The glass fell to the floor and broke. Despite her emotion, this shocked her. She flung her hand up to her mouth, not sure whether to apologize for her clumsiness or to rate this impossible man for his insolence. Her anger won. She cried out, "Certainly not! How dare you say such a thing?"

"Oh," he said, quite unimpressed, "these things

happen, it's the way of the world. And you are a very attractive young lady. I assure you, ma'am, that I have seen stranger things in my life. And I was never one to stand by convention."

"Well, I stand by it," said Margaret. She crouched down to pick up the shards of glass, but the Captain made an impatient noise and kicked the fragments away with the toe of his boot.

"Sit down," he said. "If I've offended you, I apologize. There. You cannot ask for fairer than that. And never mind that damned glass. I'll replace it. So you're not his lover. That pleases me fine. But you know him. You can't deny it."

She answered more calmly, though the color still flamed in her cheeks, "Yes. We met many years ago. My father gave English lessons in Paris. It was long before that dreadful Revolution." She added, almost in defiance, "It is strange that we should meet here. But these things happen. I assure you, it is nothing more than that."

She could see from his expression that he did not believe a word of this, yet, after all, it was true, even if most of the truth had been left out.

He said only, "If that is so, you'll not resent what I have to say. Don't trust him, ma'am. Don't trust him an inch."

"What do you mean?" Then she was aware of how her raised tone betrayed her, and subsided into a flushed silence.

"Look," said Captain Ross, in a grave, heavy tone that compelled her to listen. "I am in charge here. I am responsible for your life, for all the lives in Adeney Cross, and more beside. It is my duty to deal with the prisoners, and therefore equally my duty to

see that they do not betray me. I know nothing of
your Monsieur Sansterre, except that the escapes
started during his stay at Elchester, which is only a
few miles away. And now he has come here. I know
that he is a most peculiar man. He is a nobleman
and an officer, he is on parole, yet he is willing to do
the most menial tasks, apparently so that he can stay
in the village. Why, I've put him to the test myself. It
was I who made Colonel Walters order him to cut the
grass and tidy the garden. Do you not find that extraordinary? Do you imagine if I myself were a prisoner
on parole I would accept such orders? No, ma'am, let
me speak. It is, at its mildest, odd, and I am searching
for oddities. I am not accusing this gentleman of
anything; I am simply keeping an eye on him. I am a
Highlander. I left my country thirty years ago, when
the English overran it and massacred the greater part
of us. I was only a bairn then, when that Polish
fellow came over to lead us to perdition."

"That Polish fellow?" repeated Margaret, bewildered.

"Oh, the romantic English, who wished to hang
him, called him Bonnie Prince Charlie. Never mind
him. He's best forgotten. A deal of my family died for
him, and such of us as were left near starved. But
that's no matter. I only know that the Highlander,
however misguided he may be, regards himself as a
gentleman, and he'd rather have the skin flayed off
him than become a servant. Do you believe your
Marquis . . . did you know he was that?"

"Yes," said Margaret in a whisper.

"He's out cutting the lawn now, our Marquis. I
find that very, very strange. It appears you do not,
though I do not quite believe it. But we'll leave our

Monsieur Sansterre to cut the grass. Only, you are not French, my lass, and you look to me like a person who could be brave and loyal. He may be a friend of yours, and he may be more to bring up that pretty color every time I speak his name, but even so, you'd not want the villagers here to have their throats cut, their women raped, their crops burned—"

"They cannot be as bad as that!"

"A true feminine protest. All invading troops are as bad as that. And so are escaped prisoners, which interests me more. Ask my fellow countrymen in 1746, and that's only just over forty years ago. Human nature don't change in forty years."

"I think," said Margaret angrily, "you are a very pompous man."

He laughed again. She thought it really was a most unpleasant laugh, but she still could not bring herself to dislike him entirely, despite what he had said about Philippe. With one small section of her mind, she could see that he had some reason.

He said, in quite a coaxing tone, "Will you keep those bonnie hazel eyes open, Miss Margaret? Not only for Monsieur Sansterre, but for everyone else. If you hear something odd, see something, find something where it should not be, you just tell me. I am here most days; if not, you'll find me at the prison, for I live in a small cottage just by. Remember, my dear, there's a cache of arms somewhere to cut your throat with, a cache waiting for the day when the French troops land. And somewhere too there's an underground tunnel that goes beneath the prison, and I swear I'll find it if it's the last thing I do." He paused. For the first time, he looked almost embarrassed. "There's something else, ma'am—Margaret. May I not call you that? It's a good Scots name."

She was on her feet again. It was high time she got on with her work, and no doubt in her absence Thomas would have managed to remove a few eggs, a piece of bacon, and a slice of the cheese she had so carefully chosen in the village. She said suddenly, ignoring the last remark, not with a wish to rebuff him but simply because her mind was elsewhere, "How much should one fight against people?"

He looked disconcerted and angry. "What the devil are you talking about?"

"Oh, I'm sorry. I have no right to burden you with my personal problems. Only I was thinking, it is so difficult here. Until I came, everyone went his own way. Now I wish them to go mine, and of course they are all angry with me. It seems to me that perhaps I am wrong; it is not after all so important to get my own way. I believe that sometimes one should turn a blind eye. Or do you not believe that?"

"Oh," said Captain Ross, "maybe, maybe. But not when it really matters. Not when it is to do with prisoners escaping, to fight us again. Don't forget that, Margaret, whatever you do."

"Thank you, I won't." And she was thinking that Thomas might as well have his bit of bacon and cheese—it would at least save him a broken head, and Colonel Walters would never miss it. Perhaps the servants would then grow more friendly toward her. The thought of this made her a little happier, and she moved toward the door, only to swing around, startled, at a sudden roar from Captain Ross, who really was a most uncontrolled gentleman.

He shouted at her, "It's the devil of a business when a man is about to propose and he's given a lecture on how to manage the servants."

She could not believe her ears. She stood there,

scarlet, her mouth a little open, her hands flat against the door.

"Well," he said, now calm again, as if this were the most natural situation in the world, "I've been observing you, Margaret, and you seem to me a fine, douce little body, you're neat and tidy in your ways, and the servants, for all you talk of turning a blind eye, respect you and do your bidding. You cook us food we can eat, you keep the Hall clean, you see that the two young misses keep tidy without half their garments hanging torn behind them. I like the look of you, Margaret, though you could do with a wee bit more flesh.on those fine bones of yours, and it has struck me for a long time that I sorely need a woman about my home. This, after all, is not work for you here, for I can see you're a lady. Indeed, you're more of a lady than our little Albertine. I'm not much of a catch, my lass, with my one arm and a face that they used to say kept the bairns awake o'nights, but I'm not a bad fellow, I should not misuse you, and I'd give you the half of everything I have. Now, what do you say?"

"I don't know what to say," stammered Margaret, torn between tears and laughter. In her youth she had had her fair number of proposals, but never one remotely like this. Yet somehow she could not be offended, for this was offered in the utmost sincerity, and perhaps, if the circumstances were different, she could surely have done worse than accept this dear, ridiculous man who offered her marriage much as he might have displayed his house to a prospective buyer.

"I can tell you," said Captain Ross, who was plainly a most literal man. "You can say ay, or nay. It is as easy as that."

She said apologetically, "It must be no. Oh, I'm sorry, but we do not know each other at all, I have scarce spoken to you, and . . ."

"And there is, of course, this Monsieur Sansterre."

Her face grew bleak and old. She said coldly, "I assure you, that is nothing to do with it at all. It would not matter to Monsieur Sansterre if I married —married Thomas Lee."

Captain Ross broke into that loud laugh again. "Why, Margaret, Mrs. Lee would cut your pretty throat."

Then he stopped laughing, and she knew that involuntary moment of bitterness had irrevocably betrayed her. The Captain might be awkward in his proposing, but he was anything but a fool, and his favorite phrase, "I have been observing you," applied to a great deal else. Those dark eyes missed nothing.

And because she was now committed, because the day had already disemboweled her, she said what decency and sense forbade her to say.

"I would make no fit wife for you," she said, "or for any man." She looked at him with a proud defiance as she spoke. "I had a child, Captain Ross. The child died. It was born out of wedlock. I think you should know that, and now you will be thankful that I have turned you down."

And that, she thought, amazed at her own folly, is the end of my work here, the end of all hope and security, and the end of Philippe. She waited for the broadside—Captain Ross surely would never do anything quietly—and, because she was feeling a little sick and faint, closed her eyes. The hand that came down on hers brought her staring, wide-eyed, almost in tears.

He had clasped her hand in his. He was looking down at her, and was so close that she could not see his expression. He said, "You did not have to tell me that. But I appreciate it, I appreciate it very much. I knew you were an honest lass. But I do not give a damn. Why should I? It makes no difference to me. What is past is past, and I am concerned with the future, which I should like you to share."

She stammered, for she had never met anyone like him, "You surely cannot wish to marry me after what I have told you."

He had moved away again. He said, quite contemptuously, "You're a fool, Margaret. You're a good girl, but you're a fool. But I'll not pester you, though I warn you, I am a most persistent man. We'll forget this conversation for the moment—for the moment. And you are to feel free to come to me when you have anything to tell me. I'll not deave you with protestations and offers. Maybe later on you'll change your mind. I doubt I'll change mine."

She said, in a choked voice, "I think you are very kind. I've never met anyone like you."

He only said, as if she had not spoken, "But take care, lass. I mean that. These persons, whoever they are, are not the kind to show pity or mercy. They'll not hesitate to kill. I'm sure of that, indeed, I've seen it already. Watch, Margaret, observe and listen, but do nothing, nothing at all. Is that clear?"

She said, "Have you no idea who they are?"

He said somberly, "Ay," then turned away as if the interview was ended, as if there was no such thing as a proposal of marriage, as if what she had told him was unimportant. And so, bewildered, and still appalled by her own outburst, she went back to the kitchens, so that she could take what she needed for the day's meals. Her eye observed, as Captain Ross had instructed her, but it did not observe a cache of arms or a sinister look, simply that a corner of the cheese had vanished, that the eggs seemed a trifle loose in their box, and that a section of the side of bacon was more pink than the rest.

Thomas's sullen and self-conscious expression would in any case have enlightened her. However, as she began to sort things out, she simply smiled at him. When she had finished her task and instructed Mrs. Beeston in the preparing of vegetables for the midday meal, she went in search of the Frenchman.

She was not at all pleased when Miss Flora came running down the passage to her.

Flora was beautifully dressed in a gown of the softest wool, a fine gold brooch and earrings to match, but, as always, a button was missing, and there was a glimpse of a torn petticoat beneath the skirt. Margaret sighed. She was not at all in the mood for this foolish young girl, who had been given so much beauty and was squandering it on a young man who would never make her happy. Besides, being quick-witted herself, she found the childishness trying to her patience.

She said quite sternly, as if speaking to a small child, "Miss Flora. You have a button missing. You cannot meet your betrothed like that."

"Oh!" Flora, pouting a little at being scolded, looked down at her bodice, pulled vaguely at the empty buttonhole, then, fixing her blue eyes on Margaret, said, "Then you will have to sew it on for me."

Margaret thought, *I am become a nursemaid,* and her gaze wandered for a second, as if to see if there was any sign of Philippe. She said, a little wearily, "Have you the button?"

"I think it's on my dressing table. It fell off when

I put the dress on. It's not my fault," said Flora, quite crossly, "It was badly sewn on in the first place."

"Then I'd best sew it on for you now. I'll come to your room in a few moments."

"No." Flora's face lit up as if struck with a sudden and wonderful idea. "I'll come to yours. Oh, that would be fun. Do let me come, Margaret."

It was not fun for Margaret, who was longing passionately to find the Frenchman, and who had no wish for the company of this silly beauty. However, Flora, filled now with the excitement of coming to the cousin-housekeeper's minute room, was already flying down the stairs to collect her button, and presently she sat on Margaret's bed, while the latter sewed it on impatiently, glancing in some exasperation at the fine silken petticoat, which was indeed torn, with a flounce hanging down.

She said, "You should take more care of your clothes, Miss Flora. They are so beautiful."

"Oh, don't be tedious," snapped Flora, banging her hand down on the bed. "You're quite a scold, Margaret. I dare say that's why you've never married. Men don't like scolds."

Margaret could have answered that they did not like ninnies either, but she only smiled, remembering the strange proposal that had been made to her so short a time ago. When she had fixed the button, she lifted up the skirt of the petticoat and tacked down the flounce, saying as she did so, "I'll do that properly tomorrow. You cannot leave it like that. You'll only catch your heel in it."

She watched as Flora stepped into her dress again, saw how she pulled unnecessarily at the sleeve and fastened the buttons with an impatience which would soon end in another one's falling off. She shook her head at her. The child was quite absurd, but she was so lovely that it was hard to be cross with her. It was even harder to believe that she and Albertine were sisters—the one so beautiful and so stupid, the other as sharp as a knife.

Flora said, "Why are you looking at me like that?" She had sat down on the bed again. She showed no signs of going.

"I was thinking," said Margaret tartly, "that you are a very naughty girl. When I was young, I would never have been allowed to misuse my clothes so, and they weren't half as pretty as yours."

Flora did not seem offended, only giggled. Margaret prayed she would go, but she was looking around the tiny room, reaching out to fiddle with the things on the dressing table, picking them up and putting them down again. "Did you have many beaux when you were young?" she asked.

Margaret had used the phrase herself, but could not help resenting being thus pushed into old age. She replied in an austere fashion that yes, there had been gentlemen, and was about to say firmly that she had work to do when Flora cried out, "We are going to the prison at three. We can cross the sands then. Oh, I know we could go round the other way, but I like walking on the sands, because they are so dangerous. I love things that are dangerous, don't you?"

Margaret had hoped she would forget. She said, in a last faint protest, "Miss Flora, I am so very busy, and I am sure it would be better if your sister accompanied you."

"I don't want my sister to accompany me!"

I shall end by slapping you, thought Margaret, but

she only said patiently, "I still don't see why Monsieur Sansterre—"

"I don't want Frenchy. Why do you call him that stuffy name? I want you. And," said Flora, rising to her feet and making a portentous kind of face, "you are just the housekeeper here, and you have to do as you are told. If I say you are to come to the prison with me, you must come, otherwise I shall make sure you are sent away without any money or references."

Margaret looked up at the flushed, defiant face and said, rather grimly, "Ma'am!" At this Flora burst out laughing and, flinging her arms around her, kissed her on both cheeks. "Oh, Margaret," she said, "I do love you. It's all been so much better since you've been here," and with this was out of the room, the door slammed.

Margaret listened to her running down the passage. Flora, like the child she really was, could not move slowly. She sat down for a moment on the end of her bed (there was no room for a chair). She looked a little grimly at her reflection in the mirror. Perhaps it was the inevitable comparison with the glowing young beauty who had just left her, but she thought she had never seen herself so tired and pale and old. Perhaps that was why Captain Ross had proposed to her. Perhaps he wanted a sensible woman to be his housekeeper, someone who would not pester him with feminine whims and fancies. Margaret scowled hideously at herself, and turned away from this ridiculous creature who would so have loved a flounced lace petticoat and a beautiful dress. She turned away too from the thought of this wretched excursion to the prison—how extraordinary that it should be considered amusing to look on angry, suffering human beings—then realized that despite everything she must find Philippe.

What in God's name had made her tell him the one thing she had sworn never, never to utter to a single soul? This was indeed the end. If there had ever been any hope of his forgiving her, it was now finished for good and all. Perhaps he did not believe her. Perhaps he believed she was threatening him. Beneath her closed lids, from which the tears were already rolling down, she saw again the sad little creature, so unmistakably like his father, for all the face was white and wizened. Then the thought of the interview before her terrified her so much that she could have picked up her skirts and run, anything to get away.

But she did not. She dried her eyes and blew her nose, tidied her hair, and made sure her apron was clean, then set out in search of Philippe.

He seemed to have finished with the lawn, which looked bare, cropped and brown. The pile of bottles had been removed. Albertine would have to find another hiding place—her drinking could be secret no longer. Margaret wondered why she had to drink. After it was all over for her and the baby was dead and there seemed to be no future, she had thought she might well turn to the bottle herself, but a curious kind of pride had restrained her: She might be the lowest kind of creature, but she was damned if she were going to become some raddled, gin-soaked old harridan like the old woman in the village, who was never sober and whom everyone avoided and despised. But Albertine surely had no reason. She was, in her strange way, attractive, she had money and fine clothes, and surely there must be some young man who would long to protect so defenseless a little creature. Perhaps her drinking was one of the things that should be passed on to Captain Ross.

Margaret had no intention of passing it on. She detested the thought of being a spy, but then, she disliked even more the thought of being a traitor, and this was what she was now planning to be.

She walked swiftly down the passage, knowing now where she would find Philippe.

The Frenchman had been given a small study of his own, so that he could prepare his lessons in peace. It was a bare little room at the back of the house which might once have belonged to the gardener or the butler in the old days when the Hall was properly serviced. It had never been much of a room, and the small stove in one corner barely heated it, but it was light and quiet. Margaret, who came in without knocking, saw that he had set his books and papers on the table; the place looked tenanted.

He was sitting there, his head bent over a pile of papers. There was a dictionary at his side. The young ladies must have been doing their exercises for him. Margaret had to wonder what on earth Flora's homework could be like, and it was as if he had read her thoughts, for, without more than a brief glance up, he flicked at one piece of paper and said, "What do you think of this, pray?" Then he read out, "*Je suis vingt-quatres années vieux.*"

"What!" Despite her emotion and the wicked words that had passed between them only a short while back, she choked into a laugh. "What does that mean?"

"It means," he replied gravely, "that Miss Flora is twenty-four years old and an idiot."

"Oh!"

" 'Oh' indeed. If this continues, I shall have to buy

myself a ferule, or else a cap for my head to prevent me from tearing out my hair."

Then he looked fully at her, setting the papers down, with a paperweight neatly placed upon them. If she had not been so confused and distressed, she might have noticed that there was a flush on his pale face, and that he too was disturbed. But she was too overcome by her emotions to read his expression, and she stood there pleating her apron nervously.

He rose to his feet. She thought he had grown enormously thin. He said, in an expressionless voice, "I am glad you have come, Margaret. If you had not done so, I would have come to you. There is something I have to say to you."

She looked at him without speaking. She was thinking, *This is it, this is the end,* and her face grew weary and a little angry. She deserved everything, perhaps, but she had taken so much, and she felt as if she could endure nothing more.

He said quietly, "I owe you an apology."

She had been prepared for almost anything but this. She had thought to answer his reproaches with bitterness, or perhaps to walk out silently with what remained of her dignity. She had expected insult and anger, not this, and it took her breath away, left her standing there so overcome that she did not know what to say or do.

He went on, "I wish I had not spoken to you like that. It was unpardonable, under any circumstances." He broke off, then exclaimed, in a rush of words, "Why didn't you tell me?"

She answered, almost inaudibly, "What would have been the use?"

"But you should have done. I thought . . ."

"I know what you thought," said Margaret. It should have been her moment of triumph: This was her chance to hurt him as badly as he had hurt her. But she could feel only defeated; there was no anger left in her. She said, "Henry never touched me. But I don't blame you for believing the worst of me. After all, I could scarce have behaved more foolishly. And it don't matter any more. It's a long time ago. I should never have told you. I didn't mean to."

"I am glad you did."

"No. It was very wrong of me. I meant to keep it a secret to the end of my days. Please believe that, Philippe. And forget about it."

"Forget!" he said. "Forget! Are you out of your mind? Is this the kind of thing that anyone can forget?"

"Oh yes," she said, and gave him a small, bitter smile. "Do you know, I had almost forgotten. I didn't want to remember. Only, when we met again . . . But it cannot be helped. I shouldn't have told you. I'll never forgive myself."

"Will you forgive me?" he said. He had sat down again. He was no longer looking at her, only fiddling with his papers.

She tried to answer, but could not, though she knew he accepted her silence as an unforgiving reproach. The words she wanted to say choked her, and so she too looked away, praying that she would not cry, wanting desperately to move away, yet unable to do so.

He said at last, "It was a foolish question. But I hope you accept my apology. I would have made it in any case. I have behaved like a boor and a bully." Then suddenly he spoke in French. "We are con-

demned to stay here, Margaret. Neither of us is now
in a position to leave. Whatever we feel about each
other, we are like prisoners, we have to meet every
day. There is no point in recriminations, none at all.
As you yourself say, it is all over and done with, there
is nothing we can do about it, it certainly will not
help if we quarrel every time we meet. I know the
quarreling is my fault. To speak to you as I did . . .
You talk of forgiving yourself. I'll never forgive
myself, never. I don't know what possessed me. But it
will not happen again. We will pretend that we are
strangers, and speak to each other civilly like strangers." He looked up at her. "Perhaps we are strangers. I am beginning to believe I have never known
you. But you must forgive me my cruelty, Margaret
. . . I can only repeat, it will not occur again."

Then, almost as if this had been a set piece he felt
compelled to speak, he fell to fiddling again with the
papers. Perhaps Miss Flora's appalling exercise acted
as some sort of exorcism for his guilt.

She still could not answer, for she had to say what
was in her mind, and it was so at variance with everything that had passed between them that the words
fell over each other in her heart and none of them
would come out. She was thankful that he was no
longer looking at her, and she struggled to pull her
thoughts into some kind of coherence. However, what
jogged through her mind was not the warning she
was compelled to utter but the phrase "civilly like
strangers."

Then she said, in a clear, harsh voice, "There is
something I have to say to you too. That is why I
am here. You will not like it. I don't like it myself.
But . . . but . . ." Then she stuck again, after this

brave opening. She began once more to pleat her apron. After all this, it was so impossible to say; besides, she felt as if Captain Ross were there, listening to every word.

He suddenly shouted at her, "I wish to God you'd stop doing that!"

The roaring voice made her jump so that she backed away from him. She whispered, "Doing what? What terrible crime have I committed now?"

He mimicked her gesture. "You look like a kitchen maid. Must you always wear that confounded apron? Take it off. Take it off!"

She said coldly, "I have no idea what you are talking about," though she flushed as she said this. She moved her hands to her sides.

Then she saw that everything was going out of control, and if she did not speak her mind now, she would never do so. She said rapidly, "You must listen to me, Philippe. You say we—we are condemned to stay here. You imply we both came by the purest chance. I don't know. Perhaps it's true. But—I have no right to tell you this, but I must—Captain Ross thinks you are a spy."

He had risen to his feet again. He was not laughing now. His eyes fixed themselves on her with an intensity that terrified her. She went on in a rush, "He thinks you may be responsible for the escapes from the prison; perhaps that you are helping to plan an invasion. I cannot believe this is true, but—but if it is, you must leave at once, you are in great danger. If you are the traitor . . . But I could not bear you to be shot. I'd rather betray everyone than have that happen, even if it makes me a traitor too."

He said, "So you do believe I am a spy, that I

came here solely to betray everybody in this village?"

She said, beginning to cry again, "I don't know what to think anymore." Then she ran from the room. Once she glanced frantically over her shoulder as she fled down the corridor, thinking he might be coming after her. But there was no sign of him or of anyone, and at last she reached the kitchens, where she collapsed into a chair by the table, so panic-stricken at her own behavior that for a while she could do nothing but sit there, her hands clasped before her.

Chapter Six

*W*hen she had recovered, Margaret went up to her room to change and tidy herself for the outing. As she did her hair, she suddenly remembered Flora's gift. If it was a brooch, she could wear it to cheer up her drab clothes. She unwrapped it from the handkerchief—how typical of this young lady that the handkerchief, creased and crumpled, was of the finest cambric, with her initial embroidered in the corner—and set it on her dressing table to examine it.

It was not an ornament at all. It was a little bone

box such as the prisoners made at the Cross Prison.
The bones were leftovers from their dinners which
were boiled clean and then shaped and fashioned into
all kinds of things, including models of churches and
ships. If one could forget that this originally was part
of a joint of beef or mutton, one had to admit it
was charming. Margaret, swiveling it round in her
hands, marveled at the pains and ingenuity that must
have gone into its making. As she did this, the box fell
open. Inside was a piece of paper, which, when she
unfolded it, held simply the initial "C." This, she
presumed, was the artist's mark, and she tore the
paper up and threw it away.

She tied her bonnet—her second-best one now that
the other was gone—fastened her cloak, and made her
way to the front entrance. She saw as she passed that
the Frenchman was hard at work preparing his lessons. She walked by quickly without a word, and
when she reached the front door she sat down there
to wait.

The angry words hit her ears, and she looked out of
the window to see what was happening. The two
Walters girls were plainly having a blazing quarrel.
She had always suspected that they did not get on, but
this was the first time she had witnessed such a scene.
She saw that Albertine was afire with fury, but it was
the sight of Flora that disturbed her, for the young
woman who was normally so sweet and placid now
wore a look of barely controlled rage that was alarming in its ferocity. The beautiful face was so full of
hate that Margaret wondered if she should intervene.
Before she could make up her mind to do so, Flora
said, in a clear, high voice, "I was not to know it
was yours. It is only a common thing after all. You

can buy them by the dozen every Sunday. You are just making mischief, Bertie, as usual. There is no reason why she shouldn't have it. It's not important. You just love making a fuss so as to be the center of attention."

Albertine muttered something obviously venomous in reply, and Flora instantly pushed her aside, with a violence that nearly knocked her off her feet. Then, very pink in the face, the golden hair falling over her cheek, she swept into the hall, where, at the sight of Margaret, she at once became charming again. She insisted on taking her arm, and kept up a nonstop flow of chatter as the two of them made their way down by the sea wall to the Loving Sands.

Margaret, realizing that the quarrel must be over her little box, resolved to return it the moment she came home again. She too could not understand why it was so important, for similar objects were sold to the villagers of Adeney Cross every time they visited the prison. But she was careful not to mention it, and presently the two young women were clambering down the steep steps that led onto the sands, with the Cross Prison at the far end.

It was the first time since her arrival that Margaret had actually set foot on the sands. She paused for a moment to look about her. The sea, gray and white-horsed, was far in the distance; the sands were smooth and white beneath her feet as she began, a little nervously, to move across them.

"It's all right," said Flora cheerfully, "we have at least another half-hour." She looked, a little maliciously, at her companion. "You're frightened, aren't you, Margaret?"

"A little," admitted Margaret, and knew she would

be thankful to be off this treacherous surface, for all it seemed so crisp and firm. It was hard to believe that it could suddenly engulf one as if in a whirlpool.

She asked, "What makes them like this?"

"Oh, I don't know. They're a kind of quicksand, but only when the sea is near. A lot of people have been killed," said Flora. The idea did not seem to disturb her. "There was little Bobby Lee. They say Mrs. Lee has been touched in the head ever since it happened. And, of course, strangers don't always know about them, and think they look pretty and take a walk. And then . . ." She waved her hands and made a kind of hissing sound. "Like that! No more strangers."

"But that's horrible! The poor things!"

"Why should I worry? I don't know them. It's not my fault if they're so silly. The bodies turn up weeks later, sometimes here and sometimes as far as Elchester. They say the flesh is sucked off the bones."

"Miss Flora!"

"I think it's rather amusing myself. I think the Loving Sands are fascinating. Nobody else has anything quite like them. If we are invaded, the French will have a very difficult time."

She uttered these words in a gay and happy manner, as if she were discussing some coming ball. Margaret glanced at her but made no comment, and turned her attention to the Cross Prison, now looming blackly before them.

Like all buildings of its kind, it wore a grim and foreboding air. It had once been a workhouse orphanage, and the poor children must have wilted inside the thick, blackened walls enclosing the small barred windows and the bleak courtyard, where perhaps they were allowed to play. Even if in those days there had been a more cheerful air to the place, it was hard to see it as welcoming. Margaret thought of the stories she had heard: of the gamblers known as *les Romains* who gambled away the very clothes on their backs, of the races run with the rats that infested the prison, and of how, in the overcrowded quarters, there would be a cry of "Spoon!" in the night, so that the men could turn over at the same time.

Despite the cold, the prisoners were all out in the courtyard, displaying their wares. They were dressed in yellow suits and caps, with red waistcoats. They seemed cheerful enough, though the guards with loaded pistols were there to keep an eye on them, and some of them held dogs by the leash—savage animals whose reddened eyes and slavering jaws made Margaret shudder and keep her distance.

On the tables were straw and bone toys, including several little boxes like the one that Flora had given her. The villagers had already arrived and were making their purchases. Despite Mr. Clay's forebodings, most of them seemed on good terms with the prisoners, laughing and chatting with them, while the younger women flirted with sideways glances, giggling loudly and pretending to be offended when an impudent Frenchman caught at their skirts or tried to kiss them.

Margaret stood a little back from the others, for the sight of these men distressed her. They were, after all, captives in grim conditions, not because they were criminals but simply because they had fought on the enemy side. Philippe, were he not an officer, would have been one of them. It sickened her to think that he might be sitting cross-legged there, a peepshow for the village, surrounded by desperate men, waiting wearily for the end of a war that seemed to be going on forever. Flora, however, was evidently enjoying herself, though her eyes occasionally wandered to the officers' barracks at the side. The prisoners knew her by this time, and were enchanted by her beauty, addressing her as *ma belle* and using sometimes more familiar expressions that, fortunately, she did not understand.

Je suis vingt-quatres années vieux, indeed! Papa would have gone mad, but then, he had never been a patient teacher, and many times he had boxed Margaret's ears for making some much less elementary mistake.

She moved aside in the direction of the barracks. Flora whispered, "He'll be off duty in twenty minutes. You can go home then, but not by the sands, for the tide will be coming in. You'd best cross the prison by the barracks—that's where *he* lives!—and come out by Captain Ross's cottage. Such a horrid man, I detest him. He swears so, and he drinks too much. I can't imagine why Papa puts up with him."

Margaret was at this moment hoping that Lewis would be sober when his betrothed arrived, and started guiltily. But it seemed that Flora would not notice unless he was flat on the floor. She now decided that her duty as chaperone was done, and walked away, pausing for a moment to speak to a sad-looking young man who sat apart from the others, and who seemed to have nothing to sell.

She spoke to him in French, feeling happy to talk in Philippe's language. He brightened up at this, and she asked him where he came from.

"Provence," he said, and his vision turned inwards,

as if he was seeing not the bleak, sweating walls but the green fields and vineyards of home.

She was enchanted by this, for she knew that was where Philippe came from too, and for a little while she talked with him, hearing about his mother and his sisters, what he did as a civilian, how long he had been a prisoner. "Perhaps you will be exchanged on one of the cartel ships," she said, wishing to comfort him, for his youth—he could not have been more than eighteen—saddened her, and she was touched by the look of him, with his long, dark hair and eyes set deep in a face that was too white and too thin.

He gave her a strange, intent look. "Perhaps," he said.

"There are a great many exchanges. And you are very young. I think it is mostly the young who are sent home."

He looked almost as if he wished to tell her something, then changed his mind. He did not refer to the cartel ships again. He said only, "Good-bye, mademoiselle. If you ever come to France, you will stay with my family, they will make you most welcome. I will give you my name and address."

And this he scribbled down on a piece of rough paper. She thanked him and said perhaps they would meet again.

To this he did not reply, only again wished her good-bye, using the word *adieu* instead of *au revoir*.

She looked back at him once. He was again huddled in that dejected attitude. His name was Christian, and she wondered if she should mention him to Captain Ross. She entered the prison by the side door that led to the barracks and from there out on the other side. The guard on duty saluted her and gestured her through.

The barracks, at least, were clean and in order. The windows were unbarred, and the fresh air was allowed to blow through. She looked about her with interest and, filled with the curiosity that Papa always said would be her undoing, peeped through a window in one of the cubicles, to see what the officers' quarters were like.

Then she gave a gasp before she could check herself. She was so astounded that she did not even back away, but only stared in horrified amazement.

The room was a cell, small and bare, with one chair, a small chest, and a bed. On the bed lay Captain Lewis Moore, and beside him, with the half of her clothes on the floor and her dark hair wild, was Albertine, clasping him to her and kissing him with a kind of desperate passion. It was evident that they were lovers of long standing, and as Margaret, suddenly realizing her own deplorable behavior, swung around to be away as quickly as she could, Albertine raised herself from Lewis's arms, and her dark eyes met the hazel ones. Then Margaret fled along the corridor, anxious to put as much distance between the two of them as possible.

Various young men gazed with interest at this young woman running at top speed, but she ignored them—indeed, did not see them—and paused for breath only as she reached the back entrance. The sentry saluted her, wondering why she looked so white and aghast, asked her if she knew the way back to the Hall and added politely, "You don't go near the sands now, ma'am, they're at their most dangerous."

Margaret was too shocked and distraught to answer him. She simply stared, and then went out of the doorway.

There she stood still for a moment, trying to quiet

her thudding heart. The most fervent prayer that she was uttering to herself was that she not meet Captain Ross. She saw the cottage that was his, and had no difficulty in recognizing it: It was small, white, neat, and military, with a stiff, regimented little garden, a beautifully cut lawn, and a coat of arms over the door. She began to move on quickly, determined to avoid the owner, but her prayer was ignored, and the well-known voice brought her angrily to a standstill.

It said over her shoulder, "Are you doing an act of charity, Miss Margaret, or are you observing as I bade you? I trust you will honor my humble home, and take a glass of wine with me."

She disliked the foolish turn of phrase, and she had never wanted to speak to Captain Ross less, but she could see it would be a waste of breath to argue, for somehow he was at her side, taking her arm and steering her down the little path to his front door.

A far less observant man would have instantly noticed her disturbance. Her haste had tipped her bonnet askew, her hair was coming down, and she was flushed and breathing fast.

However, he made no immediate comment, only took her into what was plainly his study. Like the rest of the cottage, it was immaculately tidy, with papers piled on a desk, shelves of books, and an imposing portrait above the glowing wood fire, which must have been Ross Senior, for there was a marked resemblance.

The only incongruity was a sleek Persian cat, asleep before the fire. It seemed to Margaret, still hot and dizzy with shock and confusion, that a wolfhound would have been more in keeping. However, as she had always felt that animals and children were useful in social emergencies, she kneeled down beside the beast to stroke it and at the same time hide her face.

"Well?" said Captain Ross, with his usual alarming directness. "And what have you got to report?"

And he poured her out a glass of wine, for which, for once, she was sincerely grateful. He set it on a small table by her chair, putting a little lace mat beneath the glass. She noticed, as she sat down, that even the cat slept on its own white rug. These odd spinsterish touches in so rugged a man somehow moved her, so that she felt a little better. But she was still a little hysterical, torn between a desire to laugh and to answer, *Why certainly, I have just seen Miss Albertine in bed with Captain Moore, and from the air of her it is by no means the first time. I have also warned Monsieur Sansterre that you think he is a spy, and I seem to be involved in some strange business with a little bone box that I do not understand at all.*

However, she said only, "Nothing, sir," righted her bonnet, retied the strings, and took what was virtually a gulp of the wine.

"You are a damned bloody liar," said Captain Ross, with the utmost amiability, and poured himself a drink from another bottle, a clear, whitish liquid with an acrid smell. He ignored her look of outrage, which was, in any case, simulated, for his direct speech struck her as friendly and warm. "Whisky," he said, waving the glass at her. "Usquebaugh. Far better for you than that red, foreign stuff, but I dare say your ladylike constitution would not stand it. Would you perhaps care to try, Miss Margaret?"

She declined hastily, not caring for the smell.

"Ah, we'll have to be educating you. So there's nothing to report?"

"I'm afraid not."

"But surely you've warned your gentleman?"

She flushed scarlet, and he broke into one of his horrid, barking laughs, taking a great swig at the whisky as he did so. This so angered her that she spoke the truth.

"Yes," she said, "yes! Did you expect otherwise?" Then she saw the derision on his face, and her temper broke. "You wanted me to tell him. You cannot deny it. And of course I did. He may be all you say, but I am not a spy, and—and he was once a friend of mine. I do not betray my friends, whatever they have done. Of course I warned him. I would do it again." She looked at him as she spoke. She was shaking all over, but her face was proud and determined. "You never for one second believed I would betray him."

"No," said Captain Ross, and refilled his glass as he spoke. Miss Flora was right in this—he certainly drank far too much. He gave her a smile which, she thought, resembled that of a tiger. "You're a good lass, Miss Margaret. You have done precisely as I wished. Am I not a good judge of character?"

This left her with nothing to say, and for a moment she fell silent. Then she rose to her feet, saying, as composedly as she could, "I think you should be ashamed of yourself. You are a most devious and unscrupulous man. You just use people for your own ends. I have no doubt that is why you proposed to me."

"No!" The word came out in a roar. "No, in Christ's name." And he gripped her shoulder with his one hand, so hard that it bruised her. "Margaret," he said, dropping the prefix, "do you not see how serious this is? There may after all be an invasion, and we don't want the bloody French back, with

Boney at their head. We had all of that with William
seven centuries back. Mind you, I do not think this will
happen, but certainly there will be a grand escape,
and that is almost as bad. Oh, I agree, I should have
been more frank with you. But I cannot entirely trust
your Monsieur Sansterre. He is French, he is here,
and that is enough for me. He may have all the vir-
tues of a canonized saint, but I do not know, and
neither do you. I wanted him put on his guard, so that
he dare not wait much longer. If he is as innocent
as you suppose, it don't matter. If he's not, he'll have
to do something about it, and quick, too, because he
knows I am observing him. Why do you look like
that?"

She said bitterly, "You are always observing, Captain Ross. It's your favorite phrase."

"Well," he said, quite smugly, as if she had paid him
a compliment, "it's what I am trained for. Now, sit
down, lass."

"I must go."

"Not quite yet. You have been observing too. Tell
me." His face, as he spoke, grew somber and grim.
"You must tell me."

She hesitated, then told him about the little bone
box with the initialed piece of paper inside. She could
not bring herself to recount what she had seen in the
barracks, but managed to say, "I find Miss Albertine
a strange young lady."

"She is that indeed."

"She—she drinks a great deal of wine. I do not
know," said Margaret with some candor, "why she
should not, but it is unusual in a young girl, especially as she then seems to throw the bottles out of the
window." This, as she recounted it, sounded remark-

ably silly, though Captain Ross was listening with the greatest attention, but somehow she was compelled to go on. "I think perhaps she is a little in love with Miss Flora's betrothed. I—I have no real reason to say this, but I have observed . . ." She broke off, flushing, and the abominable man laughed, as she might have expected. "Well," she said crossly, "it is what you have asked me to do. I am probably wrong. I have no real grounds for such an assumption."

And with this gross and monstrous lie, she prepared to go once again, and this time he did not stop her, but only said, as he opened the door for her, "I asked you to marry me because I wanted you to marry me. I don't pretend to be head over heels in love, Margaret, like the poetry, for I am not that kind of person, but I have a great respect for you, and if you despise that, you are more of a fool than I believe you to be."

She looked back at him, half wanting to laugh, yet aware of almost a tenderness for him, impossible as he was, smelling of his whisky, the ugly face scowling at her. She said, "I don't despise it. You must believe that."

"But you are in love with that French fellow."

"Certainly not!"

"I think you are quite a liar, Margaret," he said, then, "Take care, lass. Take care."

"Why," she said, almost pertly, "what do you think will happen to me?"

"I do not know," he answered, "but I am beginning to think you'd be better away."

She did not tell him that the Frenchman had said almost the same thing. Instead, she said, "I have nowhere to go. And I do not like to run away. Besides, Captain Ross, if I left you'd have no one to observe for you."

And with this she stepped into the hallway, which was, she noticed, shining with beeswax, and out onto the path. She began to walk swiftly back toward the Hall. There was no sign of either Flora or Albertine, and the dark was beginning to fall. She had to wonder what could possibly have happened. Could the handsome captain be so barefaced as to make love to one sister after another? Though Miss Flora would never allow him such liberties—she seemed to Margaret a conventional girl. But what was Albertine thinking of to behave in such a way with her sister's betrothed? And what indeed was Captain Moore thinking of, for though there might not be much beneath that golden hair, Miss Flora was something of a catch for a young captain without much money. Margaret knew nothing of the family finances, a matter which did not interest her, but it was plain enough that there was no lack of income.

She came at last to the sea wall by the roundabout path from Captain Ross's cottage. Despite the cold and the wind rising from the sea, she had to pause to look down at the Loving Sands, for these sands fascinated her as much as they frightened her. She wondered once again what extraordinary currents were responsible for the devouring whirlpool that lay beneath them. She could see now in the moonlight that they quivered in a strange, live way as the sea swept up to them. It was as if some animal stirred underneath; it was almost as if they rustled. The prison too looked ugly and black. The courtyard would be empty now, and the men back inside, perhaps eating their meager supper. The memory of Christian induced another memory, of another Frenchman, and the sorrow came down upon her again. Indeed, it was always there; it stirred beneath

the surface of her mind like the demon of the Loving
Sands—a vast regret for something magnificent that
she herself had willfully destroyed.

She thought she heard a footstep. Something made
her turn around, and at that moment a blow caught
her on the shoulder so that she fell sideways down
onto the rocky path. If she had not moved in that
one moment, she would have been hurtled over the
wall onto the Loving Sands.

She was momentarily stunned. When a second later
she managed to pull herself up, there was no one
there, nothing but the wind and the sea and the faint
humming of the sands.

Her first reaction was anger and humiliation, for it
was not dignified to fall flat on one's face. Her bonnet
was dangling by its strings, and her cloak was stained
with sea water and sand. Her next reaction was one of
sick terror, so that she had to sit down on the wall and
bite her own hand to stop herself from fainting. This,
she knew, she had to know, was not some chance
thing—a running child not looking where he was
going or some person blind with haste or drink. No
one had stopped to help her up, and the blow had
been a savage one; she could feel that her shoulder
was bruised and sore. But for that one instinctive
movement, she would have been swallowed up in
the sands.

Someone has tried to murder me.

And only one name came to her mind. Could he
really want to kill her? What good would it do him?
He might be the spy that Captain Ross expected him
to be, but why kill her, his avowed ally?

Margaret, a little recovered from her dizziness,
managed to rise to her feet. There was no one abroad.

This was the hour when Adeney Cross settled down to its supper. Not even a fisherman would be out on so bitter a night.

Take care, lass. That was what Captain Ross had said. *Take care* . . . If it were not Philippe, and she still could not believe him capable of murder, who then?

Yet she could not doubt the malevolence of that blow, and when at last she summoned up enough strength to walk back to the Hall, she took care to keep well away from the sea wall, and even when she was going up the hill, she swerved around to make sure there was no one behind her.

She went straight to her room, and in the reality of that small place that was now home to her, she began to wonder if it had not been a chance accident after all. Her shoulder, when she examined it in the mirror, was red and bruised, but the responsible party might still have been some drunken villager unaware of what he had done.

She still felt a little sick with the shock, but she tidied her hair and brushed down her cloak. Then she realized that something was missing. The little bone box that she had been going to return to Miss Flora was gone.

"I think," said Margaret aloud to herself, "I am going mad. I am beginning to imagine things. This is all perfectly ridiculous." And, having spoken so sternly to herself, she looked under the dressing table and under the bed—the only places where the box could be. There was no trace of it. Then suddenly the answer came to her. Miss Flora, after the quarrel with her sister had decided to take it back. It would never strike her to ask permission to go into the housekeeper's room. She would simply act on impulse, as she always did, run in and snatch up the box, without considering the matter important enough to be mentioned.

Margaret, a little relieved, though still shaken by the incident at the sea wall, went down to the kitchens to make sure the dinner was ready.

Mrs. Beeston—really, one could not leave her on her own—had made her usual muddle. The meat was already done, the pie was not, and the pans full of vegetables were without salt. However, all this could be remedied quickly enough, and at least the old woman, however lazy and incompetent, never seemed to bear a grudge. When Margaret gently scolded her, she simply smiled and agreed, and when told to salt the vegetables, she did so at once.

"I think I bully you," said Margaret, and smiled as she said this, for it was impossible to dislike this old silly, who was fortunate to be employed in the Hall. Most people would have refused to put up with her.

"Oh no, miss," said Mrs. Beeston cheerfully, "I don't mind, I'm sure. I don't really listen, miss, it just goes in one ear and out the other."

This Margaret could well believe, but she only laughed as she moved the pie into the hottest part of the oven.

"Not like some as I could mention," went on Mrs. Beeston, who when awake was a great one for talking. Margaret could have echoed her companion's remark about not really listening, for the old woman's conversation was like the humming of the sands: It went on and on, with no answer or comment required. But the next words brought her head sharply around.

"That Miss Bertie, and that Captain Lewis Moore," said Mrs. Beeston, and for the first time her placidity was ruffled. There was quite an edge to her burring voice, and the wooden spoon now stirring the salted vegetables positively quivered. It was the first time Margaret had ever seen her so animated. The red face was even redder, the lower lip pouted like that of a child, and the eyes that swiveled around to Margaret were angry with the heavy anger of stupidity.

Margaret, overcome by curiosity, repeated, "Miss Bertie? What has Miss Bertie done to upset you?" And she quickly removed the spoon from Mrs. Beeston's hand, for it was stirring with such temper that some of the vegetables were being whisked over the side of the pan.

"I likes my mug of ale," said Mrs. Beeston sullenly.

"Why, yes," said Margaret, astonished, and began to believe the old woman was gone in the wits. "You make a delicious spiced ale. I like it myself." And as she spoke, she began putting the food into dishes, which two of the village girls would then carry to the Colonel's table.

"I don't see why I shouldn't," said Mrs. Beeston, more crossly than ever. She looked up at Margaret out of her small eyes. "It's all a poor old woman has left in the world. It's not as if I ever takes too much, like some as I could mention. I'm sure I don't harm nobody. You'll bear me out in that, Miss Margaret."

"Of course I will," said Margaret soothingly, more bewildered than ever. With the serving done, she fetched the old woman the pot of this ale she was talking about off the stove, and then said, "Mrs. Beeston, what is the matter? I can see something has upset you. Why don't you tell me all about it?"

This Mrs. Beeston had obviously been waiting to do for some time. She waddled up to Margaret, made her sit down, then filled two tankards with ale and prepared to speak.

"Miss Bertie," she said, after clearing her throat several times and draining half her tankard at a gulp, "she comes creeping into my kitchen without so much as a by-your-leave, goes down into the cellar, and comes up with a dozen—a dozen, mark you!—bottles of wine."

Margaret said, after a pause, "Well, really, Mrs. Beeston, there is no reason why she should not. Perhaps Colonel Walters asked her—"

"Since when has the Colonel asked his daughter to do his errands for him? There's Thomas, ain't there? It's Thomas's place to bring up the bottles and suchlike, not that little lame-legged bitch."

"Now really, Mrs. Beeston!"

But one could no more check Mrs. Beeston than the tide coming over the Loving Sands. It was growing plain to Margaret that this was not an isolated incident. Perhaps Mrs. Beeston was not quite the simple soul she imagined; perhaps those sleepy eyes saw more than a cosy fire and a mug of ale. As for Albertine, she saw her so little these days that she sometimes wondered if the young woman were deliberately ignoring her. But this situation seemed to her ridiculous. Obviously Albertine would not be expected to cart up bottles from the cellar, so why she should want so many for herself was beyond comprehension. But then, of course, if she were taking them for Captain Moore . . . It was evident by now, if only from what had been concealed in the uncut grass, that she enjoyed her wine also, but it would surely be easier to remove the odd bottle from time to time, for that wouldn't be noticed by everyone.

"I spoke to her about it," Mrs. Beeston went on. "I said to her, I said, 'What do you want with a dozen bottles, miss?' And do you know what she answered? She told me to mind my own damned business— swearing like that, a lady!—and if I didn't, she'd get me sent back to the village and turned out of my cottage, which is the only home I have in the wide world, Miss Margaret, ma'am, as she well knows, with my dear husband dead these past ten years, and no children to look after me. 'Miss Albertine,' I said, 'there's a lot going on I don't like to know, and what you want with a dozen bottles of wine, I cannot imagine, nor do I wish to ask, but I've seen things,' I said, 'and I think it's time you learned how to behave yourself. If you was my daughter,' I said, 'I'd give you a hiding you'd remember to the end of your days!' "

"Mrs. Beeston!"

". . . 'carrying on like that and drinking yourself silly o'nights!' Oh, I sees things, Miss Margaret, ma'am, I'm not so daft as you all like to believe, and there's things goes on here that ain't right, not right at all, and the vicar'd turn in his grave if he knew about them, so would the poor Colonel, too. I told her off good and proper, and she slunk away; she didn't say another word. And that Captain Lewis threatening to fire me."

And with this final volley, Mrs. Beeston seemed to return to her usual self. She subsided into her chair, with the tankard of ale in her hand, smiled sleepily at Margaret, as if this had been the most normal conversation in the world, and presently dozed off. After a brief snooze, she would retire to her cottage.

Margaret had been half disposed to tell her of the incident by the sea wall, but probably the old woman would not even have listened. And she herself was cold and exhausted, still a little chilled with the shock.

When the washing up was done, she went up the stairs to her room. She passed the Frenchman, but only wished him good night. The sight of him sent a strange shudder through her, for at the back of her mind was the dreadful suspicion that it might have been his hand that had nearly hurtled her to a horrid death. It was almost impossible to believe, but then, the whole situation was impossible, and she had, after all, virtually accused him of being a spy. She looked after him as she was closing her door. He was going down the stairs, obviously to his study. She only saw the tall leanness of him, the broad shoulders and the dark hair. The love filled her so that she almost ran after him to cry, *Was it you? I do not mind, I only want to know, I have to know . . .*

Once, a long time ago, she had played hide-and-seek with her friends, and suddenly she had been unable to endure the suspense. She had run out of her corner, crying, "Find me, oh please, find me!"

But she said nothing, only closed the door. And for a long time she sat on the end of the bed, staring out the darkened window, and it seemed to her that this was a sick house—murder lurked in its shadows. It was not only Bluebeard who said, Madam, you must die.

Some days later, the Frenchman sat in his small study. It was not the lessons that took him there. Certainly, the correction of those shocking exercises took up a great deal of his time, but now he had finished them, and had even prepared for the next week. He sat there to wait until his pupils arrived for the evening lesson. He chose to be in the study rather than in his little bedroom, because this, plain and chilly as it was, represented the nearest thing to home.

He could have told the Colonel that the lessons were an utter waste of time and money. Miss Flora was hopeless; she would never learn anything. She was a most beautiful girl, though the golden hair and a milk-and-roses complexion did not interest him. The blue eyes were lovely, and as bright as sapphires, but there was no intelligence behind them. She was as charming to look at as a work of art, but the Frenchman had grown impatient these days, and sometimes when she made a more than usually inane remark, he wanted to bang his book down and order her from the room as if she were a tiresome child. He sometimes believed she simply did not listen to him. Her mind, such as it was, no doubt was with the handsome captain. The wretched girl would have a poor sort of life with him, once the initial passion was over, but it would have been no good telling her— indeed, it was no good telling her anything. She sat there dutifully enough, her chin on her hand, her eyes fixed on him, and whenever he met her gaze she smiled. Plainly, however, she did not remember one rule, her accent was atrocious, her vocabulary was nil, and her exercises, when she remembered to do them at all, a nightmare that one had to laugh at for the sake of sheer sanity.

Only, for the past few days he had noticed that she had grown even more silent. The soft, delicate pink of her cheeks had faded, and the bright eyes wore the hurt look of a child astonished by an unkind world. Yesterday he had suspected she had been crying, and on an impulse said to her, before her sister arrived,

"You seem tired, Miss Flora. Is there anything the matter?"

She gave him a strange, wild look. She did not, as he had expected, giggle in that soft way of hers that exasperated him, nor did she grow coquettish. She only said, in a dull voice, "I do not know."

This implied a certain sense, almost as if she had been reflecting, and it so surprised the Frenchman that he looked at her more kindly, then said, "May I be permitted to help you in any way, mademoiselle?"

He regretted this instantly. God knows, he had enough on his plate without Miss Flora's woes. But she answered, with a kind of detached despair, "No. There is nothing you can do." Then, because she was a polite girl, she added, "Thank you very much."

And that was all he heard from her. It seemed both pointless and unkind to disturb her further, so he left her in peace and concentrated his energies on Miss Albertine.

Albertine troubled him more deeply than Flora, and he had by no means missed the way she sometimes looked at Margaret. The dark hatred in her eyes astonished and alarmed him, for he could see no reason for it. Certainly, there had rarely been two sisters more dissimilar. Normally there was some dim family likeness, even if coloring and features were different. But there seemed to him no resemblance whatsoever between this lovely, golden idiot and this dark little changeling, with her big, watchful eyes, her pointed little face with the wide, toothy mouth, and the minute body. The one was as quick as the other was slow. Albertine gobbled up his French lessons with an avidity that startled him. He never had to tell her anything twice, often in her queries she was ahead of him, and her exercises were intelligent, shrewd, and always most dutifully ready.

He remarked that evening, when the two sisters were seated at the table, "You have quite a natural gift for languages, Miss Albertine."

She raised the great eyes to his. They were like the eyes of a lemur—vast, round, opaque. The malice in them pricked his blood. There was no kindness or gentleness in this little creature, despite that deceptively soft, high voice. One could never imagine her with children, or gentling some small animal. Love for her must be a thing of sensual passion, stripped of tenderness. She gave him her little sideways smile, and he noticed again the predatory tooth, which protruded a little at the side of her mouth. "It must be," she said, "because I have such a good teacher."

He did not trouble to reply. He knew perfectly well that she did not mean it. Albertine was good at French because she wanted to be good at it—all she needed was to be directed. Sometimes he could not believe that she had never spoken French before, though she constantly assured him that this was so. "Except for the prisoners at the Cross," she said, "I have never even met anyone from your country. Of course I listen to the prisoners, and sometimes I try to answer them. But I have never taken lessons."

Flora remarked suddenly, "You can quote from Bluebeard in French."

He thought Albertine looked briefly disconcerted. She answered sharply, "That is different. One of the prisoners taught me, and I learned it by heart. You did too."

This meant nothing to Flora, who had relapsed once more into her dream, but Albertine smiled and said, "It is a rather amusing tale, don't you think, Frenchy? I do enjoy quoting from it. I like to say, *Il faut mourir, madame, et tout à l'heure.*"

Madam, you must die. The words jarred the Frenchman, and shot through him an inexplicable pang of fear. There was no reason for it. It was a child's tale. Perhaps children a century ago were tougher little beings than now, perhaps they took headless corpses and bloodied keys in their stride. But what nonsense it all was—the eleventh-century room had been given the name simply out of foolishness. He finished his lesson, and Albertine made no more strange remarks, but only sat there meekly, answering his questions and inclining her head with its shining dark hair so as to write his instructions down in her notebook.

Flora said nothing more, nor did she take any notes. Once the Frenchman saw Albertine shoot an angry look at her sister, but no words were exchanged between them.

They left on the minute, as they always did. Flora sailed out, and the little sister hopped behind her, dragging her deformed foot. She stopped at the doorway. She said, "Why don't you eat with us this evening?"

"I have not been invited, mademoiselle."

"But I invite you, Frenchy!"

He answered coldly, "Thank you, but I have work to do."

She said in a jeering way, "You will, of course, dine with housekeeper Margaret. Have you not met before, Frenchy? I have seen her looking at you. I think she is *éprise*. We use that word too, you know. Do you like Margaret, Frenchy?"

He had learned by this time that direct rudeness was his only weapon. What was more, she seemed to enjoy it. He spoke to her with a brutality that years ago he would never have employed to any woman. He found that he almost hated her, and in some odd way was afraid of her, not personally but for the malice that emanated from her. He said, "I do not care for this kind of conversation. I find you a very impertinent young lady."

"Oh, Frenchy," she said in mock horror, "what would Papa say if he heard you talking to me like that?"

"I am more interested," returned the Frenchman calmly, "in what he would say if he heard *you* talking to *me* like that. May I remind you, mademoiselle, that I am only the French tutor here."

"And the gardener!"

"If you wish. But it is not my place to conduct such conversations with you. I do not like it, and, to be frank, I do not like you either."

"Oh, Frenchy!" she said again, apparently quite undisturbed. Her eyes moved over him, and her mouth trembled as if she wanted to laugh.

"It is time you joined your father for dinner, mademoiselle."

"And you your Margaret."

He made her a bow in silence. He thought she wanted to stay, but Flora called out, "Bertie, where are you?"

She said, "I'll be seeing you again, Frenchy. We must finish this conversation. You see, I don't dislike you at all. I like you. You are not so very handsome, but you are attractive. And I love tall men, I feel so ridiculous beside them."

And with this she hopped off, casting a little provocative glance at him before she disappeared down the corridor.

Chapter Seven

The Frenchman, coming out to get his own meal, met Margaret, also on her way to the kitchens. Normally, he would have stopped to exchange a few civil words with her, for he was still ashamed of what had passed between them, ashamed too that he had caused her so much unhappiness. She paused as she saw him, and he looked directly at her. He could not help thinking of Albertine's words, and his brows met at the thought of this little watcher whose large eyes saw so much, and who, it seemed to him, made mischief as easily as she breathed. And, thinking this, he said nothing, while Margaret, who had kept quiet for so long, could hold herself in no longer and burst out with the words she had sworn not to say.

"Was it you?" she said, her voice high with hysteria. "Was it you who tried to kill me?"

The look of incredulous anger he gave her checked her hysteria and at the same time filled her with a chill conviction that her suspicion was true. She backed a little away from him, and her face changed, grew cold and still.

He said at last, "Are you out of your mind?"

She could not answer, only shook her head. Her hand went out as if to ward him off.

He said more quietly, "What are you talking about, Margaret? Why should you believe I tried to kill you?" And then, urgently, "Margaret! What is this nonsense? What has happened? You must tell me!"

But she could not speak, because the fear and grief were choking her. At last, she managed to say, in a voice he had never heard from her, "It don't matter, Philippe. It's not even important." She gave him a half smile. "I always seem to say things to you that I have promised myself not to say. It's just, I think, that I like to know. Are you coming down for your supper now?"

He said, keeping his voice as calm and controlled as he could, "I want to know who has tried to kill you. Will you please tell me?"

She said, "Oh, it's best forgotten. I'm sorry. I always say the wrong thing."

And with this she was running down the stairs, leaving him standing there, staring at her.

He did not follow her. He decided to forget about

the supper, for which he now had no appetite, and returned to his study.

And there, deliberately, and for the first time for many years and months, he opened wide the door of his memory, looked at Margaret within his mind's eye, and recalled in dispassionate detail the quarrel that had separated them for good and for all.

Like most quarrels, it started with nothing. The acute crises come when one is unprepared; there is no warning that the events of an ordinary day can change the whole course of a life. The sun shines, everything goes well, and then comes the one wrong word, the one wrong act, and nothing is ever the same again.

The Frenchman, on that ordinary day, was then a Marquis, and a most personable young man. He saw Henry before Margaret did, but did not for one second trouble himself about him. Older than his fiancée in both years and experience, he recognized an adventurer when he saw one, and that was all Henry ever was. He had a great deal of charm, startling good looks, of the kind that other men cannot abide, and all the effrontery in the world. He had no money, of course, but his air and presence persuaded various unhappy tradesmen to provide him with all he needed. He swaggered into the salon of a silly middle-aged lady who should have known better and proceeded to examine the company for the most likely dupe. The Frenchman did not know this, but for a while the young man could not make up his mind whether to set his sights on the middle-aged ninny who had provided the entrée or the remarkably pretty young lady who was attracting so much attention, and whose escort, Henry recognized, was wealthy, a nobleman, and very much the kind of person he wished to avoid.

He decided it would be safer to make a set for the middle-aged lady, and he would have been a great deal better off if he had done so. She was wealthy, widowed, and stupid, and would probably not have resented the fact that her new beau was nothing but a gigolo. Unfortunately, she was extremely ugly, and Henry was extremely young. Later on he was not to be so fastidious, but then the thought of making love to this fat old woman with her bad teeth and raddled face was more than he could stomach, for all she was so rich and could have introduced him to a number of other potential suckers. And Margaret, then eighteen, was entirely ravishing. She was aglow with love and life and the excitement of it all, she was wearing a new and becoming gown, and she was perfectly aware that none of the titled ladies about her could hold a candle to her. She was, however, piqued, because Philippe, instead of remaining at her side, as she thought he should, had crossed the room to greet some friends, and she was by now sure enough of her power to grow sulky, toss her head, and look away from him.

The fact that he paid no attention to this display did not improve her temper. She began to realize for the first time what this strange, glorious, and unexpected marriage would entail. There would be endless and tedious social responsibilities, she would have to entertain lavishly people who despised and resented her, and she would have to observe the brittle, demanding protocol of the French court. She fell to sulking in good earnest, refusing to smile at anyone who approached her, glowering at the distant Marquis from beneath her lashes.

The young Margaret dearly loved her Marquis, and would not normally have even glanced at the handsome young man who bowed to her and asked for the honor of a dance. If the Frenchman had smiled at her only once across the room, she would instantly have recovered her temper; she was not a bad-natured girl, only a spoiled one whose good fortune had gone to her head. But the Marquis continued to ignore her, by accident rather than by intention. He too was in a difficult position, marrying so much beneath his rank, as his friends would see it, and he was exerting his charm mainly to induce his companions to be kinder to this little girl they so obviously despised. Margaret, suddenly in a blazing rage, bestowed her most brilliant smile on Henry, and permitted him to lead her out on the floor.

The Marquis was astounded that his betrothed should dance with a person who made his living by putting other people's money in his pocket, and who would eventually be kicked into the gutter, where he belonged. This was a sign of ill-breeding that he had never suspected in her, and it was confirmed by the bright, defiant smile she flashed at him as she danced by. He simply looked at her without speaking, and, indeed, did not mention the matter to her until much later, by which time he had drunk too much wine and she was bitterly ashamed of herself, especially as Henry, already too familiar, had indicated that he would like to see her again, and had even pushed a note with his address into her reticule.

The quarrel started in the carriage on the way home, grew and fed upon itself, and in Margaret's drawing room—her father, unaware of all this, had retired for the night—it turned into a storm.

Margaret was ashamed and, knowing herself to be

entirely in the wrong, hysterically angry. The Marquis
was hurt, astonished, then furious. He had drunk too
much, and she had brooded too much—the situation
was instantly out of control. The difficulties that had
beset them became mountains. Margaret had suffered
from endless snubs from elegant ladies who muttered
audibly to each other that she was just a little English
miss out for money, and the Marquis was always being
warned by friends that she was a fortune hunter who
would ruin his life by her ill-breeding and bad
manners.

They shouted at each other as if they were ordinary,
common people.

"In England," she cried, "we are permitted to dance
with other men, even if we are engaged."

"In France," he shouted, "we are not!"

"Then I think it is very stupid."

"You are living in France and it will be your
home. Your behavior was unpardonable. And with
such a man—could you not see what kind of person
he was?"

"He was very charming. He was more polite than
you."

The Marquis was still drinking. He was used
enough to wine, but now he poured himself out
another glass with a shaking hand, and Margaret
exclaimed, "At least he didn't drink. You have drunk
far too much, Philippe. Is that your idea of good
manners?"

He looked at her, suddenly silent. His face was
very white. She was terrified, longed to make it up,
could think of nothing to say, and said the unsayable.
She stammered, "He may have been all you say he is,
but at least he was warm and friendly, he didn't

despise me. He treated me like a woman, not just one of your horrid bits of porcelain. He said he loved me. I think—I think we'd better end our engagement. I could never be happy with you. You would always be criticizing me and telling me how to behave. You would never accept me as another human being, because you're not human yourself, you are so proud of belonging to a famous family and having lots of money that you never consider other people's feelings . . ."

He still said nothing, only came up to her, standing so close that his body pressed against her. He hated her, and yet he still wanted her. She was so beautiful —so dear to him—and now she had ended the relationship. He wanted to take the ultimate revenge on her, and hurt her as she had hurt him. She wanted to scream for her father, but could bring no sound out. When he pushed her back onto the settee, she hardly struggled, only waved at him feebly with her hands. And when he had done with her, she lay there staring at him, then turned her face against the cushions. She did not hear him go. When at last she managed to drag herself up, he was gone.

For a little while, she was out of her mind. Nothing in her life had prepared her for anything like this. She did not go up to her father, or call for the servants. She mechanically righted her clothes, pushed back her disordered hair, and walked out of the house, into the street, where Henry, moved by the odd sixth sense that was so invaluable in his profession, was waiting around the corner, in a carriage he had not paid for.

The Frenchman knew nothing of what happened between them, only learned the next day, when he woke up, appalled and ashamed, that she had gone to this gigolo. His friends were sympathetic and delighted. The scandal rocked his world for a full three days, then was replaced by something more intriguing. He could see now that his world had vanished, many of the scandalmongers were headless, and it was all mainly his fault. His behavior, unprecedented and unbelievable, had been entirely disgraceful, and if Margaret had been older and possessed more common sense, she might have known that this was her moment of victory—that her own wrongdoing would be utterly forgotten in his shocked contrition.

He still could not understand his behavior. He was a great believer in self-control. And because he could not bear himself, he had turned his self-hate on Margaret, and for a long time now forced himself not to remember.

And now he remembered.

The house was asleep; across the garden a light still flickered, the lamp in Mrs. Beeston's cottage. He wondered vaguely and without interest why the old woman was up so late, for it was past midnight, and countryfolk kept early hours. Perhaps she left the light on to keep the ghosts away. He dismissed the matter from his mind, and the memories beat upon him; they cut and tore him. He heard his own angry, drunken voice. He saw Margaret in tears and temper, the angry color blazing in her cheeks, the eyes bright with weeping. And he saw the face she turned upon him at the last—a strange, old face, almost imbecilic in its lack of expression, with an incredulous, hurt look, as if she could not believe what had happened to her.

"Oh God!" said the Frenchman aloud, and again,
"Oh God!" He pushed the exercise books violently
away; they fell to the floor. Miss Flora did not even
know the verb *avoir,* and it was clear that she would
never be able to speak a word of French that any
Frenchman could understand. Miss Albertine, on the
other hand, had done neat, intelligent homework,
with only two small mistakes, everything written
clearly with neither correction nor blot. He thought
he could not bear, simply could not bear, to take these
lessons again, with the two girls facing him, one so
golden and silly, the other so dark and—the word slid
into his mind—bad.

Je ne peux pas le supporter, je ne peux pas! Lessons
for ever and ever and, Please Frenchy, how do you
say, and Frenchy, I don't understand . . .

And the Provençal vineyards would be green, and
he could be among his own again.

And Margaret looking up at him.

He put his hands over his eyes. He had never in his
life felt so isolated, alien, and desperately alone.
When, out of the corner of his eye, he saw the shadow
by the door, he spoke the only name that came into
his mind. "Margaret . . ."

Then he saw who it was.

He rose to his feet. He said coldly, "Miss Albertine,
what is this? It is well past midnight, and you should
be asleep." Then, as she made no attempt to obey him
—indeed, came nearer, so that the sleeve of her gown
brushed against him, and he could smell the strong
perfume she always wore—he forgot himself altogether. It fitted in too well with his ugly memories.
He could remember the touch of another body, the
feel of her flesh beneath his angry hands. He cried

out, "For God's sake, girl, leave me alone. I do not want to see you. I do not want to see anyone. I have done my work. I am entitled to my privacy. Will you please go away."

She answered, smiling, "I think you want to see Margaret."

He looked at her, almost in disgust. She wore some kind of house-gown, a loose woollen thing that both covered and revealed her. The dark hair was piled high, as if for a party, and the look on her face of such frank invitation that he could not pretend to miss it. He was filled with fury, and with helplessness too. The Colonel could have no idea of how his daughter behaved, but certainly, if he learned about this, the full blame would fall on the Frenchman's shoulders.

He tried to control his mounting temper for the memories had disorganized him, and he felt dreadfully out of control. He said, as calmly as he could, "Miss Albertine, we are both tired. You should go to your room, and I will go to mine. Whatever you want to talk to me about can wait till the morning." He added deliberately, "I presume this is some query about your lessons. I appreciate your desire to learn, but it is very late, and I would prefer to leave it till tomorrow."

She began to laugh. One could hardly blame her. She did not wear the air of one concerned with learning. "Oh, Frenchy," she said, "you know perfectly well that I do not give a fig for my exercises. I have come down because I want to see you. Why are you being so unkind to me? Is it because of Margaret? Margaret is asleep. I peeped in to see. She is all alone in her bed, Frenchy. Don't you want to join her? I think you

should join me instead. I am much more exciting
than Margaret, and I'm younger, too. Don't be cruel
to me. I like you so much. I have always liked you
from the very beginning. It would be quite all right.
Papa has drunk too much wine and is dead to the
world; besides, he lives on the other side of the landing. No one will know. You do like me a little, don't
you? Oh, say you do, Frenchy, do!"

He felt as if he were enmeshed in a nightmare.
There was something remorseless about this well-
brought-up young woman who was inviting him to
her bed like any whore. He said grimly, "Miss Albertine, you are going to listen to me."

"Oh you're not going to lecture me again, are you!"

"I am going to do precisely that. What do you
imagine you're doing? Have you no sense at all?" She
was smilingly adoring all this drama, but he went on,
ignoring the fluttering lashes and pulling his arm
away from the hand that lay upon it. "I am simply
the French tutor here."

"So you keep on saying, Frenchy. It's so boring. I
know you're the French tutor. That is why I like you
so much."

This time there was no pretense, as there had been
that first evening. She was pressing herself against him
so that he was forced to back to the wall. It was obscene
and absurd, and he pushed her away, but she did not
seem to mind. She reminded him of a cat—it was as
if she wanted to rub herself against him. He would
not have been surprised to hear her purr. She said in
her quick, high voice, "You were so nasty to me
last time, but you see, I don't bear grudges, Frenchy,
and I'm sure you really like me, you must do, all
men do. Oh, I know Flora is prettier than I am, but

she's so stupid, isn't she, and men don't really care for silly girls, except just at the beginning. Lewis is tired of her already, and they are not even married. But you and I, Frenchy, have so much in common."

He could only stare at her and wonder what the devil was coming next. He found the strange, protruding tooth oddly distracting: It gave her an animal look; it was greedy and lascivious.

She said, her voice now very soft, "Forget about that silly old Margaret, she's so plain and stupid, she's not nearly good enough for you. You need someone clever, like me. You won't end up like that boy from the prison who got killed trying to escape—I have good friends among the officers, you see. Aren't you pleased with me? I can be a very good friend, you know. Papa don't trouble his head about anything, and as for Flora, she's just a ninny. But I'm different. Oh, Frenchy," cried Albertine, her voice shrilling out, "love me a little. I've always wanted you, so much, so much. Be kind to me. Don't make an enemy of me. Now you're going to say something nice to me, aren't you? I think you might be going to kiss me. I should like that very much, and I think you'd like it too."

The Frenchman had recovered both his composure and his temper. He surveyed Albertine as she stood there, holding out her hands to him. He saw her with the utmost clarity. He realized that in her excitement—and she was shivering with it—she was almost beautiful. The eyes had grown enormous, the lips were shining and parted, the hair gleamed in the lamplight. Only the hands that reached out for his were a predator's hands, thin and sharp-nailed. There was no love in those hands, and the thought of their

touching him made him shudder. And at that
moment he understood why she was there. If she
wanted him in her bed, it was from greed and the
pride of possession. Whatever came from her was not
love. Love did not grab and demand, love did not
cajole and threaten, love did not denigrate the rest of
the world. She did not want a lover, she wanted a
whipping-boy. He could feel only contempt for this
young woman who was so eager.

He looked her up and down, and his expression
made her smile vanish, made her back away.

He said at last, "I have no intention of kissing you
and I am not interested in you. And I am not afraid
of you, my girl. Oh, I have no doubt you make a bad
enemy, but certainly you would make the poorest of
friends. I could never trust you or respect you. You
are only behaving like this because you love power."
And here he advanced on her, so that this time it was
she who was forced to retreat, her lip curling back,
like the wildcat she was. "It is the only thing you do
love, isn't it? Apart from yourself. When you first
spoke to me, I could not believe that anyone could
behave with such vulgarity. Now I see it is some kind
of game you are playing. But you are unwise to try
such games with me. One more word of this and I go
straight to your father. I am not your dupe like that
drunken English captain. You don't love me, you
don't even want me, you are simply making use of
me. And now we will end this stupid talk. Tomorrow
you will come here with your exercises, and we will
discuss French grammar. Apart from that, I want
nothing more to do with you. In my country, it is the
men who offer love, not the women; if it is the
women, we call them whores. Go back to your room,

please, and we will both try to forget that this conversation ever took place."

Albertine was not by nature one to take a rebuff kindly. She made no more pretense of being seductive. She was snarling at him, all her beauty gone. Then suddenly she made a rush at him, and her nails raked down the side of his cheek. She would have aimed at him again, only he caught at her wrists and held her at arm's length, his fingers pressing so cruelly into her that she hissed with the pain, and the tears started to her eyes.

He did not relax his grip. To him she was no longer human, and he surveyed her with a cold detachment.

He said quietly, "You remind me of the fishwives from Les Halles."

And as he said this he knew it was true: This was a creature who would rend and torture, tear another human being to pieces, joyously parade a head on a spike. This was someone who would sit beneath the guillotine and delight in death and suffering. The thought of what he had seen in the past brought the sickness up in his throat, and past and present elipsed in the person of this little savage who, white with pain and rage, was glaring murder at him.

He could stand the sight of her no longer. He released her violently and swung around. When he turned, she was gone.

Mrs. Beeston's lamp still flickered. The old woman must simply have forgotten to extinguish it. The Frenchman put his handkerchief up to his cheek, where he could feel the blood trickling down. That would require some explaining in the morning, but he was too exhausted to consider it now. He was thankful that he had stored a bottle of wine in his room. He thought with a cèrtain satisfaction that Mademoiselle Albertine, who so liked her wine, would probably fall to the bottle the moment she arrived upstairs.

On the landing he paused for a second outside Margaret's room. It seemed she thought he wished to kill her, and this he could not understand, but he wanted to speak to her and tell her that this evening had purged him of resentment and anger. He wanted to say, *What happened is past, it was mostly my fault, I'm sorry.* He did not say any of this, he did not so much as touch the handle of her door, but he hoped in a sleep-bemused way that somehow she would hear his thoughts, that he could communicate peace to her. This evening he had not only lived through ten years, he had seen hate in action and recognized it for the ugly, useless, destructive thing it was.

And then he shut his door, poured himself out a glass of wine, and swung himself onto the bed without undressing. Presently he slept, more calmly and deeply than in a long time, and so he lay until the dawn gleamed through the small window.

Chapter Eight

The Hall and the village hummed next day
with news of another escape from the Cross Prison.
Margaret was engulfed in the excitement the moment
she came downstairs. By this time, the servants had
begun to accept her and had grown much more
friendly, and they gathered around her to tell her what
had happened. She could not help smiling a little, for
the escapes did not entirely displease her. Besides, she
felt unusually well and happy this morning, having
slept surprisingly well, with pleasant dreams.

"Six, Miss Margaret, ma'am! Six! The impudence of it! One of them was killed, and serve him right. They say the others thought he was a spy. I think the whole lot of 'em is spies." This was from Thomas, filled with his usual righteous indignation. "They should be shot, every one of them. Coming here, living at our expense, eating the very food from our mouths, good-for-nothing bastards. The only good frog is a dead frog, that's what I say. Begging your pardon, sir, no offense meant," he added unconvincingly to the Frenchman, who had at that moment made his appearance. Then he saw the marks on the Frenchman's cheek, and his mouth dropped open.

Margaret saw them too. She could hardly avoid doing so. Scratches of that sort, like a black eye, were difficult to explain away. She opened her mouth to ask him what on earth had happened, then quickly turned away. She could hardly believe her eyes, and he was so very pale. He must have been involved in some dreadful brawl. In an effort to tide the conversation over the uncomfortable silence—for everyone was gazing at him—she said, a little too loudly, "What's happened to Mrs. Beeston this morning? She's usually here by now."

And, certainly, the old woman was punctual—it was her only virtue, though the reason was certainly that she enjoyed sitting by the hot stove and wanted her early-morning mug of ale.

Half an hour later, she had still not arrived, and Margaret, who had had to prepare the breakfast, grew suddenly angry. It really was too bad of her. She did little enough work as it was, and she should at least be helping with the hot chocolate and rolls, and seeing that the Colonel had his great slices of roast beef, with which he always started the day.

The Frenchman, drinking his chocolate, said, "Her light is still on. It was on all last night. Perhaps she's ill. If you wish, I'll go and see if anything is the matter."

"Oh, yes, please do," said Margaret thankfully, and went on slicing the beef, after setting aside the dish of kidneys that the Colonel would require as an entrée.

The Frenchman crossed the garden. The wind had dropped. If the invading fleet were ready, this would doubtless help them. And if the ships did come over, he was in a damnable position. He did not go immediately into the cottage, only stood for a moment on the newly cut lawn by the Bluebeard Room. He remained motionless there, wondering, with a certain bitter humor, which country he was expected to betray, his own or this strange place that he now lived in. Once he would have said that he had little feeling for either. His own had driven him out, compelled him to be a fugitive when one spying word would have sent him to his death, and he had only survived because his own people jealously protected him. Provence was home, France the enemy. When the final heads had rolled and the war come, he had joined up not from patriotism but simply because he could no longer endure a life of inaction. Victory or defeat did not matter a damn to him, and when he was taken prisoner he was entertained by the situation—the hero imprisoned for the sake of a homeland that was no longer home.

And now his eyes moved over the bare lawn, brown in the winter cold, then up to the window of Albertine's room. It was shut tight. He frowned, touched his smarting cheek, then at last made his way to the cottage.

There was no sign or sound of life. The lamp still burned and flickered. A faint mewing attracted his attention, and he stooped down to stroke the small black cat that weaved toward him. This was the old woman's adored companion, so now he knew that something must be very wrong.

He called out, "Mrs. Beeston!" And then, "Mrs. Beeston, are you there?"

The cold was shuddering through him, but it was not entirely the cold. He walked up the path, banged at the door, then pushed it open. It was unlatched. He looked first into the parlor, where the lamp was shining. The room was cluttered with far too much furniture, and everything was dusty, floor unswept. He called out the name again, then stepped into the other room across the small passageway.

Mrs. Beeston lay face down on the bed, one plump hand dangling down. Someone had thrust a knife through her shoulders. There were dried patches of blood everywhere, as if there had been a struggle, but somehow she had managed to reach the bed to die. She had obviously been dead for a long time. Her murderer must have been waiting for her when she came home.

The Frenchman did not attempt to move her. He had seen a great deal of death in his time, in the Paris streets and on the battlefield. But it brought the vomit into his throat, for somehow violent death in this fusty little room was indecent. What harm could this poor, silly old woman have done to anyone, passing her life by a warm stove, drinking her ale and going to sleep?

He came out of the cottage, the little cat following after him. He made straight for the breakfast room, where the Colonel would be devouring vast quantities of beef and kidneys. He would certainly be alone, for the young ladies preferred to take their hot chocolate in their beds.

Colonel Walters was not pleased to see him, and showed it. He had no complaint to make against the fellow—he was quiet and unobtrusive, and the girls seemed to like him. Albertine said he was *très charmant,* presumably to indicate how her French had improved, and Flora said vaguely that he was always so kind, he never shouted at her even when her exercises were wrong. Moreover, he did as he was told without grumbling, even down to cutting the lawn. Of course, one could never be quite sure of him, as these frogs were always after anything in petticoats, and had neither morals nor scruples.

He glared without enthusiasm at the tall, composed gentleman who stood in the doorway, swallowed a vast mouthful of beef, then barked, "Well, what is it now? Don't tell me those girls have been misbehaving themselves."

"Oh, no, sir," said the Frenchman, but for a second his mouth twisted.

The Colonel then burst out with what was uppermost in his mind. "You've heard about those bloody escapes? Six of them! The incredible impudence of it! I gave Captain Moore a piece of my mind, I can assure you. I cannot abide inefficiency, and I know that if I had been there, not one of those blackguards would have got away. Fortunately, one of them was killed, did you hear?"

The Frenchman, growing impatient, began, "Sir, I—"

But the Colonel never really listened to anyone else, except Captain Ross, who shouted him down, and he went roaring on in his usual way. "They say it was the other fellows killed him, he didn't have the right pass or something—don't understand a word of it myself. Some outlandish name or other—Christian. That's it. Christian. Fine name for a heathen bastard."

None of this meant anything to the Frenchman, and he could endure all this nonsense no longer. He took a step nearer the Colonel and said, in a firm, loud voice, "Sir, there has been a murder."

"What, what?" The Colonel could hardly ignore this, but, as his mind was still on the prisoners, he roared again, "Are you telling me those damned *parlez-vous* have killed an Englishman?" Then, though the word "tact" was not in his vocabulary, he perceived that this was an odd thing to say to the *parlez-vous* standing in front of him, and said, more quietly, "I don't know what the devil you're talking about."

The Frenchman told him, only by this time he was so exasperated that he made it as brief as he could and did not follow it up, as he had intended, with a request to speak to Captain Ross. He took advantage of the Colonel's staggered silence to leave, and he went to his study to calm himself and recover his temper.

When he came back to the kitchens, half an hour later, he found that the news had preceded him. They were all white and aghast, the little maids were crying, and Margaret, very pale but in control of herself, was dealing as well as she could with the hysterics around her.

It was Thomas who had found the body, some ten

minutes after the Frenchman had gone. He had forgotten some of his tools in the garden, for he had left
that morning in considerable disarray. Mrs. Lee, in
one of her manic moods, had got it into her head
that there would be an invasion at any moment, and
would not let any of her family depart before they
had armed themselves against the enemy. A fine
array of weapons now lay on the Lee parlor table:
carving knives, hammers, scissors, an ax, and a couple
of ancient pistols which, never having been oiled,
certainly would not work. By this time, Mrs. Lee was
in a frenzy, and the family, driven to panic, rushed
around doing nothing, as if by this means they could
rebuff the so-far-invisible invaders. And Mrs. Lee
shrieked and swore and stormed, boxing the girls'
ears, shoving her enormous sons away from her, and
creating a chaos that resounded through the village.

"The old bitch is clean out of her mind," said Mr.
Clay, whose inn was across the road, and who was
watching the distracted horde of Lees rushing here
and there, while their minute demon-mother almost
brought the roof down with her yelling.

His wife said crossly, "I don't know what's got into
her. You'd think she had special information from old
Boney himself." And she stared out at the sea, half
expecting to see the invading fleet. There was nothing
but the wind and waves and a few desolate seagulls,
though on the Loving Sands, now at low tide, there
was considerable agitation, with prison guards running up and down.

She remarked, "They say there's more prisoners
escaped."

"Of course," said Mr. Clay, with the air of one
who knew all about it. He added, "What did I tell
you? The *parlez-vous* coming here, and that young

woman—I never liked her. I told you so at the time.
They say she's a real bully up at the Hall, and poor
Thomas don't know how to call his soul his own."

"Thomas's soul never has been his own," said Mrs.
Clay, and at that moment Thomas shot out of the Lee
cottage as if from a catapult, and they could see him
tearing up the hill toward the Hall. She said, "I like
the girl. There's nothing wrong with her. I dare say
she has her work cut out, what with those silly girls
and that old drab, Mrs. Beeston, who never bothered
about anything in her life." And, unaware that Mrs.
Beeston's working days were done, she added, "That
Miss Margaret is a lady."

"They're always the worst," said Mr. Clay.

"She has a sad face. I fancy some gentleman let her
down. And I'll tell you something else, Ted. She's
sweet on the Frenchy. I saw them together once, and
she looked quite different." Then she saw that her
husband was now confirmed in his view that both of
them were spies, and smiled, for he was a harmless
man, and a good husband in his own way. One might
say that invasions and spies were simply his hobby.

Mrs. Lee was now standing in her doorway, looking
like the minuscule wrath of God. She held an ax
across her flat bosom, and at this sight Mr. Clay, forgetting about the *parlez-vous* and the uppity young
lady at the Hall, burst out laughing. She heard the
laughter and understood immediately that it was
directed at her. She released hold of the ax to shake
her fist at him, then shouted in that thin, high voice
of hers, which was like the whistling of a hurricane,
"They're coming. They'll be here any day now, Ted
Clay. The day of wrath is at hand. We shall all
perish."

The Clays looked at each other, shrugged, and

hastily retreated into the inn. Mr. Clay instantly poured himself out a tankard of ale, while his wife said reflectively, "It was the boy's death as did it. Sucked down into the sands, he was, not a chance in the world. Mind you, she never was what you might call sweet-natured."

And with this remarkable understatement, she set about preparing for the midday drinkers, and all thought of invasion was forgotten.

In the Cross Prison, security measures were being tightened (as always, only after the need had passed), and Captain Lewis Moore was very drunk indeed, so that his fellow officers grinned and shrugged at each other, nd the prisoners imitated his stagg ing gait and sl rred speech. And in the village Mrs. Lee, having reduced her family to a state of nervous prostration, laid down the ax and began to cook her own midday meal as if nothing had happened. She firmly believed in the coming invasion, and disaster and death were the breath of life to her. She could never have endured living in peace—a born Cassandra, she needed drama, and if it had not been invasion she talked of, it would have been flood, plague, or fire.

The Frenchman drew Margaret aside. He saw that, despite her surface calm, she was shaking from head to foot. He made her drink a glass of wine and sit down at the table. This she agreed to do, chiefly because her knees were giving way beneath her, but her gaze kept on sliding to the empty rocking-chair by the stove, and her lips quivered.

He said calmly, "It would have been all over at once. She could never have known what happened."

And this was not true, for it was plain that the poor

old woman had struggled for her life, but Margaret would never see the body, which was now decorously laid out, waiting for its final resting place, and covered with a sheet.

She whispered, "Who could do such a thing? She was the most harmless old soul imaginable. Her only fault was being lazy, and if one is to be killed for laziness . . ." The tears came to her eyes, and she fumbled for her handkerchief. "I was always nagging at her. I am so ashamed."

He said roughly, "Don't be stupid. You had your work to do, and so had she. It was your duty to scold her, you probably did not do so often enough. You could not, after all, foresee her murder."

Margaret said, "You are very heartless."

"I have seen a great deal of death during the past ten years."

"I don't think one has the right to grow hard."

"One becomes accustomed," said the Frenchman dryly. He eyed her, wondering how to say what he had now decided he must. But before he began, he tried once more to calm her.

"Why don't you drink your wine?" said the Frenchman.

"I can't," said Margaret. She turned her head away, but not before he had seen the tears rolling down her cheeks. She said, in a choked voice, "It has been such a shock. I still can't quite believe it. But I must get on with my work, it will certainly do me more good than sitting here." She half rose, supporting herself on the table as she did, so, but his next words made her sit down again, very suddenly.

"I think you should leave at once," he said.

She answered with some spirit, "Oh, not again,

Philippe. This becomes tedious. And I have no intention of doing anything of the kind. Why should I?"
She added, flushing, "We have discussed this so
many times before. If you find my company so unendurable, I suggest you leave yourself."

He looked at her defiant face, wanting to shake her.
He said suddenly, "What is all this about someone
trying to kill you? Of course, you believe it was me,
but—"

"No," said Margaret quietly.

"But you said . . ."

"I know I did. I'm sorry, Philippe. I don't think,
whatever happened, you would do such a thing to
me. Somehow . . ." She looked away again, her voice
low and subdued. "It was very strange, but somehow,
when I woke this morning, I saw how silly and unjust
I had been. I hope you will forgive me. It has not
been easy lately, and I think perhaps I was a little
hysterical."

He did not answer this directly, only said, after a
pause, "Will you tell me what happened?"

"Oh, no. I think perhaps I imagined it. It was
someone in a hurry, or . . . I don't know. It's not
worth discussing."

"It's very much worth discussing. I want you to tell
me."

She was on her feet now. "Later. There is so much
work to do."

He saw that she had no intention of telling him,
and the fear within him was now so strong that he
dared not urge her too much, as he might communicate his own panic. He said, as calmly as he could, "I
cannot imagine why you want to stay. You cannot
possibly enjoy it here."

"But I do. I have grown used to it. It was difficult at the beginning, of course, but then, I imagine it was for you too." She bestowed on him a small, ironic smile. "I am even quite fond of the place. And the servants have grown quite friendly. But you are still trying to get rid of me, Philippe, aren't you? I think you are unreasonable. I keep out of your way. I doubt we meet more than two or three times a day. You have your duties and I have mine. I am sorry if my presence is so offensive to you, but I must remind you that not only have I no home to return to but also I have no money. I have had no chance to save more than a few guineas, and I cannot starve, even to save your feelings."

He said dryly, "You've developed quite a shrew's tongue, Margaret."

She said, in a sigh, "I have grown older."

He was silent for a moment. Then he said, in a strained voice, "We have come a long way since our first meeting."

"Yes."

They looked at each other, and for that brief instant in time there was a shifting and a retreat. The young and pretty girl was transposed onto this exhausted woman whose eyes were still filled with tears, whose brown, curling hair had streaks of gray. And she saw before her the elegant young man with his powdered wig and his youthful, unlined face, who had mocked her a little, loved her a great deal, and who had once proposed to marry her.

Then it was over. There were left a tired young woman, her face remote with sorrow, and an angry, disturbed gentleman in shabby clothes who was look-ing at her as if he hated her.

Yet she was reluctant to leave the memory. She moved her hands out a little as if somehow she could retain it, prevent its leaving. "Your clothes." she said. "We dress plain in England now. Grand finery would seem absurd, but those clothes were so wonderful then. And I had such a pretty gown . . ." Then she realized the idiocy of what she was saying, flushed scarlet, and flung her hands up to her cheeks. She said, trying to smile, "Oh, forgive me. I don't know what is the matter with me. This horrid news must have overturned me. A fine gown was never important, and it was all ten years ago, almost a lifetime. I think I am become a silly old woman romanticizing over her lost youth."

He exclaimed, "For God's sake! You talk as if you were a hundred."

"At this moment, that is exactly how I feel."

He glanced at her, then away. He said at last, "Margaret. If I give you such money as I have, and the address of someone in Elchester who would, I believe, help you, will you go?"

"Are you providing me with a protector?" asked Margaret. She had recovered herself. Her voice was brisk and derisive.

He answered stonily, "It is an old lady. She was very kind to me. She said if ever I needed help, I was to let her know. I do not believe she would turn you away."

"Perhaps," said Margaret, "I could become her companion. Do you not see me as a companion Philippe? Taking her little dog for walks, preparing her hot possets, reading to her in the afternoons from the latest three-volume romance out of the circulating library. Perhaps she will like the Gothic romances, and we can frighten each other with skeletons and ghosts."

The Frenchman had passed a difficult day, and his temper had never been his strongest point. He shouted at her, "You damned stupid girl! I want you away from here, and now. You are in danger. Do you not see that?"

She stared at him. Her hands were folded before her. She said quietly, "I don't know why you always imagine I'm in danger. And would you really care if I were?"

He answered, forcing himself to be calm again, "I am asking you civilly. And I do care. I would scarcely trouble myself if I did not. Will you please go?"

"No!"

"It is nothing personal. It is simply that this place is not good for you, or anyone. I wish you would try to understand. Go and pack your things and leave. I'll explain it to the Colonel."

She said, almost sadly, "I cannot go, Philippe."

"I could kill you!" said the Frenchman. Then he realized the absurdity of this and, for the first time during this conversation, burst out laughing. He said, "What am I to do with you?"

"I do not know," replied Margaret, "what you will do with me, but what you must do with yourself is to take your two pupils for their French lesson." Then she exclaimed in dismay, "Oh my God, how quickly one forgets. There will surely be no lesson. Not even Miss Albertine could consider such a thing after what has happened, and Miss Flora, who is so gentle, will be prostrated. I must go and see how she is."

"I assure you," said the Frenchman, "that the two

young ladies will be waiting for me. Neither invasion
nor a new Flood would stop them. Miss Flora will
not be prostrated at all. She will, I am prepared to
wager, say, *Oh poor Mrs. Beeston, what a shame,* then
produce for me the usual intolerable mistakes. As for
Miss Albertine, she will be enchanted by the drama
and expect full details of what has happened, down
to the last drop of blood."

"Oh, don't!"

"That is how it will be. I know my pupils better
than you do."

Margaret, now beginning to chop up the vegetables,
looked at him without speaking, and the Frenchman
made her a little derisive bow before turning toward
the door. But the look in his eyes was not derisive,
and he paused as if to beseech her again, only she was
stooping over her work and did not raise her head.

As it happened, the Frenchman's prophecy was
wrong: There was to be no lesson.

He came up the stairs and walked down the corridor to his study. Like most men, he did not notice
much the state of his surroundings, but he had to
remark the vast change since Margaret's arrival at the
Hall. The dust no longer lay powder-thick, there were
lamps set at the darker corners, and even the unused
rooms were dusted and polished and swept. And
because he was gravely disturbed and in no mood for
the young ladies with their soft, silly voices, he loi-
tered a little, opened doors that were normally closed,
peered into empty rooms, wondered if the Hall had
ever been lively and full of light and gaiety.

There were more than a dozen such rooms. The
Colonel used only his library and the breakfast room,
the two girls had their own apartments, there was a
drawing room, where the Sunday parties took place,

and a small dining room, where the family ate. The remaining rooms were hardly furnished at all, and cold with the chill of emptiness. The Frenchman opened the door on a vast ballroom, where dancing feet had not touched the floor for God knows how many years. In this, as in the others, there was little: a few pictures on the wall, some battered-looking furniture, and a china cabinet.

This interested him, and he stepped inside to see what treasures had been abandoned. What extraordinary people the English were! But, of course, the Colonel would not be interested in such trivial things, and the two girls, though they wore expensive and fashionable clothes, seemed without interest in things that did not affect their personal adornment.

Suddenly, as he came up to the cabinet, he perceived that he was not alone.

Miss Flora was huddled on the settee. He had never seen her in such a state of disarray. She certainly was the stupidest young woman he had ever met, but she was very beautiful, and perfectly aware of her own beauty. The remarkable hair, so astonishingly golden, was always glossy and well-arranged, and her clothes were magnificent, especially since Margaret had taken charge of her wardrobe. Flora might have little in the way of brains, but she was entirely feminine, and loved to adorn herself. Now she sprawled there, the hair half out of its pins, her gown open as if she had clawed at it, her skirts crumpled, and her face swollen with crying.

His immediate reaction was to back away. He had no wish to be involved in what was doubtless some lovers' tiff, and besides, she would hardly wish to be seen in such a deplorable state.

But his feet sounded on the uncarpeted floor, and

she raised her head. She did not seem to mind his seeing her. She merely brushed at the tears on her cheeks and pushed a lock of hair away. She said, in a thick, choked voice, "I am glad you are here, Frenchy. I want to show you something."

He was beginning to think that all the Walters family was mad. But she gave him no chance to escape, for she was instantly at his side, and her hand clutched his.

He was about to ask her if she had forgotten about the lesson. Then it struck him that she was more sensitive than he had realized: This grief was perhaps due to the news of the old woman's murder. But she at once destroyed this illusion by bestowing on him a strange, savage smile. He had never seen her look anything but sweet and foolish, and the transformation was horrifying. For the first time, he could see a resemblance between her and Albertine. The smile was Albertine's smile, and was all the uglier for its appearance on that vapid, charming face.

"I think," she said, as if reading his thoughts, "there will be no lesson today." The hand on his tightened. "There will be no wedding neither. Do you not find that droll, Frenchy? No lessons, no lessons— never no more. And no wedding, not if I have anything to do with it."

He really believed her wits were turned. He had once seen an aunt who had become insane, and the wild look of this girl and the roughened voice were very much the same. He said, "Mademoiselle, I am going to fetch Margaret."

"No!" It was almost a shout.

He insisted, now really alarmed. "Miss Flora, you

are not well. Permit me to escort you to your room. Perhaps the doctor . . ."

She began to laugh. The laugh was as crazed as her appearance. It was hard to believe that this was Miss Flora, whom till now he had never seen in any kind of mood. Occasionally she grew impatient, as a child does, but mostly she was foolish, vague, and apt to dream. She stopped laughing as suddenly as she had begun. She said, more calmly, "I want you to come with me, Frenchy. Now. There is something very interesting for you to see. You'll not believe your eyes. I could scarce believe mine."

And with this she proceeded to lead him out of the room. He felt remarkably foolish, yet consumed with a lively curiosity, for he could not understand what all this was about. They walked down the corridor to a room at the far end—another of the unoccupied ones that he had not so far seen.

Flora flung open the door, crying out in a shrill voice, "Look! Look, Frenchy! Look at the play."

Albertine and Captain Lewis Moore were sitting on a sofa by the window. Their arms were about each other, their mouths touching, their faces flushed and blurred and blind. At the sudden opening of the door and Flora's loud cry, they instinctively fell apart. Lewis was aghast, but the next instant Albertine had flung her arms about him again, turning on the Frenchman and her sister a visage filled with spite and triumph.

The Frenchman was too taken aback to know what to do. He was furious at Flora's humiliation, and he thought, as he had often thought before, that the English had the oddest manners. In the sophisticated world that had once been his, sister could rob sister, friend could despoil wife. But it was done with discretion, behind locked doors. This open war was something he had never witnessed, and, though he disliked and despised Lewis, he could not entirely restrain a sneaking sympathy for the young man entrapped by Albertine into such a situation.

Then he realized that Lewis was again very drunk. Perhaps, to do him credit, he would not, if sober, have conducted himself in such a fashion. He was indeed drunk since the early morning. He tried now to release himself from Albertine's arms, and managed to stagger to his feet. His face was red and swollen, and his voice, when at last he spoke, so thick that it was difficult to understand him. The Frenchman, staring at him in angry disgust, suddenly understood why so many bottles had been thrown out of the young lady's window. No doubt she too enjoyed her wine, but certainly the liquor had provided a means for seducing Lewis.

Lewis, now leaning heavily on Albertine's supporting arm, for all that she was half his size, said, "I was just—just coming to find you, Flora. I—I looked for you everywhere." Then, as he turned his bemused gaze on the Frenchman, seeing, no doubt, three of him, his voice grew haughty with the dreadful pomposity of the drunk.

"What are you doing here, fellow? You should be at your work. You are spying on us. If you don't go away im-immediately, I shall take my horsewhip to you."

"By all means," said the Frenchman, and stepped fully into the room. He had forgotten that he was the tutor. He had forgotten that he was in England, where dueling was no longer encouraged, and where killing one's opponent might mean hanging at the end of a rope. Indeed, for that moment he was almost back in the days when the young French nobles disported themselves in the Jardins des Tuileries, ready to skewer one another for a sneeze or a cough. He came up to this drunken boor, but before he could say another word, Albertine stepped between them, turning a smiling face on her sister, her eyes snapping at all this wonderful excitement.

"I'm glad you have seen us, Flora," she said. "It's time you did. I am tired of all this silly pretense. He's not for you. You're too prim, too virtuous, too missish. He's mine. He's always been mine. Oh, we used to pretend that we disliked each other; it was just a game, it was so amusing, it made us laugh. And we let you have a little while with him, but at night he used to come to me. He is my lover. He has always been my lover.

"You despised me, didn't you? You thought a little plain thing like me—with a lame foot, too—I was nothing, and you, of course, so beautiful, so sure of yourself. But you're a stupid goose, Flora. Men don't like stupid geese. Sometimes your stupidity nearly drove him mad, did it not, my darling? He would never have married you. He just pretended because, well, we didn't want to be seen together too much. But now it no longer matters, and in a few days it will not matter at all. I love him so much, sister, and he loves me. Tell me you love me, Lewis. Tell me. Tell me now."

The gallant captain was too drunk to know fully

what was happening. Through his thick mind, which
fairly bubbled with wine, there stirred a vague realization that this was not as it should be, but Albertine's hand touched his cheek and Albertine's lips
were suddenly pressed against his own, so instinctively
he put his arms about her again. The gesture nearly
sent him headlong, but the sofa at his back saved him,
and he began to mutter, "I love you."

Then Flora sprang forward, before the Frenchman
could restrain her, her hands groping for her sister's
face, her own face wild with grief and fury.

The Frenchman caught at her wrist to pull her
back, but not before Albertine screamed in mock terror, "Oh, Lewis, help me, she's going to kill me. Please
stop her, pleasé! I'm so frightened. She's as fierce as a
cat, she always has been, and you know how weak I
am. My balance is so shaky and—Lewis! Please stop
her."

Lewis glared savagely at the distraught young
woman who had been his betrothed. He reached out
his hand, set it against her shoulder, and pushed her
away. He said in a growl, "Don't you dare touch her,
you bitch. Threatening her like that! If you set a
finger on her, I'll wring your neck. My poor little
Bertie, she's never done anyone any harm."

This was about as much as the Frenchman could
take. He had trained himself to some self-control
throughout these bitter years; he was no longer the
hot-blooded young man he had once been, but
Flora's face, which betrayed her astonished fear and
bewilderment, and Albertine's palpable delight were
not to be endured. He caught at Flora and put her
behind him. Then, so close to Lewis that there was
barely an inch between them, he slapped him hard on

both cheeks, then knocked him down with all the force that sheer black anger could give him. He would dearly have loved to do the same to Albertine, and she must have sensed this, for as she gave a little cry and stepped back, the smile vanished.

The captain went down like a stone. In his drunken state, he would have collapsed from a far lighter blow, and the Frenchman had hit as hard as he could. Lewis lay there on the floor, the blood from his cut cheek running into his mouth, and in a moment, what with the drink and the beating he had received, he sank into oblivion, eyes closed, the snores beginning to bubble forth from his open mouth.

Albertine, now white with temper, hissed at the Frenchman, "Oh Christ, you'll pay for this—I'll kill you. I swear I will. By the time I've done with you, you'll wish you'd never been born." And she sank to her knees by her prostrate lover, trying to revive him, which, naturally, she could not do; even her kisses produced nothing but louder snores. She screamed out, "At least you can help him up!"

The Frenchman said, "Help him up yourself, mademoiselle," and turned his back on her, for the sight of the two of them sickened him so that he only wanted to shut the door on them. He put his arm around the shoulders of the weeping Flora, and led her from the room. It seemed to him, as he slammed the door, that the air at once was sweeter.

He said gently, "I'm sorry, Miss Flora. I had no choice. You must try to forgive me. You must go to your room, and I will send Margaret to you. Perhaps your father—" He broke off. The Colonel could no more deal with such a situation than he could have delivered an infant. The only hope would be that he would instantly shoot Captain Moore, and that would hardly help this poor, deceived young woman.

Flora, however, had stopped crying. She was surveying him with a white, still face. She did not answer him, only walked away, very upright, apparently in full possession of her senses.

Chapter Nine

*T*he Frenchman watched Flora walking away. He felt it would be an impertinence to offer to escort her. In her anger and disillusion, she had acquired a dignity he had thus far never seen in her. He watched with a kind of rage and despair. He had never liked her, having little tolerance for stupidity, but now he felt in himself something of what she must be feeling, and he was aware of real hatred for the little sister who was prepared to betray everyone, including her sister. And then he thought of Captain Lewis Moore, seduced perhaps more by a bottle than a female, and at long last realized what he had to do.

But first he went down to the kitchens in search of Margaret, for surely that poor girl must not be left on her own. He saw as he came in that nobody was working. The servants huddled together, eyeing Mrs. Beeston's empty chair, and even Thomas Lee, usually so vocal, looked stricken and dumb. They had none of them particularly liked the old woman, but now she was sanctified by death. They could speak her name only in hushed tones.

They stared at the Frenchman. He saw the instant suspicion in their eyes. There was a murderer about, and here he was, the foreigner, the enemy. His face was scratched; they would soon remember that it was he who had found the body; soon no doubt they would be suggesting he had killed her. He gave them a bitter smile. He was not afraid, but it was a trifle ironic that he, who had discovered so much, should be accused of murder.

He asked where Margaret was, and they all started, as if he might be proposing to murder her too.

"She's gone down to the village," said Thomas at last, and the girls all peered and giggled nervously.

The Frenchman nodded and set off, as he had intended, for Captain Ross's cottage. There was now no indecision left in him, and he felt quite light-headed with relief at having at last made up his mind. When, on making a detour by the sea wall, he saw Margaret's little fat pony ambling along, with her sitting very upright in the cart, he waved his hand to her in a friendly fashion, and crossed over to her side.

The pony obediently stopped, being a lazy animal who preferred stopping to anything else. Margaret

looked down at the Frenchman. He saw that she was
still very pale, but she had obviously done all her
shopping, and was surrounded by bags and boxes.

She remarked, gazing across him at the Loving
Sands, "They talk of nothing but invasion in the village. I could get no sense out of any of them. It was
all I could do to get my supplies. They seem to think
that Mrs. Beeston was killed because she knew about
it. Surely that's nonsense. What could an old woman
like that know about anything?"

"I think," said the Frenchman, "she knew too
much, and not necessarily about the invasion."

"But how could she? She never went out. She
walked across to the cottage at night, and the rest of
the time she spent snoozing by the stove. She wasn't
interested in anything but her tankard of ale and a
fire to sit by."

"Perhaps she was more observant than we thought."

"I cannot believe it," said Margaret. She looked at
him, then said, "Mrs. Lee is prepared to kill all the
invaders single-handed." A hint of laughter crept
into her voice. "She has an armory of weapons. You
have never seen anything like it. If I were an invader,
I should be terrified. She says they will all be killed
because the wind is changing and will drive them
onto the Loving Sands. I can't tell you how blood-
thirsty she looked."

"She is a true *tricoteuse*," said the Frenchman.
Then, as if this reminded him of something, he said
once again, "Be careful, Margaret."

"Oh, you are always saying that." Her voice was
haughty, and she flicked the reins against the pony's
plump side. He started to amble on again, and the
Frenchman walked at his side.

"When you get back, I want you to go to Miss Flora," he said.

"Why? Is she ill?"

"She might well be. She has received a great shock. I think she will be in her room. She needs help very badly, Margaret, and for God's sake, keep that little sister of hers away from her."

"But what has happened?"

"I think it is better she tell you herself. And be careful, girl. You are foolish not to listen to me. Do you take me for some old grandmother?"

"Oh!" It was an impatient sound, but he fancied that a brief look of fear crossed her face. He had a sudden urge to go with her, but decided this was unnecessary, and what he had to tell Captain Ross could not wait. He saluted her and continued on his way to the cottage. When he arrived there, he paused for a second to look out across the sea.

There was nothing to be seen. The sea was gray and still. Only the scurrying clouds indicated the possibility of a rising wind. But he found that his apprehensions were almost choking him and, when the Captain answered the door, he pushed past him unceremoniously, without a word.

Margaret came a little breathlessly into Flora's room, for she had run up the stairs. She could see at once that something was very wrong indeed.

The room was in its usual state of chaos. The two girls, when changing or undressing, simply threw everything onto the floor. Flora had taken off her dress, and was sitting on the edge of the bed in a wrapper that was badly soiled. The soft wool dress, which must have cost a packet, lay in a crumpled pool at her feet. One earring had rolled toward the window, and she must have broken a flask of perfume, for there was glass everywhere, and a powerful smell of scent.

Then Margaret saw Flora's face, and forgot about everything else.

She thought, as she ran to her side, that the young woman resembled Ophelia. She was still beautiful, for she could not be anything else, but it was as if for the first time the reality of the world with its pain and grief and suffering had descended upon her. The golden hair was down and tangled, and her face was a strange, pale mask, with the blue eyes vacant and horrified. She did not seem aware of Margaret. Only when her hand was taken did she at last turn her head. She bestowed on Margaret a faint smile that seemed to hold no recognition.

In her lap lay a pistol. Margaret recognized it: It was one of the brace that were normally in a box in the library.

She tried gently to slide the pistol out of Flora's hand, but the young woman was not so distracted as she at first seemed, and her hand descended on Margaret's wrist with surprising strength.

"No," she said, and again, more insistently, "No!"

"Miss Flora, what can you want with that?" Margaret, now very frightened indeed, kneeled before her, looking up into the lovely face, now so wild and distraught. "I don't know what has happened, but I do know that, whatever it is, it will pass. Everything passes. I can see you are terribly unhappy, and— please forgive me, I don't mean to be impertinent, but I feel this is something to do with the heart, and I can only think that you have perhaps quarreled with your betrothed."

"Quarreled!" Flora burst out laughing and crying

at the same time, and Margaret was thankful to see the pale calm broken, though she still could not remove the firmly clasped weapon from the girl's hand. "No," said Flora more quietly, "we have not quarreled, dear Margaret. We have finished. I am no longer engaged to him."

"Oh, come now!" Margaret rose to her feet, then sat beside Flora on the bed and put an arm around her shoulders. She said, in a brisk voice induced by something near panic, "I think you are exaggerating. You have always seemed so happy with him, and I cannot believe this is really serious. Certainly not serious enough to consider taking your own life. Please give me that pistol. I am sure you do not know how to handle it, and these things are very dangerous."

"But I do know how to handle it," said Flora. The tears were gone, and she was smiling again. The look of her appalled Margaret, who was beginning to believe that her young cousin was crazed in the wits. Flora went on, in a small, calm voice, "Papa taught us. You see, he always wanted a son, and he was very angry that he only had two daughters, but he said even if we were girls we should know how to shoot. We are both good shots, Bertie and I. Shall I show you?"

And she raised the pistol, only Margaret managed to restrain her, saying as quietly as she could, "I'll take your word for it. And I am sure your Papa would not want you to use it. You cannot really mean to kill yourself because you have broken your engagement."

"I have no intention of killing myself," said Flora, turning the wild, blue eyes upon her.

"Then give me the pistol."

"I am going to kill Lewis first, and then my sister."
Then Margaret understood. She did not answer
for a moment. She saw again that scene at the barracks. She said at last, "Miss Flora, I was once very
much in love. I suppose it may seem strange to you,
but I was very pretty as a girl, and very silly, too. I
met someone I fell in love with, and he loved me,
and we were going to marry, and it was like all the
fairy books. I had the chance of being happy, which
is more than happens to most of us, and because I
was so stupid, I threw it away. It was all my fault. I
don't know what has happened, Flora"—she was
agitated enough to omit the "Miss," but neither of
them noticed—"and it is certainly not your fault,
but . . . Oh, how can I know? It is Lewis who has
thrown away his happiness. You should pity him. He is
a fool. I don't know if you can forgive him, or even if
you want to forgive him, but to talk of killing is completely foolish. It will help nobody, least of all yourself.
What will you achieve? So you kill Lewis, and perhaps
your sister. That will be the end of all three of you.
Give me that pistol and forget about revenge. I know
this will mean nothing to you now, but you are very
young and very beautiful, and there are other young
men in the world. Couldn't you go away for a while? I
am sure your father would be willing to arrange a
holiday for you. You cannot stay in this gloomy house
while you are so upset, with your—with Captain
Moore so near, and your sister next door."

Flora had listened to this patiently. She said simply, "You don't understand at all." Then, "What
happened, Margaret? Did he try to kill you?"

"Oh, no. He just went away."

"And you never saw him again?"

Margaret hesitated, wincing a little, for this conversation was painful to her. Then she said, reluctantly, "Once."

"And did you make it up?"

Margaret was too distressed to consider what she was saying. She forgot that Flora, though childish, had a certain animal acuteness, and she did not see where this was leading. She said bitterly, "No. We did not make it up. He has never really forgiven me. I think he hates me. I cannot blame him. I could not have behaved worse. A girl from the streets would have had more sense and more decency."

Flora cried in triumph, "I knew it. Oh, I knew it. It's Frenchy, isn't it?"

Margaret looked at her, sighed, then said, "Yes. You are perfectly right. I did not know you were so observant."

"You see, I'm not as silly as you think."

"I've never thought you silly. But—"

"It was Bertie who noticed it first. Bertie," said Flora, uttering the name with a startling savagery, "don't like people to be in love with anyone but her. You don't know Bertie at all, Margaret. She is so little and so plain, but she has a way with her, she is very determined, she always gets what she wants. You should be careful. She don't like you. She never did like you from the very beginning. And when Bertie dislikes people, she does terrible things. However," said Flora, after this unusual display of interest in someone other than herself, "you need not worry, poor Margaret, because I am going to kill her. After Lewis, of course. I want her to see Lewis dead. I don't care what you say. Why should they treat me like that? Besides, I do observe, though no one thinks I

do—you were surprised I knew about Frenchy, but
then I saw you looking at him . . . and there are
other things. All kinds of things."

"What other things?" asked Margaret, regarding
her steadily. It seemed to her that, despite all this
talk of killing, Flora was now in a healthier state of
mind. The wild, desperate look had disappeared,
though it had been replaced by a strange air of malice
that sat oddly on such a gentle and foolish girl.
However, anything was better than the former despair, and Margaret still hoped she would have the
opportunity to take the weapon from her. She managed not even to glance at the pistol, though she
could see out of the corner of her eye that Flora still
held it firmly. She repeated, "What other things?"

She thought Flora was not going to answer, but
presently she said, in a vague, bored voice, "There
are things in the Bluebeard Room that should not be
there. I think Lewis would not like me to know that."

"The Bluebeard Room!" repeated Margaret in
bewilderment. She had forgotten all about this mysterious room, for during the past weeks there had
been a great deal else to occupy her mind. She said
with a smile, "That is just a fairy tale, Flora. There is
nothing there. What do you expect to find? The key
and the headless corpses are just something written in
a book. They say the real Bluebeard was called
Gilles de Rais, but I don't suppose he really did such
dreadful things."

She was discovering that the best way to make Flora
talk was to contradict her. Like the child she was, she
could not bear to be crossed. There was certainly
more to this gentle, foolish young woman than she
had ever realized. Flora might not have the brains of

her sister, nor, perhaps, her tenacity of purpose, but there was certainly an obstinacy, and even a curious ruthlessness.

She grew angry now, and in her anger forgot about the pistol, which fell noiselessly onto the sheet. Margaret, with a sigh of pure relief, saw to it that a fold of her skirt covered it; then, as Flora was talking, she gently slid it into her apron pocket.

Flora cried out, "There is something there. There is, there is! And I think I know what it is."

"Oh, come, you are imagining things," said Margaret, grown suddenly cunning, for she was anxious to learn the truth, and was beginning to suspect that there might be grounds for Flora's suspicions.

Flora said, with great dignity, "I think you are being most impertinent. After all, you're only the housekeeper here. I know you are a cousin, but a very distant one. We all think of you as a poor relation, which is dreadfully dull."

Margaret, unmoved by this outburst, which was like that of a naughty child, eyed her expressively but said nothing. Presently, Flora, apparently forgetting what she had said, went on.

She said, in the way of one telling a ghost story, "I have seen Bertie there at night, and there's a key to the door. You never knew that, clever Margaret, did you?"

"I am not as clever as you," said Margaret meekly, then thought, *Really, I am become quite horrid to play this silly child in such a way*. But she was too curious to stop now, and she waited with downcast eyes, one hand always on the pistol in her pocket.

"You are not clever at all," said Flora, then giggled like a little girl. "I know where the key is, too. Bertie would be wild with fury if she knew I had been

watching her. But then, cunning people like Bertie
always think everyone else so silly, and that makes it
easy."

Margaret saw that there was considerable truth in
this, and promised herself not to take other people too
much for granted in the future. But she made no
comment, and Flora said, "Shall I tell you where the
key is? Then you and I can go and have a look. I
would be too frightened to go by myself, but you are
very brave, aren't you? And you would be protecting
your Frenchy, too."

Margaret, a little bewildered, said, "I am not brave
at all, Flora. And I would be terrified of going into
that room, for I have a great fear of being locked up.
But I don't suppose there is really a key to the room
at all."

"There is!" said Flora in a sudden temper, "and if
you don't open the room, your precious Frenchy will
probably go to prison and be thrown in the Black
Hole. Lewis will make sure of that. Oh, how stupid
you are, Margaret. I really don't know why we put
up with you. Of course there is, and it's in a bottle
in Bertie's room."

"A bottle!"

"I've just told you. She hides the bottle in different
places, but I dare say we could find it. There are
always bottles there. I think she drinks a lot of wine,
and now I know why she does. I think Lewis does too.
Would you like me to tell you about it?"

"If you wish," said Margaret, now past all shame, for
somehow this seemed connected with Philippe's safety,
and she was determined to learn as much as she could.
But then the triumph and spite on Flora's face vanished, and she began to cry again, covering her eyes
with her hands. Margaret, overcome with remorse,

tried to comfort her, but Flora pushed the consoling arms away, sobbing, "I didn't know, I didn't know. I thought he loved me. And he was drinking with her all the night so that she could find out everything she wanted to know, and then I suppose they made love. I can't bear it," wailed Flora. Then, for her moods changed as suddenly as the wind, "Why don't you go away? You're like Bertie, you're just spying on me. Go away! I don't like you. I'm not going to tell you any more, it's none of your business. It's like that little box. You stole it from me!"

"Miss Flora, that is simply not true," said Margaret, rising to her feet, astonished and angered by this undeserved accusation.

"It is true," said Flora sullenly. "Bertie was furious. She said I had no right to give it away, so I told her you took it, and then that boy was killed, and it is all your fault. Bertie said it was all your fault."

"What boy? Miss Flora," said Margaret indignantly, "you are talking nonsense. You know very well I never stole that box. You gave it to me yourself. And what could it possibly have to do with a boy being killed?"

But Flora would not answer, and at last Margaret went away, thankful to have the pistol, which she instantly took up to her room and put in a drawer beneath her underclothes.

She stood for a while by the window, staring out at the Bluebeard Room. Of course it was all nonsense, a disagreeable fairy tale. There could never have been a room filled with the corpses of over-inquisitive wives, but certainly the old building had a formidable air to it. What could there be in there, and what had it to do with Philippe? Her curiosity suddenly overcame her, and she forgot that she was behaving remarkably like one of Bluebeard's ladies. What could it be? They did dreadful things in the olden days—perhaps some wretched woman had been walled up there, or some unhappy prisoner. Once she had visited an old castle and seen the oubliettes where men were thrown down to starve to death in the dark and cold. The very thought of this made her dizzy with fear, and the childhood terror returned, so that she visualized herself behind that solid door, shut in forever.

But nothing would ever induce her to go in. She would simply open it to look inside.

No doubt that was what the wives had said. *I won't go in. I'll just open the door and have a peep, no one will ever know. When dearest Bluebeard comes home, the door will be locked, the key on its hook, and I'll make him an extra-nice dinner so that he'll suspect nothing.*

And the bloodstains on the key would not wash off. That must have been an appalling moment, unimaginable in terror. Scrubbing wildly at the key, the footsteps coming up the stairs, and that shocking vision painted on the eyeballs of the headless bodies of the disobedient wives . . .

And *Il faut mourir, madame, et tout à l'heure.*

Oh, poor things, poor things! Nobody deserved such a punishment, even for disobedience, and, after all, what woman could resist such a challenge? Margaret, half laughing at herself and shuddering at the same time, was convulsed with pity for these innocent girls whose only crime was folly. She knew then that Bluebeard would have found in her another victim. She had now made up her mind to find the key and open the door, if only to save Philippe from prison.

She went down the stairs to the kitchens. She would have to look for another cook tomorrow, and this time it must be someone who really worked. But this reminded her again of Mrs. Beeston, and she set doggedly to preparing the food, set the still-whispering servants to their various tasks, and presently stepped out of the back door to throw away some vegetable peelings.

She raised her head, to see that Albertine was crossing the garden, and Albertine turned at the same moment, so that their eyes met. Then she walked toward Margaret, with her odd limping gait.

Margaret, her own face a little set, thought that Albertine had in some strange way changed. Perhaps it was simply the bitter cold, but the pointed cat's face was taut and sharp and old, the dark eyes glittered, and the wide mouth, with its one twisted tooth showing, was set in a grim, fierce line. She was wearing a fur cape and bonnet, as if she were about to take a walk, but the hand that shot out toward Margaret was ungloved, and red with the cold.

"I want you to go," she said, the small voice trembling up and down the scale with rage. "I want you to leave now. You are no good. We never wanted you here. You are grossly incompetent. You do no work, you are stupid and lazy, and you are always meddling in other people's affairs. Go upstairs and pack your box. Go this instant."

Margaret stood there, looking at her. It seemed to be the day for people telling her to go away. Once Albertine had frightened her, if only because that small frame held so much ferocity. At times she was like a wild cat, and she was like a wild cat now. But now she sensed something else—she knew that Albertine was afraid.

She said quietly, "Why do you hate me so?"

"You interfere too much," said Albertine, in a more normal voice, the sweet high voice that was so at variance with her nature. She raised the magnificent dark eyes to Margaret's pale face. "We were happy here before you came, you and your lover." She saw Margaret's countenance flicker, and laughed in a shrill, trilling way that made her cousin long to slap her. "Oh, we know all about that too. Why do you think yourself so clever? We've laughed about it many times, except that it is not amusing, it's rather disgusting."

Margaret said dryly, "You all seem to have knowledge that I don't possess." And she could not help thinking how angry the Frenchman would be to be credited as the lover of an old flame he now despised.

Albertine did not follow this, and an exasperated look flashed across her face. She said again, "You must go. If you are wise, you'll go this very moment. It was a pity you ever came here in the first place. I told Papa so, but of course he would not listen."

"I think," said Margaret, "you are a stupid and interfering young woman."

"How dare you speak to me like that!"

"Oh, I dare," said Margaret in a sigh, and wondered secretly how she did so. But it was plain that her days here were numbered; it scarcely mattered if she spoke her mind at last. She said crisply, "You are a mischief-maker, Albertine. You have made mischief for your sister, and you will doubtless do the same for me. I think you must lead a very boring life, for you seem to have nothing better to do than upset everyone, indulge in silly intrigues, and—and drink too much wine."

Albertine received this broadside with surprising calm. It was almost as if she enjoyed it.

Margaret stared into that wicked little face, only a few feet away. Suddenly she knew who must be instrumental for what had occurred. This minute creature could hardly be strong enough to push her over the sea wall, but certainly it was her design, whoever had been her dupe and tool.

She cried out, "You tried to kill me!"

Albertine did not attempt to deny this. Perhaps she would never deny anything that provided drama. She was silent for a moment, and then fell into what seemed to Margaret a kind of child's tantrum. She stamped her foot and waved her hands; tears of rage were falling down her face. She swung round and made for the garden, hopping and dragging her twisted foot behind her. She hissed over her shoulder, "You'll see. Oh, you'll see, you and your lover . . ."

And then she was out of sight, the side gate to the garden swinging behind her.

Margaret watched her, and then returned to the kitchen. She felt a little sick, for violence always disturbed her, and, despite her own words, she was afraid, though the threat had been childish and without meaning. She would at that moment have given anything for a sight of the Frenchman, but he was not to be seen. By this time, he was in Captain Ross's cottage.

Captain Ross regarded his visitor without enthusiasm, yet with the air of one who had expected his company. He said in a surly manner, "You have taken your time, Monsieur le Marquis."

Nobody had addressed the Frenchman in such a

way for nearly ten years. He opened his mouth to protest fiercely, then saw the absurdity of such a gesture. He raised his hands in the foreign fashion that had also been alien for a long time; then, because he was exhausted, unsure and apprehensive, he stepped over the cat lying before the fire and sat down, without waiting for an invitation.

Captain Ross did not offer him wine. Instead he poured out a liquid white as water, and when the Frenchman took a mouthful of it and nearly spat it out in sheer surprise, he said, "I might have expected it. You foreigners spend your time drinking wine. I'd swear you've never tasted good whisky in your life."

The Frenchman nearly answered that he hoped he would never do so again, but was discovering that the acrid liquid, for all it burned his gullet, descended with an unusually invigorating warmth. He took another sip—more cautiously this time—and waited, not knowing how to begin with this gentleman who had always been so hostile to him.

Captain Ross did not begin either, or at least not in the way that might have been expected. He glanced at his visitor, who, being even taller than himself, and sitting there with his long legs outstretched, took up a great deal of room. The Frenchman considered Captain Ross from beneath his lashes, and thought that he was not an agreeable-looking man, but, like Margaret, he recognized the strength and honesty in that ugly fighting face, and knew he had come to the right place. This was the kind of man one would want at one's side in battle; this was someone uncompromising and dependable.

And then he spoke. The Captain, of course, had heard of Mrs. Beeston, and did not seem much interested, even in the story of the bottles, but when the Frenchman told him about Margaret and how apparently she had nearly been killed, he swore and banged his own glass down.

"She will not tell me the details," said the Frenchman. "But I have tried to persuade her to go. I know she is in danger. I feel it in my bones. And she won't listen to one damned word I say."

"She is a good lass," said Captain Ross. "She's a fool to be in love with you, but she's a good lass." He ignored his visitor's outraged expression. He was probably a man who could ignore anything. However, when the Frenchman jerked himself upright with such violence that he spilled some of his whisky, the Captain at once sprang forward to right the glass, and scowled admonishingly.

He said, "What ails you, monsieur?" He had an excellent French accent, and now, to the Frenchman's astonishment, slipped quite naturally into his visitor's tongue. Somehow one would have expected from him the most appalling British-accented French, but Captain Ross did not hold his present post for nothing, and spoke French as easily as his native Scots. He said, quite casually, "I have offered for her myself. She's turned me down. Oh, I am not surprised. I'm not much of a catch for a beautiful young woman— have you never looked at her, sir?—with my one arm gone and a face that makes the young misses swoon when I ask them for a dance. But I did not know at the time that she was taken elsewhere." He used the word *éprise*. "It was very unobservant of me. When I looked properly, I saw that she had eyes for no one else but you. Will you kindly sit down? There is no call for Gallic temperament. I am only speaking an

obvious truth that you must be fully aware of yourself."

The Frenchman was filled with a confused urge to
seize this arrogant blockhead by the throat and shake
him to death, or else to storm from the room. He
realized that the first was unlikely to help the situation and would probably land him in the *cachot,*
while the second was both childish and ridiculous.
He stood there, struggling to control his temper, his
chest rising and falling with his emotion, but Captain
Ross merely stooped to wipe up the spilled whisky
with a spotlessly clean handkerchief, then refilled his
glass and said, "If you are not aware of this, it is high
time you were. Sit down! You cannot challenge me to
a duel. This is not Paris, where you spit each other
like chickens; in this country we are more civilized."
Suddenly he smiled. On such an ugly face, the smile
was surprisingly charming. "Ah, sit down, Marquis.
I'm an old man, and I have only one arm. You cannot fight me, and much good it would do you if you
did. Relax and drink your whisky, and be thankful
that I have now changed my mind about you. For a
while I believed you to be the spy I was looking for."

"And how do you know I am not?" demanded the
Frenchman. He gave the Captain a slightly shame-
faced smile, and sat down again. He really could not
continue to stand there looking dramatic, and it was
plain that this was to be a prolonged session.

"Because I'm a good judge of character," said the
Captain, speaking always in his fluent French. He
must have read the look in the Frenchman's eyes, for
he added, "You are astonished that I speak your language so well? You should not be. I was at school in
Paris, though that was a long time ago, and my mother,

a remarkably tiresome woman, was French. She survived to a great age, which made life difficult for all of us—I have four sisters—and she never lost her mind or her evil tongue. However, I dare say that could have arrived in a Scotswoman, so I am not reproaching your nation, in case you are due for another bout of patriotism."

The Frenchman did the only thing left for him to do—he laughed. With that laugh he looked a great deal younger, though this fact would not have interested him. At the same time, he discovered that he liked this damnably impertinent man, who, having bestowed on him the unnecessary information about his tiresome mother and sisters, turned again to the attack.

He said again, *"C'est une brave fille.* You're damned lucky, sir, to have such a woman to adore you."

The Frenchman said carefully, "You are completely mistaken. The young lady in question no longer has the least feeling for me." He broke off, a faint color coming into his cheeks. Damn the man, he would notice the slip of the tongue immediately.

But Captain Ross, whether he noticed or not, made no comment, but only repeated, "She loves you. Do you imagine I would not notice? I'll not pretend to be sick with love for her, for I am too old, but I asked her to be my wife because I admired and respected her, because I know she would do me credit even if she did not feel much love for me. It is rare to find such a woman. You should count yourself lucky, sir." And then he said once more, *"C'est une brave fille."*

The Frenchman could perhaps have thought of a time when Margaret had warranted neither admira-

tion nor respect, but he did not do so. He only saw
Margaret as she was now, and he saw too that she
was as beautiful as the Captain had said, pale and
composed as she was. She stood up to the insults he
had thrown at her, and had taken upon her slender
shoulders the full burden of running the Hall and the
Walters family, for all that she was unaccustomed to
such work and hardship. He made no reply to the
Captain, only idly stirred the cat with his foot. The
animal, taking this for a caress, instantly fell into
noisy purring.

"She would do better with me," said Captain Ross.
"But then, all women are fools, even the best of them.
The worse a man treats them, the more they love
him. It is something I shall never understand."

The Frenchman did not answer this either, and
only raised his eyes for a second to this extraordinary
gentleman who in moments of crisis had nothing better to do than discuss women and love.

Then Captain Ross, speaking English once more in
his usual brisk voice, said, "Well now, what else have
you to tell me, Marquis? Or would you prefer that I
tell you?"

"As you please," said the Frenchman.

"I think you had best tell me. Apart from the old
woman, what else is there you have observed?"

Margaret could have told him that this was the
Captain's favorite word, but the Frenchman did not
notice it. He said slowly, "There are many strange
things happening. Miss Albertine plays some secret
game of her own that I do not like. I think she is a
very dangerous young woman, and she has done her
best to make me part of whatever it is she plans."

"She is a bitch," said Captain Ross roughly. "She

is at the heart of the whole matter. I've warned her father time after time, but naturally he pays not the least attention. I believe she is behind all these escapes. I have thought so for a long while now, but I have no proof. I thought, as I have told you, that you were with her, but now I suppose I must admit to being in the wrong. I can see from your look there's something more. What is it?"

The Frenchman rose to his feet and stood by the mantelpiece. The cat followed, rubbing itself against his legs. He took a deep breath, then related what had happened to Miss Flora. When he said he had knocked Lewis down, the Captain positively roared with delight, and insisted on pouring him out another whisky. The Frenchman did not smile back. He said grimly, "You of all people must see that I am in a damnable position. I believe your young captain is a traitor. There is all this talk of invasion. But I am a Frenchman, sir. Not only is England not my own country, it is also my enemy. I am, after all, a prisoner of war. In coming to you, I am virtually betraying France. I never thought I could side against my own land. It is not that I think myself a particularly loyal person, but this, even though my own people have persecuted me, is something that will always be on my conscience. I cannot really understand myself, only for some reason I find I do not want disaster to fall on the house and the village." His voice suddenly rose. "You expected this of me! And you thought me a spy. Perhaps it would be more honorable if I were. Your spy is my patriot. I am beginning to find it intolerably impertinent that you should accuse me of betraying your confounded goddamns, and now expect me to betray my own people."

"You are a most inconsistent man," said Captain
Ross calmly. "Why don't you drink your whisky? All
this is just havers."

"What!"

"Ah, that's a good Scots word that you ignorant
foreigners would not understand. Talk, man. Just
talk. Windy words that mean nothing. You are speaking nonsense. You owe nothing to your country.
Your compatriots would have chopped your head off
if you'd not run for it." He grinned at the spasm of
fury that crossed the Frenchman's face. "Of course
you ran. I'd have run too. No one but a fool would
stay to put his head under the guillotine. You may
detest the English—I don't care for them much
myself—but you cannot love this Boney, who has
only spared you to fight for him. And I'm not asking
you to betray your own country. If you are betraying
anyone, it's that Miss Bertie, and she'd sell the whole
wide world, including her lover, to the highest bidder,
and will doubtless do so in due course if he sur-
vives that long. Besides, Marquis, you are doing none
of this for—what were your words now?—the house
and the village. You are doing it for your Margaret."

"That is not—" The Frenchman broke off. He did
not attempt to finish the sentence. He reached out for
his glass and drained it, while the Captain watched
him with some satisfaction.

The Captain went on, "Miss Bertie's lover, however, will not survive." A strong emotion came into
his voice, and his face set like a rock. "Did you believe
I did not know? I have been watching young Moore
for a long time. Apart from everything else, I have no
patience with officers who are foxed morning, noon,
and night. It is bad for discipline. But I could not be

sure. I knew there must be someone in the Cross Prison who . . . However, there will be no more escapes."

"But there will be an invasion," said the Frenchman, uttering at last the words he had really come to say.

"No."

"Are you out of your mind? What is all this for if not—"

"There'll be no invasion," said Captain Ross, almost wearily. "Oh, maybe a few little boats will one day appear on the horizon, but if so, it'll not be here, it'll be on the west coast, more like, where the Polish boy landed a few years back. I know there was a handful of troops landed at Fishguard last year. They crawled onto the rocks and turned one of the farms into their headquarters. It didn't last long. From a military point of view it was a waste of time. I doubt they'll do it again. If they do, the Loving Sands will get them, and if the sands don't, I will. There are plenty of loyal men here. We are an island, Marquis, we have the sea, and we have Nelson. There is no chance of a successful invasion. There's many have tried it and failed. The nearest we got to it was when the Highlanders came to Derby. And we turned them back, and they scuttled home so fast they left half their kilts behind them. I am a Scot and a Highlander. But I have no patience with such nonsense. You could say with as much sense that Robespierre was a Frenchman and you owed him loyalty. Robespierre was a scoundrel. The Polish boy was a scoundrel too, and a fool into the bargain. Because I am a Scot don't mean I have to back all the riffraff spewed onto our shores, with a gallon of foreign

blood in their veins. Why, I'd dirk a Stuart as soon
as a Frenchman any day."

The Frenchman sighed, and made again that faint
foreign gesture with his hands. He reflected that he
would never understand the British, and certainly not
Captain Ross. He only said, "If there is not to be an
invasion, all this is incomprehensible."

"You don't begin to understand Miss Bertie."

"That is true enough."

"She is a born intriguer. Perhaps it is because she is
small and lame, with a beautiful sister. I do not know.
But she loves power. She likes to move people like
chess pieces on a board. She decided it would be
amusing to seduce one of my officers, who is her own
sister's fiancé. She has beside a kind of passion for
General Bonaparte—God alone knows why—she
wishes to go to France, and she is planning a mass
escape from the prison. That's why there is this talk
of invasion, to get everyone out on the streets at the
crucial point. Invasion there will not be, but a small
war there might, for there is somewhere a cache of
arms, and until I know where that is, I cannot arrest
the lady and her companion. There is also a carefully
concealed underground escape route, which leads, I
imagine, onto the sands. Do you know anything of
that?"

"I do not."

"Then find out!"

The Frenchman, who was beginning to understand
him better, gave him an expressive look and said,
without anger, "You presume to ask such a thing of
me!"

"Why not? There is nothing here to offend your
patriotism. Maybe you wish the prisoners to escape,

but you should not, for they will all die, either on the sands or at the hands of my officers or be slaughtered in the village. You underrate Adeney Cross. Mrs. Lee," said Captain Ross reflectively, "will certainly manage a small massacre on her own. I should hate to fall into her hands. But other people will be killed, and that must be prevented. After all, as you have made plain to me, your Margaret in some way knows more than she should, and that last attempt to put her out of the way will not necessarily be the last."

The Frenchman did not answer this, though the words beat upon him, stirring all the fear within him. He turned toward the door. He said harshly, "So you expect me to find out about this passage and the cache of arms. And each time I ask you why I should do this, you talk of Margaret. I consider I have done more than my duty in coming to you at all. You say the prisoners will be killed. I have only your word for that. I do not feel I have the right to prevent them from escaping. They, at least, are not hampered by a parole. Sometimes even then I think that kind of honor is outdated." He broke off, then said, "This cache of arms. How do you know it exists?"

Captain Ross was watching him patiently enough, but there was a glitter in his eye. He said, "Because the man we captured and killed was fully armed."

"Then interrogate Captain Moore!"

"I prefer to know before I interrogate him."

"Interrogate Miss Albertine, then."

"I have already told you, I wish to catch the she-devil redhanded. And I doubt she'd answer, or if her father would let her. Don't you see, sir, I must stop this for good and for all. The war will be going on for a long while yet. Maybe it is not so important to have this small center of treachery, yet it is something

I will not endure, and I'll not be happy until the
whole boiling lot of them are safely tucked away,
somewhere where there'll be no escape, perhaps
beneath the sands. You," said Captain Ross, speaking
to the Frenchman, who had opened the door,
"whether you like it or not, Marquis, were always the
one little pebble in the way, and—though this is
something you have not so far mentioned—I'll lay a
hundred to one that Miss Bertie has tried to seduce
you. As I surmise she has not succeeded, she will soon
try to cut your throat, much as she dealt with that
poor old limmer who's now in her grave."

The Frenchman was surprised enough to swing
around. "You think it was she who murdered Mrs.
Beeston? But she's such a little thing."

"It may not have been her hand," answered Captain Ross, "but it was certainly at her direction. I do
not think Captain Moore drinks entirely for the
pleasure of it. But, to come back to yourself, I
know that Bertie was not best pleased when you
arrived. I imagine she had hoped to learn French
from one of the prisoners and have free entry into
the prison whenever she chose. But I do not know.
You do my work for me, Marquis. Tell me where the
cache is, and, if you wish, I'll see you home on the
next cartel ship, with your lassie by your side."

"Are you trying to bribe me now?" asked the
Frenchman quietly.

"No. You need no bribing. You'll do what I want.
You have the best inducement in the world. Oh, I
know you fall into a temper whenever I mention her
name, but, after all, Miss Margaret has come athwart
Miss Bertie, and that young woman has never cared
for her own sex, being the kind to be jealous of all
the rest, whether they're eight or eighty. I tell you, as

I've told you already, there might well be another accident, and a final one. I think you'd not like that over-much, Marquis."

"I wish," said the Frenchman in a sudden fury, "that you'd not address me in that ridiculous way. My title was taken from me ten years ago."

"Very well, *citoyen!* But I think you'll do what I want."

"I think," said the Frenchman, "you'll do your own dirty work."

The Captain called after him, "You pretend not to believe me. Tell me, then, why did you cut the grass for me?"

The Frenchman looked at him in a furious silence; then, the next moment, he was out the door. He thought as he stormed down the path that he had never met a man who trampled so implacably on other people's feelings, and for a while he paced up and down by the sea wall, trying to calm himself and gather himself into some kind of coherent thought.

The one question remained with him: *Why did you cut the grass?*

And the answer to this foolish question was clear. *Because I did not want to leave, because I would rather perform an unsuitable and humiliating task than leave.*

And why did you not want to leave?

Because, deep in my heart, I did not want to leave Margaret.

And then the Frenchman, now confronted with the inevitable, sighed, turned up his coat collar against the cold, and made straight for the Hall, where he went upstairs to Margaret's room.

He pushed open the door without knocking. The room was empty. Then he saw that she had gone

away. The drawers were all open and untidy. Some
of the clothes were still there, as if Margaret had
packed in a frantic hurry, as if she had been so desperate to go that she could not take everything with her.
The apprehension settled within him like a lump of
ice. She was a tidy and methodical girl. She would
never behave like this unless driven by real despair.

He sat down on the bed, trying to think what he
should do. His eyes moved over the room, which he
had never before entered. The dressing table, wooden
with a small, stained mirror, was stripped of whatever
had been upon it, and it looked as if somehow she
had swept her hand across it, for there was a broken
portrait on the floor, the buckle of a belt, a few
hairpins. The Frenchman picked up the article which
had caught in the hinge of the mirror. His face was
almost broken in the emotion of realizing what it was.

It was a silk handkerchief, of the kind that fops
used to wear for some grand occasion. It was not the
kind of thing he had normally indulged in, but it had
been fashionable, and he had worn it attached to his
wrist for that celebrated ball when Henry had appeared, when Margaret had quarreled with him, when
their life together had been smashed like glass. It was
of the finest silk, with his initials and family crest
embroidered in one corner.

He turned it over and over in his hands. It brought
back a vanished world, and, like that world, it was
faded and stained. He could for a strange moment
hear the music, the voices, smell the perfume, feel the
heat of the overcrowded room.

And Margaret had carried it with her for ten
years. It must have dropped to the floor that evening,
and she had picked it up without a word.

He continued to hold it, smoothing the silk with

his fingers. Then he pushed it into his pocket. He was cold with grief and anger and remorse. Perhaps it was he who had driven her away by his ill manners and harsh words. This frippery of an age past and gone was all he would now have of her.

He wondered if he could find her. Presumably, she would have gone home. Then he remembered that she had no home, since before coming to the Hall she had sold the cottage. Perhaps the Colonel would have some address for her, or a reference. The Frenchman, cursing himself for the stupidity that had brought all this about, rose violently to his feet and nearly tripped over something that was half concealed under the bed.

It was Margaret's reticule. It was closed. When he opened it, he saw that it contained her housekeeping keys, a little money, and a small, cheap, cotton handkerchief.

The Frenchman knew something about women, and one thing was certain: No woman, however desperate, however much in a hurry, would set out on a journey without her reticule. Anyone who could remember the ornaments on the dressing table would hardly forget something far more indispensable.

He looked around the untidy, denuded room. The fear, which had dwindled at the thought of her being away and safe, smashed down on him again. He had no idea what to do, but certainly something had happened to her. Something perhaps had terrified her into flight. Then he saw that he must go back again to Captain Ross, the only person who could advise and help him. And because he was now badly afraid himself, he did not go straight to the cottage, but took himself to the Loving Sands, in the hope that the cold night air might somehow clear his bewildered thoughts.

His fingers touched the silk handkerchief as he walked. In his ears were the foolish words *Why did you cut the grass?* He should have known a long time ago, and perhaps now it was too late. He came at last to the sea wall and climbed down onto the sands, now safe at low tide. The garden wall was too steep for him to manage, and he sat down on a rock at its foot. Once he glanced up, as if to see how he could make his escape should he fall into a reverie and the tide catch him unawares. There was not much foothold, only the odd jutting stone here and there, with hanging creepers to aid him. No doubt he would manage, for the prospect of so dreadful a death would make a legless man agile.

And there he remained for a while as the tide slowly turned.

Chapter Ten

Margaret did not go to Albertine's room immediately, for she was too disturbed. In any case, she knew that it was safe for she had seen the young woman walk out of the garden after that horrid, ridiculous scene. Besides, she was fully entitled to enter the girls' rooms whenever she chose, in her role of housekeeper. But now she had to admit that she was spying. Her curiosity with regard to the Bluebeard Room—she now never thought of it in any other way —was intense, and apparently it held danger for

Philippe, though this she could not begin to understand. But she did not like the thought of creeping around to find that mysterious key, and she quailed a little at what she might discover when the door was opened, though God knows, she did not expect to find headless corpses.

It seemed to her almost as if she had come here for the sole purpose of finding out what lay behind that heavy door. The room was somehow the center of the mystery. Confused pictures flashed through her memory: Flora distraught and crying, Albertine savage with frustrated rage; invasions, escaping prisoners, a drunken captain, and an atmosphere of desolate evil that hung upon this house like a sea fog. And Philippe. If she could only open the door and find that there was nothing there at all, the mystery and evil would depart. She would see that this was an ordinary house with two foolish, obsessed girls and the Colonel, who, poor silly man, never had concerned himself with his daughters, except to buy them what they asked for, and see that they were housed and fed.

There was no one around but herself. The kitchens were empty. Albertine was out on her own errands, Flora still lying on her bed, and Philippe had disappeared, which was possibly just as well, for he would certainly try to prevent her from doing what she proposed to do.

She went at last, a little shamefacedly, to Albertine's room, the room that overlooked the Norman ruins and from which she used to throw her bottles into the garden.

It was entirely different from that of her sister. It was equally untidy, with the garments strewn about

the floor, but it wore a sluttish air, and might have
been some dissolute nightwalker's den. Its atmosphere
was unpleasing. Margaret stood on the threshold, her
hands folded over her apron, as if indeed she were
nothing but a housekeeper making sure that all was
well. Then she suddenly saw why the room was different. It was entirely impersonal. Flora's room was
decorated with a vase of flowers, a pretty ribbon—the
souvenir of some party—tied over the mirror, a dance
program, even a romantic novel, though neither of
the Walters girls was much given to reading. Here,
however, there was nothing to indicate the owner. It
was all bare, except for the clothes on the floor. There
was not a flower, not a paper, not a book. Except for
the quality of the discarded garments, it might have
been a servant's room. There was not even a picture
on the wall.

Only the bed had character. It was rumpled, with a
pink quilted eiderdown oddly at variance with the
owner. There was a flask of perfume lying on the two
pillows which lay side by side. It had an air of occupa-
tion. Perhaps this was the heart of Albertine's power.

Margaret did not have to hunt far for the bottle,
for it was at the back of the cupboard, concealed by
the hanging dresses. Albertine had not shown much
subtlety in her hiding place, or perhaps she did not
believe anyone would trouble to look for it. She was
certainly not stupid, but, like many cunning and
scheming people, she had her blind spots, and one of
them was that she felt nobody was as clever as herself.
Yet Margaret, holding the bottle in her hands, had
to realize with a faint chill that the hiding place was
the obvious one. Was it possible that she was meant to
find it? Then she mentally shook herself for being so

silly, and shook the bottle too, to drop the key into her hand.

She left the room at once and came out into the corridor. The house was as deserted and cold as the grave. The Colonel was as generous with fires as he was with most material things, but nothing could take the chill off so vast a house. Margaret, walking swiftly up and down it many times a day as she performed her duties, often thought that if ever she had her own home again, she would make sure it was cosy and warm. The Hall was full of beautiful things, rare books and exquisite ornaments, but it was unlived-in and unloved. She was always thankful to return to the kitchens, which were alive and filled with people.

She went to her own room first, to put on her cloak. She looked down at the key in her hands. It was simply an ordinary, if rather large, key. There was no blood on it—oh no! What nonsense was this? *I am growing mad,* she told herself quite fiercely, *I am becoming old and daft like Mrs. Lee.* A key would probably not even fit, even if she could find the lock. Miss Flora was half crazed with grief, and perhaps did not know what she was talking about. The key, this perfectly ordinary key, might well be a spare for the cellar (Miss Albertine being so addicted to the wine), Margaret knew nothing about this, for bringing up bottles was not one of her duties, and she had never even seen the celebrated cellar, which was, in its way, responsible for poor Mrs. Beeston's death.

Death. My mind is full of death. What the devil is the matter with me? I think of nothing but that absurd story, a children's story—poor little souls, it must have kept them awake at nights—but it is only a fairy story. There never was a Bluebeard. Gilles de

Rais could never have been so wicked, it is simply an invention, and here am I, brooding on headless ladies, bloodied keys, and horrid gentlemen who murder their wives for nothing but a perfectly natural feminine curiosity.

A natural feminine curiosity. At that moment her courage faltered, and she nearly abandoned the whole scheme. It would not take a minute to return the key to its bottle. Then she could go about her normal duties in the ordinary way. Philippe would be back soon, and however angry he might be, his presence always comforted her. Miss Flora would recover from her tears, and Miss Albertine return in a better temper. All would go on as before. It was really neither sensible nor dignified to ferret around in mysterious rooms at this hour. It was none of her business, and she would do far better to concentrate on the supper.

Margaret, not the most domestic of girls, longed most passionately to force herself to go prepare the supper. She dwelled on the thought of the warm kitchen, the pleasant smell of cooking, the idle gossip of the servants around her. She wanted to forget all this foolishness and discuss it tomorrow with Captain Ross, who would probably laugh at her, but who could send a couple of his men down to make the investigation properly.

Then she thought again of Philippe. Indeed, nowadays she thought of little else. If she did not go, he might, as Flora had said, end in the prison, and she could not bear that. She saw him sitting in the courtyard, his head shaven, his body clad in those revolting yellow clothes. He might be selling—the thought was quite unendurable—some ridiculous objects made of straw or bones. Philippe would be no good at all at

straw and bones, nor could she visualize him joking
and flirting with the villagers on Sunday mornings.
She remembered all the stories she had heard of the
savage *Romains* who murdered and robbed, of the
terrible overcrowding, of the disgusting meals, the
cold, the dark, the abominable punishments for the
least insubordination. Captain Ross must be a cruel
man, though he was, of course, only doing his duty.

And she sighed, swallowed hard, put the key in her
pocket, together with a tinderbox and candle, and
set off at last, feeling a little dizzy and sick with
apprehension, for the garden.

She reached the Norman walls and stood there for
a minute, trying to regain her self-control. She was
most dreadfully afraid. It was as if every kind of warning signal was flashing through her brain and heart,
though she was quite alone, the kitchen only a few
paces away, and someone—probably the Colonel—
was in the library, for she could see the dim lamplight
through the closed curtains. She nearly turned and
ran back. But common sense and shame kept her
there, and at least she had the light of a full moon,
which was just as well, for the wind was too high to
allow her to light her candle.

She moved toward the Bluebeard Room. However
much she tried not to, she could think of it only by
this childish name. She glanced over her shoulder as
she did so, for she had the feeling that she was being
observed, but there was no one and nothing in sight,
not even one of the Hall cats, who often roamed the
garden at night. The leafless trees shivered and sighed,
and she tried to find comfort in this, hoping the wind
would hinder the invaders' boats.

She crouched down by the moss-covered door, the

key still in her pocket. And there was a lock after all, and not so difficult to find. The bolt was useless, rusted with the centuries. Her strength was insufficient to move it an inch, and, indeed, nobody could have moved it at all, for it was as if it had grown into the door. But under the moss, a little above the bolt, her searching hand found the lock. It was cunningly concealed beneath the slimy green, which she had to pull away, but when at last she saw it in the moonlight, she found it was oiled and clean. It had plainly been used, and not long ago.

Her heart was thumping as if it might jump out of her body, but, with trembling hands, she managed to insert the key and turn it. It turned without effort, and she watched, her eyes wide with fear, excitement, and curiosity, as the great door pulled outward. The lock had been easy, but the door weighed so much that she could hardly move it. She moved her hands around the width of it, which was such that her fingers could only catch on the rough surface, then leaned forward to look into the dark interior.

Then something struck her violently on the shoulders so that, gripping the door so insecurely, she lost her balance and shot headfirst into the chamber, and the key knocked from her hand. Whirling round, frantic with shock, she had one glimpse of Albertine's white face, her mouth open like some kind of gargoyle, before the great door swung shut behind her.

Margaret was so shocked and appalled that for a moment she simply lay where she had fallen. When at last she managed to raise herself on her elbow, she could see nothing. The room was pitch black. Then panic overwhelmed her. She crawled to the door and began to batter on it with her fists, crying out

Albertine's name incoherently. Then, too terrified to realize the absurdity of it, she shouted, "Philippe! Philippe, Philippe, Philippe!" It was only when exhaustion and the pain of her bruised hands checked her that she managed to regain something of her self-control.

She began to talk to herself. She fought to push out of her mind the anguish of the little girl locked in the cupboard twenty years ago, convinced that no one would ever find her, that she would be discovered, dead of cold and starvation, a century hence. The screaming panic that had possessed her then descended on her now, but the sound of her own voice helped to keep it down. She realized that her hysteria would do nothing but exhaust her, for that thick door had been well fashioned, and her feeble cries would not carry to someone outside. And the only person there would be Albertine, who, now that she had done what she had set out to do, would have doubtless run back to the house, or have set out to join her lover.

"Don't be silly," Margaret said aloud. "Don't be silly. There is no point in making all this noise. No one will hear you. There is no point, either, in battering on the door. How do you imagine that one person could so much as scratch that thick, strong piece of stone? After all," she told herself, "there must be a spare key. Albertine would never dare depend on having just one, and someone is bound to miss you. The servants will be expecting you to cook the supper. The Colonel will begin to wonder what has happened to you. Captain Ross . . ." This was the most comforting of all, so she repeated his name several times: "Captain Ross, Captain Ross, Captain Ross. Captain Ross, when he finds you are missing, will probably guess what has happened—after all, he asked you to find out about things."

Then she was overcome with fury against Captain Ross for daring to put her in such a dreadful position, and the rage turned once more into hysteria, until she recognized her danger and fell quiet.

At last she began to think of the Frenchman. However much he hated her—and a little warmth filled her at the realization that he no longer seemed to hate her as much as he had—he would never let her die such a fearful death. And so she spoke to him in a foolish, encouraging kind of way as if addressing a small child: "Oh, come now, Philippe. I really am in the most dreadful scrape, and I am sure you would not want me to die in this horrid room. You must try to find some way of getting me out. You can make Albertine give you the spare key. She must have one, as she'll want to come and collect whatever is hidden here, or perhaps she will want to make sure I am dead." This last remark was not very happy, and Margaret, the tears of terror flooding down her cheeks, choked, muttering, "Please, Philippe, help me. I'm so afraid. Be kind, Phillippe. Please come and look for me. It is so cold and so dark."

Then she remembered. In her pocket were the candle and tinderbox. The relief of this discovery was such that momentarily her panic disappeared. With trembling fingers, she dug the candle out of her apron pocket and managed to light it. The small flame seemed like a blazing fire after the cold dark that had preceded it. Shuddering with relief, she stumbled to her feet and looked around her.

The room was larger than she had expected. She found that she was standing on the one clear patch of ground, a kind of pathway that led to the other end. Weapons were piled on every side of her: the "Brown Bess" muskets used by British soldiers, with their fixed bayonets, as well as rifles, pistols, and swords. Margaret's dazed eyes counted an enormous number of them. Although this would hardly suffice for a regiment, it would serve well enough for escaping prisoners. Almost calm now, she surveyed these things that might mean death for her—these lethal instruments for which Albertine was prepared to murder, which she had collected from God knows where and hidden here at dead of night. What strange pride and ambition had driven her to such excess, no one would ever know. The Colonel, so bored with his two daughters, a man who had so passionately wanted sons to carry on the family tradition, would surely have been amazed at the machinating soul and driving power of his little changeling, who looked as if she would be lost in a rough, masculine world. There must have been so much scheming done to find these weapons and have them carried here. Perhaps escaped prisoners helped, perhaps young men whose heads were turned by Albertine's wiles, certainly Captain Lewis Moore, too drunk to know what he was doing.

Margaret stared down at them. They must have been there a long time, for the dust lay thick upon them. The hysteria had gone, though her teeth were chattering with cold, and she could see almost dispassionately that she might well die with these instruments of death for company. There were no windows in the room, not even an arrow slit. This place could never have been built for living in, but was evidently intended as some kind of storehouse. And she considered this, so cold and calm and detached that she almost marveled at herself. It was almost as if she were resigned to die.

She called out once or twice more, but there was not the faintest sound in reply. She might as well have been buried. If this had been intended as a dungeon, the men who made it had known their business: Anyone here would have no sight or sound of the outside world.

Margaret vaguely felt that she did not care. Perhaps this was the last blessing allowed to those who were buried alive. It was as if a weight of apathetic exhaustion had descended on her. She no longer spoke aloud, but voices in her head were saying, *You have no chance, you will never escape, you are as good as dead.* Her fatigue was such that she might have been fettered by chains. She sank to the floor again, one of the muskets almost touching her skirts, and set the candle down beside her. It would not last more than a couple of hours at the most, but the sight of it comforted her, and she refused to think of the awful moment when it would gutter out.

She looked down at the little yellow flame, holding out her numbed hands to it, then gasped as the heat struck one of her palms. Then she saw that the flame leaned sideways, as if before a draft, and she realized suddenly something that should have struck her from the beginning: The air in this enclosed place was remarkably sweet; indeed, it smelled of salt and the sea.

This shook her into action as nothing else could have done. The fatigue slipped from her like her cloak, which had fallen to the floor. Courage and spirit flooded back into her, accompanied by a frenzy of purpose. She said aloud, "I am not going to die, I am not going to die," and with this, holding the candle high, began to walk swiftly down the little passageway between the muskets, towards the black, narrow end of the room.

She did not discover the small opening at first, but the candle flame helped her, and after a few minutes, moving her bruised hands over the rough stone, she found a space down by the floor through which she could crawl. Without the candle she would never have discovered it, for it was well concealed.

She began to move through on her hands and knees. In the confined space the candle went out, so that she was once again in the dark, but she dared not pause for even a moment, lest her courage fail her. Exhorting herself in a foolish fashion that would have given to anyone overhearing the impression that she was crazed in her wits, she continued crawling painfully down what seemed like an opening in a mine. The ceiling of it scraped her head, the walls cut into her hips and shoulders, but there still seemed no obstacle in front of her, and the air was growing perceptibly sharper. She tried to push out of her mind the fear that the roof would fall on her, or, worse still, that the passage would suddenly end, for then she would be sunk indeed, there being no space in which to turn. This was so unendurable an idea that she could not permit herself to think of it, and so she continued her wild talking aloud, the words coming in heavy gasps as she dragged herself along. For the most part she spoke nonsense, reciting little rhymes she had learned in her childhood and singing songs. And because in her terror and urgency she was indeed a little out of her mind, she took to addressing Bluebeard as if he were standing behind her. She could almost see him, dark and satanic, with a bright blue beard and glistening eyes, delighted by her terror and the indignity of her method of escape.

"You silly little man," she told him, gasping, with tears of pain trickling down as she banged her head for the dozenth time, "you don't need a wife, you just want someone to torture and terrorize. You're like a little boy pulling the wings off flies. I'm glad your wife's two brothers killed you. You're simply a monster, not a man. Your wives should have opened the door, thrown that horrid key away, and left you. To play such wicked games with them . . . I would have shot you myself," muttered Margaret. She was beginning to think she could take no more, for her arms were almost breaking, and her head was swimming. "I would have shot you with a Brown Bess musket!"

Then, suddenly, she could continue no longer, and she began to sob in despair, letting her head fall on her arms, her cheek against the tattered sleeve. For a second it was as if she fainted. Then she grew aware of the sharp, cold air against her brow. Raising her head a little, very carefully, so as not to knock it once again, she saw, almost disbelieving it, the opening at the side, and through it the pale, quivering expanse of the Loving Sands, with the tide beginning to roll in.

She did not move again—indeed, there was not much she could do, for the sands were alive, waiting for their victim. To step out would mean an instant and hideous death. She lay there, too exhausted to make any further effort, and despite the cold, the pain of her battered body, and the sick awareness of the death she had so barely avoided, she fell into a half-swooning sleep.

And it was like this that the Frenchman, stumbling along the wall, at last found her. Indeed, he might not have found her at all but for one bruised and bleeding hand that clutched the side of the opening.

The Frenchman was, of course, unaware for a long time of her predicament. He sat on his rock, looking across at the prison. He saw that the guard was changing. He supposed that the escape route was some tunnel made by the prisoners. It was extraordinary that so astute a man as Captain Ross had not managed to discover it, but he did not dwell on this, nor on the cache of arms. If the prisoners managed to escape, and the goddamns were so stupid as to let them, the best of luck to them. He was, after all, a prisoner himself, only he was fettered by his parole. These men, despite their evil conditions, were far freer than himself, and he hoped that every one of them was now safely back on his native shore. Behind him lay the Hall gardens, gray and cold in the declining light, with the Bluebeard Room rising above the rest of the ruins. And the thought came to him that this could be an excellent hiding place, for arms or for anything else, provided there was some means of entry. Perhaps the moss concealed a keyhole, or perhaps one had to say *Open Sesame* and the door would silently swing back.

Let Captain Ross work it out for himself.

His mind drifted to Margaret, and there was a deep, inexplicable fear within him as he gazed out across the sands, remote and ghostly now, still safe for a little time, until the tide turned.

He knew instinctively that something was very wrong, and he continued to stare at the sands as if somehow they held the answer. A brief terror that they might indeed hold the answer struck him, and he stiffened in panic. But she knew their danger well enough, surely, surely. The cold was intense but he did not notice it—perhaps that strange, pale drink still warmed him—and he tried desperately to focus his mind. If that smooth, still surface would only speak to him. As always, the sands looked harmless yet forbidding, somehow a reminder of a long-past primeval world. The sea, now lifted and swirled by the rising wind, was in the far distance; if he had not known how swiftly it could rush in, he would have believed himself secure for many hours. He wondered in a sick, fearful way what happened beneath that implacable surface that could suck a man under in an instant and vomit him up, even months later, a battered, fleshless thing with all the life torn from him. In the two months of his stay here, he had already heard of one body that had turned up near the prison. It was a stranger who had paid no heed to the warnings and who one night, a little drunk, had decided to take a shortcut across the sands. It had proved a shortcut to eternity. His body had been found ten days later; the time of discovery was always unpredictable.

Margaret. Captain Ross said she loved him. He knew now this was true, and knew that deep within him he loved her as he had always done. It had seemed to him the cruellest of coincidences that they should meet again in such a fashion, and the shock of it had made him savage her in a way that now appalled him. Surely he would find her again, he must find her, if only to be able to apologize, to say, *The past is done, let us forget it, let us forgive and love each other.*

Then a sudden terror hit him. It was all so terribly
wrong, and he did not know why. He did not know
what to do. Perhaps he should go down to the village.
She had always been friendly with Mrs. Clay. But
something told him that she was still here, and in
some dreadful danger. He was about to leap to his
feet, to go God knows where—anything was better
than this inaction—when a familiar high, breathy
voice spoke to him.

"Daydreaming, Frenchy?" said Albertine. "Daydreaming of your little Margaret?"

He looked at her steadily. It was as if he were seeing
her properly for the first time. He was not a fanciful
man, but she seemed to him in some strange way
a kind of human manifestation of the Loving Sands.
Like the sands, she appeared harmless at first sight,
vulnerable, pathetic, the beauty's lame little sister, the
eternal shadow of Flora's brilliance. But he knew now
she was predatory and dangerous: She could engulf
a man, strip him and throw him aside, without caring
what happened to him. Even her admiration for
Bonaparte was bogus, for by nature she could not
really love or admire anyone. It was simply that he,
like herself, was ruthless, ambitious, and—what she
always had longed to be—successful. It was the last
that would count with Albertine, and so she would
make him her hero, this stout little Corsican who was
a genius in war, yet who would almost certainly end
his own victim, at the hands of the English people
or his own. Such people were doomed by their own
egoism, as Albertine was doomed.

She was smiling at him. He knew now that the
answer to everything that was wrong lay within her.
Like Margaret, he saw how she had changed. There

was no more pretense of being the poor, innocent little miss. Albertine had not been innocent since her birth, and now her face, with its beautiful eyes, was sharp with hate and malice and wickedness. This was a face such as he had seen many times in the bad old days when the mob lurked for him outside.

He did not answer her, and then she said, "You'd best forget about Margaret, Frenchy."

He said as calmly as he could—he knew he must on no account lose his temper—"What do you mean, mademoiselle?"

"She's gone, dear Frenchy. Left. Deserted you." Unexpectedly, she made a gutter face at him, drawing her mouth down at the corners, shooting out her chin. "Perhaps for another, as the story books say. Women who take lovers are seldom faithful for long."

"That is something," he said, "you undoubtedly know about. But I do not believe you."

"Are you presuming to call me a liar?" Her voice shrilled out at him. Then, taking him entirely by surprise, she shot out her hand and gave him a great push, with such force that he was nearly sent back against the wall. But he continued to regard her impassively, and made no attempt to defend himself or retaliate.

"A fine lot we have taken into our home," said Albertine. She spoke more quietly now, and drew back from him, drawing her skirts tightly about her knees as the wind threatened to blow them up. He saw that she was dressed for a journey, with a thick shawl about her shoulders, which she was now pulling up to shroud her windblown hair. In one hand she clutched a heavy reticule, and then he noticed that even in this plain and serviceable attire she was wearing as much jewelry as a dozen young misses at a ball: at least four

necklaces, earrings, brooches, and every finger on her
little hands wore some dazzling ring. The Colonel had
stocked his children well with clothes and jewels.
Only the love and care were lacking.

He said, ignoring this last remark, "Where are you
going?"

But she paid no more attention to this than he had
to her. She said, her voice sharp with derision and
spite, "A poor, landless aristocrat without spirit or
wit and a whore. A whore!"

She must have expected him to rush to Margaret's
defense, but he did not do so. It was partly that the
accusation was too vulgar and stupid to need an answer, but it was also because he was frantic to find
out what she had been doing. Her next words confirmed all his suspicions.

She waited for his reply; then, when there was
none, the angry color rushed to her cheeks. She cried
out in a little shriek, "Shall I tell you about Margaret,
Frenchy?"

"I should like you to do so," he said very quietly,
as if it scarcely mattered. He longed to seize hold of
her and shake the truth out of her; it was plain that
she had been up to mischief, there was no doubt at
all that she was somehow responsible for Margaret's
sudden departure. But he managed to remain calm,
for fear that she would run away from him, and he
did not even keep his eyes on her, but turned a little
aside, as if the conversation bored him. He saw that
the sea was on the turn. The excitement pricked within him. He could not remember exactly how long it
would take for the sands to become dangerous, but he
knew that the time was short. Perhaps he could turn
this to his advantage.

Albertine should have been more aware of the

danger than himself, but as he knew, she could not bear being thwarted or ignored, and her vanity overrode her caution. Instead of moving nearer to safety, she even stepped back a little, nearer the sea. Her face was twisted with temper. He knew then that she was fundamentally stupid—even in her wickedness, she had to be showing off, determined that the world would cry, *How clever, how wonderful, how remarkable!*

The little soft voice was now almost a squeal of rage. "Oh, I know all about your Margaret," she cried. "I cannot imagine why you ever troubled yourself about her. She told me all about you. We had a little discussion."

Then he knew for certain that she was lying. Margaret would never discuss him with anyone, much less this little demon who grudged the whole world any happiness.

"She told me you were pursuing her," said Albertine in an affected, drawling little voice. The moonlight illuminated her countenance, making of it pits and shadows. "I must say, I found that hard to believe, Frenchy. I have always believed that she was pursuing you. She is the kind of woman who must hunt her man, but then, she is so old and so very plain, don't you agree? No man in his senses would look at her twice. Then she went on to say that she couldn't endure it any longer—that kind of boring thing—you were so unkind to her, et cetera, et cetera, she had to go. I did not try to stop her. I saw her go. She packed her things and left. It was most inconsiderate, of course, but what can you expect from a person like that? I dare say she has some of our silver in her pockets, but, do you know, I was so thankful to see the last of her, as I dare say you are too, you poor fellow, that I just let her go without another word. So she is gone, Frenchy. You'll never see her again. Never!" Then, to his horror, she began to laugh, and went on laughing wildly and hysterically, her mirth shrieking out across the sands as she rocked herself to and fro. "Never, Frenchy, poor Frenchy. It's good-bye to Margaret, the nosy little bitch, and soon it will be good-bye to ... But I can't tell you that, and you would not understand if I did. You're so stupid! How I despise you, how I despise everyone."

And the Frenchman now believed that Margaret must be dead, murdered by this evil little slut, to whom she had done no harm.

A bitter, savage anger that he had not experienced for ten long years rose in him. He cast one brief glance over Albertine's shaking shoulders. The sea was advancing, white-crested in the wind. He suddenly leaped forward and caught hold of her wrist. It took her completely by surprise. She stopped laughing. For a second she stared at him, her mouth a little open, the crooked tooth fully displayed, as in a snarling animal. Then, her eyes slewing sideways, she at last perceived her danger. He saw in the bright moonlight how the color shot from her cheeks. In an instant she was as white as the foam on the waves. He was fiercely delighted. He smiled at her, a wide, terrible smile, and tightened his grip. Then she began struggling to release herself. She was far stronger then he had expected, and she fought like a wild animal, slashing at his legs with her heels, trampling on his feet, trying to bite his hands, and then clawing at his face so that her rings ripped open again the scratches she had made before. But in his anger and despair he could have coped with a dozen of her—his grip did not so much as falter, and he spoke not a word, but, still smiling, he only looked at her with hate and without pity.

She whispered, in a kind of whistling scream, "Let me go, let me go!" And as, unmoved, he continued to hold her, moving his other hand to grasp her other wrist as well, she let fly a stream of obscenities such as he would never have believed her to know—words from the barracks room or the London gutters. And his hands tightened brutally, since, for the first time, he was beginning to feel the ground beneath his feet shift. He had never yet experienced the power of the Loving Sands: It was a strange and horrifying sensation. It was as yet barely a movement, more the faintest quivering of something soft yet living, like some obscene monster jellyfish. It made him a little dizzy, and then he was wildly afraid, for it was utterly inhuman, something from another and more evil world. But his purpose was like steel within him, and, holding her in a fashion that must have almost broken her arms, he said slowly and softly, "What have you done to Margaret?"

"Let me go, you bloody bastard!"

"Not till you tell me. You can't let well-enough a-lone, can you, Albertine? You have to display your triumph. Well, your moment of triumph is done. Now tell me, please. What have you done to Margaret?"

Her strength seemed to be going. The wrists in his grasp were limp. She whispered in a frantic voice, "We'll both be killed. You'll die as well. Let me go and I'll tell you."

"If you don't tell me now," said the Frenchman, "we'll both die, for I'll not let you go until you do."

She staggered as if she would faint, and he was foolish enough to relax his hold. She snatched one arm away and dived into her pocket. But then he saw the danger, and as her hand shot out with a pistol in it, he smashed his hand down on hers so that the weapon was hurled away. It fell several yards back. Then he saw it whirl around and disappear, sucked into the sands.

It nearly broke him, for, indeed, he did not want to die, and not in so hideous a fashion, but it broke Albertine too. She began to cry in fury and terror. She sobbed, "She's in the Bluebeard Room. She's locked in with the key. I took her things away so that it would look as if she'd left. She'll never get out. She'll die, thank God, she'll die!"

"Where is the key?" he asked, in a cold, steady voice.

"I don't know. I ran off as soon as I shut the door on her. And I threw the spare one away. I did, Frenchy, I did. I threw it away. I don't know where it is."

He knew with terror that she was speaking the truth. Why should she not? She was going away herself, as all those jewels she was wearing clearly indicated. The secret was now a secret no longer, and this was the kind of vile thing that would appeal to her: to leave someone immured there forever, to rot in the dark and cold. He almost released her so that he could somehow fight his way past that enclosing door behind which Margaret might die, but then a sudden idea struck him. He said, "You evil, detestable little bitch. There's no good in you. You would murder an innocent girl for nothing but wickedness and spite. But I do not believe there is no way out." He saw the flicker on her contorted face. "There is, isn't there?

Tell me at once. Tell me, or we'll both die, I'll be glad to take you with me."

She was genuinely near fainting now. The sands were shivering beneath them, with, from time to time, a faint but perceptible tug. In a few minutes it would be all over. She muttered in a thin whine, "There is an underground tunnel. It comes out . . . oh, let me go, please let me go! I don't want to die, you must let me go!"

Then she began to scream at the top of her voice, shrieking for help, but there was no one to hear, and no one could have come even if all the prison garrison had heard her cries. He released one wrist momentarily to slap her across the face, then caught at her again, shouting, "Where does it come out?"

But he thought it was too late. Then he looked down and saw something so extraordinary that he could hardly believe his eyes. A yard away from him in this quivering and devouring morass lay a small, battered object, hardly recognizable which lay on a patch of sand that neither moved nor rippled. He recognized it only because his senses were sharp with fear. It was so absurd, it filled him with a sudden hysterical urge to laugh.

It was Margaret's poor, battered bonnet. Never could a little village bonnet have undergone such a journey; never could there have been a more extraordinary savior. Sucked down beneath the Loving Sands, carried God knows where, with the felt and ribbon long since in the monster's belly, it had been vomited up many weeks later. Its sole purpose there seemed to be to rescue its owner's former lover.

He leaped onto it. The small area was blessedly hard and still beneath his feet. He lugged Albertine with him, holding her tight against his chest, as if they were lovers, though the very touch of her sickened him. Around them the sands heaved now, making a strange, humming sound, as if they were alive. He could feel Albertine's heart hammering away, and so, indeed, was his, for this oasis was barely a yard square, and there would be no more chance of surviving the monster outside that shivered and rippled and hummed. He said to her, "If you don't tell me where that opening is, I'll throw you back onto the sands, and God forgive me, I mean it. I think you must know I mean it."

She knew. She flung her head back from him. He saw the mad terror in her face. She did not struggle any more. She did not dare, for the safe surface was so small. One false step and they would both be dead. She could hardly force herself to speak. Her head lolled on its neck, the whites of her eyes showing. He was terrified that she would faint before she could speak, and, holding her with one hand, he raised the other and struck her again and again, hardly knowing what he was doing, so afraid for Margaret, so afraid he would die before he could rescue her.

Her words were so faint that he could hardly hear them. She looked dreadful, like a dying old woman, the bones sharp and clear, the mouth twisted to one side. She whispered, "It's near—here. In the wall. Where—where the wall comes near the prison. Where the—the sands end."

Then she fainted in good earnest, and he was left there, hoping to God he could keep his balance, with this half-dead, bejeweled little ghoul clutched to his bosom—a dead weight against him.

Captain Ross's voice came to him from above his

head. It seemed to him as distant as if from another world.

"Catch hold of this rope," it said, and so dazed was the Frenchman that he hardly understood. His whole thought was possessed by fear of the dreadful death that surrounded him.

The voice called again, "Catch hold of this rope, for God's sake!" And the rope fell over his shoulder, with a noose in it, as if for his hanging.

Then, his fingers numb with cold and fear and strain, he managed to knot it around Albertine's waist, and saw her swing away from him, so limp that she was like a doll with the sawdust running out. The ascent must have knocked her cruelly against the wall, but he no longer cared. He would not have cared if she had been sucked into the sands, and when the rope came down again, for him, he had to knot it around himself, for he had scarcely the strength to catch on to the stone wall.

Only, as he swung up, managing now to help himself with the jutting stones and the creepers, his foot for one fleeting second touched the sands. It was the most horrifying sensation he had ever experienced in his life. It was as if some cold, implacable hand caught at his ankle, pulling him down with unimaginable strength. If the rope had not been strong, and not had three of Captain Ross's soldiers at the other end, he would have gone down like a stone, without the faintest chance of survival.

He swung himself over the wall, then fell onto the grass, the grass he himself had cut not so long ago. He was so weak with exhaustion that for a while he could not even raise his head. He tasted the brandy that was held to his lips, gulped some of it down, then at last looked up at Captain Ross, who stood over him. The soldiers had picked Albertine up and were carrying her into the house. Her head hung down. Her mouth was still twisted to one side. Even though she was deeply unconscious, one hand trembled, as if with the ague. He looked at her without pity. He had never felt such hate for another human being.

Then he said savagely to Captain Ross, "You waited, did you not? You overheard us. You would have let us die if she had not spoken."

Captain Ross only answered, "I had to know where Miss Margaret was." Then he said, "Are you strong enough now, Marquis, to come with me to find her?"

The Frenchman picked himself up. He felt as if he had been beaten all over, but he was damned if this intolerable Scotsman was going to rescue Margaret all on his own. Together they made their way in silence to the end of the garden, and climbed over the wall. The Loving Sands ended here. It was like a demarcation line. A few yards away, with the tide now nearly up, the surface turned and whirled and twisted; then, suddenly, here all was calm. There were even some sea thistles growing, and a little distance away was the wall of the Cross Prison.

"That was how they escaped," said Captain Ross, almost reproachfully. "And I believing there was a tunnel beneath the prison. So simple. They only had to walk across, and then the little miss would let them out at night, no doubt armed to the teeth, and then they could make their way to the road. So simple. But then, I always was a complicated man."

At that moment the Frenchman cared nothing about Captain Ross or escaping prisoners. He walked very stiffly by the wall, for every limb was aching. Then he saw the small, stained, bruised hand protruding from the wall like a starfish.

Between them they managed to pull her out, as gently as they could in the circumstances. She was in a sad state, her clothes half torn off her back, her hands bleeding, her face cut and bruised and black with dirt. But then she pushed their hands aside. She stood there swaying, staring at them as if she could not believe her eyes.

She said at last, in an unrecognizable, hoarse voice, "I thought I would never get out. I thought I was going to die."

Then the Frenchman, forgetting about Captain Ross, forgetting about everything, caught her in his arms, and, muttering, in his own tongue, "For God's sake, oh, for God's sake," he cradled her against him, kissing the battered face, stroking the poor, bruised hands, holding her so tightly against him that she could scarcely breathe.

She whispered, "I knew you would find me."

Chapter Eleven

Captain Ross stood there for a moment, his eyes on the Frenchman and Margaret. His long mouth was turned down at the corners. He had to see that this was no moment for a dissertation; neither of them would be interested in escapes or a cache of arms. It was obvious that Margaret was now in excellent hands, so he turned on his heel and walked away. There was disapproval in every line of him, and perhaps regret, too, though this was something he would never have admitted. But then, as he told himself fiercely, he was

nearly fifty, and there were many important things to
see to, including Captain Lewis Moore, who, as his
men had informed him, was dead drunk in the barracks.

He did not even consider Flora, for the Colonel's
daughters had never been of the least interest to him
until Albertine forced herself upon his notice. He did
not even think of the Colonel, who had returned from
his duties, without the faintest idea of what had been
going on—to him it was an ordinary day.

The Colonel dismounted and came up the steps
to the Hall. There was nothing to suggest that anything unusual had been going on. He was glad to be
back. He did not expect to be greeted by his daughters,
for they were, doubtless, about their own business.
They might even be in bed, for the hour was late
and there was little social entertainment in the district. He was certain that Margaret would have a good
dinner waiting for him. She was a good girl who
performed her work excellently and kept out of
his way.

And so, thinking mainly of the wine he was about
to pour out, and thankful that the tedious visits to
his tenants were over, he came into the library, half
hoping that Ross would be there. But there was no
sign of him. Flora was waiting for him, and he was
not at all pleased to see her, so he gazed at her with
a disapproval that immediately changed to astonishment.

He so little considered his daughters that he never
really looked at them. He was dimly aware, however,
that Flora was a beauty who dressed well—and so she
should, with all the money he spent on her—and he
was occasionally amused by the way his young

subalterns blushed and stammered when they spoke to her.

Flora was now in extraordinary disarray. He actually remembered the dress she was wearing, for she had bought it in London a month back, and it had cost so much that even he had raised his eyebrows when presented with the bill. It was a soft blue woollen thing very becoming to the golden hair and blue eyes. It was now in a disgraceful state, as if she had slept in it—it was crumpled, torn, and dirty. But it was her face that shocked him. Usually so soft, dimpled, and appealing, it was now pale and distraught, angry and old. There was no coquettish prettiness left, only a strange, sullen look that almost frightened him.

He exclaimed, "What are you doing here, miss? And why aren't you properly dressed? You look disgraceful. I should be ashamed if anyone came in and saw you like this. Why, your hair is half down your back."

She did not answer. Normally, if he scolded Flora she at once dissolved into tears like a child, then ran to him, to kiss and hug him and beg for his forgiveness. Now she did not seem to care, though she automatically put her hands to her hair, took hold of a bunch of it as if to coil it up, then let it fall again.

He said sternly, "Go to your room, please. I sometimes think I am far too lenient with the pair of you, but I will not endure this sluttishness. Go to your room, do you hear me? I'll see that Margaret is sent to you. If you are incapable of dressing yourself properly, you'll have to get yourself a maid. You look like a drab. I'm ashamed of you. What would you do if Lewis came in?"

"Lewis will not come in," said Flora. Even her voice had changed: It was hoarse and harsh.

"Well, it's bad enough my having to look at you," snapped the Colonel. He was growing furious. It really was too much that a man returning after a hard day's work should have to put up with all this nonsense. "If you were younger," he told her, "I'd have you whipped. You're behaving like a naughty child. Do as you're told, and go to your room. I do not wish to have to speak to you again."

"I've come to say good-bye, papa," said Flora. She was moving back towards the door, like an actress in a sleepwalking scene.

He roared at her, "What confounded nonsense is this?"

She continued her silent retreat to the door. There she stood, pale but apparently collected, looking up at him. There was something in the blue eyes that was almost an appeal, and the Colonel, who had never really troubled himself about her, was for the first and only time in his life moved. He took a step toward her.

But the next moment she was gone. The door shut quietly behind her.

He was so disturbed that he did not even pour himself wine. He went over to his desk and sat down heavily, like an old man. He felt vaguely that this was all quite unfair. His daughter had no right to worry him like this. No one could ask for a better father. Why, he never grudged the girls one penny for their fal-lals, nor did he check on their behavior, as most fathers would have done.

He reached out, almost automatically, for his box of dueling pistols, as if they would comfort him. They had always been a source of great pride to him. Then he saw that the box was empty.

This was the last straw. He was now really outraged. He would ask Margaret about it. Margaret was a sensible girl. Margaret always knew where things were.

He rang the bell-pull.

There was no answer for a long time, and now the Colonel was in a roaring temper, although he had a dim awareness that something was very wrong. He rang again and again, almost pulling the cord off, until at last the door opened.

It was not Margaret. It was a girl from the kitchen whom he did not know, who was very young, and so frightened that she stammered when she at last managed to answer.

The Colonel, unused to considering anyone, shouted at her, "Where is Margaret? It's Margaret I want."

She was almost fainting with fright. She whispered, "Margaret can't come, sir."

"Why the devil not?"

"She's not well, sir. And please, sir, please—the Captain says, will you come to see Miss Albertine, please, sir, as soon as you can, sir."

The world was gone mad. He asked, more quietly, "What is the matter with Miss Albertine? Is she ill too?" And the words seemed absurd, for Bertie, despite her frail appearance, had never had a day's illness in her life.

The girl stammered, "I don't know, sir." She was in tears. "But the Captain says you must come, sir."

He said curtly, "Very well." And he added, "You can go now. I dare say you have plenty of work to do.

And tell Miss Margaret that when she's feeling better, I want to see her. Do you understand?"

"Yes, sir." And she fled. He could hear her running
down the corridor.

The Colonel at last poured out his glass of wine,
and drained it at a gulp. Then he set off for Albertine's room.

Lewis looked up in glazed surprise as Flora came
into his room at the barracks. He was too fuddled
with drink to see her clearly. He could only wonder
vaguely why she, who had never set foot here before,
should appear instead of Bertie, whom he was expecting, but he did see that she looked quite strange.

He had been off duty that afternoon, and he had
started drinking immediately. His black eye pained
him, and he was very stiff. He had already had two
quarrels with his fellow officers, who were laughing at
him and inquiring which husband had beaten him
up. He retreated to his room and the bottle. Once, a
long time ago, he had been more temperate, but since
he had known Bertie he had taken to drinking more
and more, and now was seldom sober. He would sneak
into her room at night, and she would always have a
bottle for him. "Wine is very good for you," she
would say, making big eyes at him, and he would
drink more and more, to end up in her arms, so confused that sometimes he hardly knew which sister he
was making love to.

And now, filled with the awfulness of what he was
about to do, he was very drunk indeed. The words
traitor and *deserter* rang dimly in his mind, though
he did not fully take them in. Sometimes he believed
he hated Bertie, and occasionally, even now, he would

look at Flora with a kind of desperate longing, as if
to bring back the days when he was a young captain
about to make a good marriage and lead a normal,
happy life. And then Bertie would come to lead him
to her bed, so that Flora, with her pretty foolishness
and golden hair, somehow vanished from his mind.

"I'll bring all my jewelry with me," Bertie had said,
"so we'll have plenty of money. And I've arranged
that silly Thomas will believe there is to be an invasion, and he'll run to tell his horrid mama, then all
the village and the garrison will know. No one will
have time to bother about the prison. The Frenchy
will of course be shot, and so will the guards on duty."

He protested at this. He was not so drunk then, and
these men were his friends.

But she overrode him fiercely, as she always did,
her little face contorted with rage. One must never
cross Bertie; Bertie could not endure it.

She shouted at him, "What a fool you are! Why
should you worry about them? They'd shoot you soon
enough if they knew what you are doing, and if you
don't listen to me, I'll see they do know." Then her
face and voice changed; her arms slid round his neck.
"Oh, Lewis, I love you so much. I love you, I love
you! Don't be angry with me. I'm doing this for you.
No more looking after prisoners and saying yes, sir,
no, sir, to that beastly Captain Ross. I must go now,
my darling, there is one thing left to do. But I'll call
for you when it's dark."

Lewis, when he had recovered slightly from his
drunkenness, and was feeling very proud of himself
(as the inebriated often do), set to doing something he
had never done in his life. He was still very drunk
and not fully aware of what he was doing, but he

felt he had to make plain to the Captain and his fellow officers what a clever fellow he was, and not
entirely under Bertie's thumb. He was not a highly
literate man, but he began to scrawl down in his
unformed, childish handwriting something of what
had happened, and how he himself was responsible.
It came out incoherently as it fell from his mind.
The murder of Mrs. Beeston, who had suspected his
liaison with Albertine, the attempted murder of Margaret. The escaping prisoners, each with his little box
with an initialed piece of paper inside so that there
could be no spies or traitors getting through, and how
he had had to kill that fellow Christian, who had not
carried the proper password. It was scarcely readable,
but he felt the better for putting it all down, and it
was just as he was describing the cache of arms that
Flora appeared.

He set his papers down, carefully placing a weight
upon them so that they should not blow away. He
said haughtily, "You cannot see this. It's private."

And then he backed a little away from her. He
could not imagine why she was there. The drink
fogged his mind. He could not even see her very
clearly, but it seemed to him that she looked like a
ghost, her hair falling over her pale face, her eyes
glittering so strangely. Something about her frightened him, and when she came nearer he put out his
hand as if to ward her off.

She said, in a soft, slow voice, "I'd like you to come
with me, Lewis."

And he was compelled to move toward her, taking
the hand she extended to him.

They came out together, hand in hand. He did not
fully know what he was doing. The other men looked

at him curiously, and were to remember afterward his strange, bemused expression. After all, though, he was off duty, and he was engaged to marry the Colonel's daughter. There was no reason why they should not walk out together, and though it was high tide and the sands were at their worst, they must both of them realize the danger.

Flora did not speak, only walked steadily on.

Lewis said, in a thick, blurred voice, "Where are we going, my darling?"

She turned her head. Her face was wild, and a pang of fear pierced him. She answered, "You cannot stay here any longer, Lewis. They'll hang you. I could not abide that. You must come with me. You'll be safe with me."

He struggled to pull his drunken wits together. He stammered, "But Bertie . . . Oh, Flora, I do not mean to hurt you, but you must see how it is." Then he thought he understood what was happening. It was quite lunatic, but then, this was his pretty Flora, his little sweet goose, who did not have a sensible thought in her head, poor little Flora, whom he had betrayed but who plainly still loved him. "You're taking me to Bertie," he said.

And even in his drunkenness this seemed absurd, but she answered calmly, "Yes, Lewis. I am taking you to Bertie."

They came to the prison entrance. The guards, averting their eyes from Lewis's battered face, saluted. He did not return the salute. Flora led him around the side, silent now, her eyes staring ahead, until they stood on the threshold of the Loving Sands.

The tide was fully in. The sands, a hundred yards from them, shivered and hummed, alive now, and hungry for their victim. It was as if a wind blew across them, making hills and craters, and the moon shone down on the white surface. There was no one there but themselves, and the fear and menace and desolation of it brought Lewis back to his senses.

He swung around on Flora, who stood there, silent and still, and the sight of her strange, expressionless face, now stripped of all emotion, shocked him into violent speech.

He cried out, "You said you were taking me to Bertie!"

She held his hand so tightly that he could not release it. She said, in the soft, sweet voice that he had once loved, "Come with me, Lewis."

And now she tugged at him, making for the Loving Sands.

He stammered, "But we can't possibly go there. We'll both be killed. Flora, you must be mad. What are you trying to make me do?"

She turned her head and then briefly pressed her lips against his. He saw that her eyes were wide and staring. It was almost like a farewell. He looked around frantically for help, but there was no one in sight. The guards on sentry duty were sheltering in the doorway around the front of the prison, and no one else would be out at this dangerous time when the tide was in. And he knew now that Flora was indeed mad. The only expression on her face was that of a childlike sweetness, as if she had sunk back into her babyhood. There was no wit in those over-bright blue eyes, and her voice was gentle, a little petulant, as if she were admonishing him for some bad behavior.

"Oh, Lewis," she said, almost pettishly, "why don't

you come with me? What is the matter with you? You must come. I'm sorry, but I insist." And then, with her free hand she produced a pistol, which had been concealed in the folds of her dress. He recognized it. It was one of a brace that normally lay in the Colonel's study. Flora began giggling in a fashion that chilled his blood. "I am a good shot," she said. "You'd never believe a girl could shoot straight, would you? But I can, you know. Now, be good, Lewis. Come with me, otherwise I shall have to shoot you, and you wouldn't like that, would you?"

He was now, too late, completely sober. He struggled frantically to free himself. He was a young man, tall and strong, and she was only a girl, but her grip was one of iron. He would never have believed her to be so powerful. He was wild with terror, striking at her, wrenching at her hand, struggling to get back to the prison—never mind if it meant the hangman's rope—anything to get away from her. And the hold of that soft, white hand never faltered. Always, relentlessly, she pulled him on, until he suddenly felt the ground shivering beneath his feet and knew that he was on the brink of the Loving Sands.

He screamed for help. The wind caught his scream, so that only a faint echo of it penetrated the prison gates, but the guards heard it and stopped talking, their faces suddenly pale. They recognized Captain Moore's voice and knew that he must have been caught by the sands. There was nothing they could do—nothing anyone could do—but they ran out. As they did so, they heard the shot. and they paused, staring at each other.

When at last they saw the sands, there was the faintest glimpse of yellow hair, then nothing more—only the shivering surface, the sea, the wind, and the full, white moon.

The Frenchman helped Margaret back to the kitchens, where he sat her down by the fire and brought her some wine. But she refused this and only sat huddled there, too exhausted even to answer the excited questions of the servants who had gathered around her. Presently one of them, responding to a sideways gesture of the Frenchman's head, took her by the hand and led her away, to put her, not in her own little box of a room, but in one of the Hall's spare bedrooms, where she lay down in a vast and luxurious four-poster bed and immediately fell asleep.

When she woke up (it seemed a century later), she blinked dazedly for a while in the morning light, wondering where she was, then saw that the Frenchman was sitting by the window.

He did not for the moment realize that she was awake. He was looking out the window. He was sitting on one of the two chairs in this vast room, which must once have been used for guests but which had been untenanted for a long time. She suspected that he must have been here all night, for there was a burnt-out candle on the windowsill. His face was drawn and pale, with ugly red scratches on his cheeks. The black hair was disheveled, and his clothing torn and stained with sand. One hand was bandaged. He was a world away from the handsome young man who had once spoken sweet words to her, but it was Philippe, and her heart was filled with such love for him that she thought it would break.

She said, in a voice husky with sleep, "What are you doing here?"

He answered without turning his head. "I thought you would like to find someone here when you woke up."

She sat up in bed, pushing her disheveled hair out of her eyes. She winced as she did so. Her shoulders felt as if they were on fire, and her knees were horribly bruised. She spoke the words that had somehow been going through her mind, even in her deep, exhausted sleep. "Why did she want to kill me?"

The Frenchman answered, "She is a poor thing. She is not sane. I think she envies everyone and everything, and she is completely destructive. She has destroyed her sister, she has destroyed her lover, and she wanted to destroy both of us. Don't ask me why, Margaret. I do not understand such things. But I believe Colonel Walters in no way knows the daughters he has bred. He imagines himself to be a good father. But it is not enough to give children money and clothes. Our children will have more than that."

She repeated in a whisper, "Our children?"

"Yes. Our children." And then he came over to her and sat beside her on the bed. "Why not? I have never believed in fate, I do not think for a long time I have believed in God, but I cannot regard it as chance that we met by that sea wall. I want to marry you, Margaret. I wanted to marry you then, and I want to marry you now. Must I compromise you to compel you to agree with me?"

She answered quietly, "I have no right to protest about being compromised. But I cannot marry you, for all I would give the world to be able to do so. You must know that. You must."

He did not, as she had expected, bring forward any argument to persuade her. He simply sat there, looking at her, and she could not read his countenance. Then he said, "At least I must talk to you. Are you well enough to listen? May I bring you some chocolate or coffee?"

"No. I am quite recovered," said Margaret, though this was not entirely so: There was a great weakness in her limbs, and she felt oddly unmoored, as if she were floating in space. But she could not endure to lose one moment of his company, and so she lay back on the pillows, watching him, her face pale and intent.

He said, "I have been both cruel and stupid. I want to apologize again. No, you must let me speak. I have always been proud and stiff-necked. Let me indulge myself and you. I doubt it will ever happen again. If we did marry, Margaret, I should probably be an autocratic husband who would insist on you doing all the apologizing while I stamped up and down our home, dictating, domineering, and possibly beating you."

She said calmly, "You are making fun of me."

"A little, perhaps. But this is serious. I do apologize. I was young and stupid then, I have been old and stupid now. You see, I now realize that I have never stopped loving you. That intolerable Captain Ross, whom I dislike so cordially—partly, I think, because I am jealous of him—was perfectly right."

"Captain Ross?" she repeated, then turned her face into the pillow so that he would not see she was crying.

"Yes, he knew. He told me I loved you. He also said you loved me. I don't know about that. But I should have known about myself, if I had had any sense at all. I was so cruel to you . . . One is only

cruel in such a fashion to people one loves. If I had
really not given a damn, I should have been cool and
polite and ignored you. But you cannot blow love out
like a candle. And if it had not been for you, I
would never have stayed here. Cutting the grass . . ."
Then he sighed, laughed, and broke off.

She said weakly, "Cutting the grass?"

"That's Captain Ross again. Never mind. What
matters is that there has never been any other woman,
my dear, except the casual ones who do not matter
—you may not approve, but then, no man can
remain entirely celibate for ten long years. They never
counted. That may not be much to my credit, but it
is true. You did count, even when I believed I hated
you. I think in my heart I always knew I would see
you again."

She said at last, "It wouldn't do, Philippe. It is not
that I don't love you. I do. I always have done. I
always will. But it is too late."

"You talk such nonsense. I am beginning to believe
all this has turned your wits. Why is it too late?"

She sat up in bed. When he took her hand, she let
it lie in his grasp, but did not return the hold. She
said, "I have thought it over so carefully. I am too old
—perhaps not in years, but in living. In some ways
we are strangers to each other. I am not the silly girl
you once knew. I would not make the right kind of
wife for you. There is too much between us. Can we
really, either of us, forget what happened?"

"It would be foolish of us to try to do so. But it is
no longer important."

"I think it might become so."

"I see," he said, "that cruelty is not my sole
prerogative."

She did not answer this, but only said, "We would be going back in time." Then, "Oh, Philippe, I am so tired, I cannot think properly. Perhaps . . . I don't know. But one thing is certain. I must leave here. You mentioned some lady in Elchester. Perhaps you would give me her address and an introductory note. It should not be too difficult to find work. And I have a little money saved. I suppose I should stay here for a few days, if only to find the Colonel a new house-keeper, but I want to leave as soon as possible." Then she said, "It's almost Christmas. Do you know?"

He had risen to his feet. He said coldly, "I shall be leaving too. My tutoring days here are certainly done. As a parole prisoner, I have to report back to Elchester. But I promise not to pursue you."

"You are not making it very easy for me," said Margaret, almost inaudibly.

"I see no reason why I should." He was speaking now in his former disagreeable fashion. He moved toward the door. He said, "You should rest. Would you not wish me to send you a doctor?"

She shook her head. He made her a little bow and shut the door behind him.

She lay there for a while. It seemed to her that the ghosts of Henry and her dead baby lay beside her. She longed to call Philippe back, but did not do so, though the effort of restraining herself brought the tears to her eyes. What sort of life could they live in such company? One day he would return home to his chateau and his family, and she would trail after him —the foolish English girl who had humiliated him. She would be there as a constant reminder of one of the worst times in his life. And her body ached for him; she could not visualize a life without him. She

felt as if she were sinking into spinsterdom, with all
the warmth and tenderness irretrievably gone; she
felt as if she had signed her own death warrant.

She said aloud, with the shocking inconsequential-
ity of her weak and foolish sex, "He might have
tried to persuade me a little more."

Then at last she managed to get out of bed, feeling
weak and a little dizzy, and presently she came shakily
downstairs.

A little while later, the Colonel stood, white and
appalled, in his younger daughter's bedroom. She
had now recovered consciousness, and he had come
back, with Captain Ross beside him, to see what could
possibly be done in this monstrous situation.

It was Christmas Eve, although he did not think of
this. He had aged immeasurably since last night. He
said only one word: "Why?"

And, as Captain Ross did not answer, he looked
again at Albertine, lying on her bed. He saw the
mouth down at one side, the palsied hand. He
thought she did not recognize him, but then the dark
eyes moved to his. There was recognition there, and a
hatred that turned him cold. He was not an imagina-
tive man, but he had a sudden and terrible vision of
the life that lay ahead. Flora was hideously dead, and
he would be saddled forever with this changeling who
hated him. They would live in this vast house
together, isolated from everyone. The doctor had said
she would probably walk again, but she would never
lose the twisted mouth or the palsy. Whatever shock
it was that she had suffered would make her perma-
nently an invalid. The Colonel did not know exactly
what had happened, but it seemed as if she had had

some kind of stroke. He could only think that she was a traitor. She would have betrayed her country, helped the prisoners to escape with that cache of weapons from the Bluebeard Room—he would have it razed to the ground, he could not bear to look on it again—and she had, he now learned, been conducting an affair with Captain Moore, whom she had seduced both from his honor and his duty.

He said once more to Captain Ross, "Why? I simply do not understand."

And the "Why?" pertained to Albertine's behavior and Flora's death, but it mainly meant, *Why has this happened to me, what have I done to deserve it? I have always been a good father to the girls, so what ill fate has wished such disaster on me?*

And again Captain Ross did not answer, for he could not. He had already promised that nothing would be done about Albertine. There would be no invasion, no further escapes, and now she was so ill, it scarcely mattered, she could do no more harm. He had read Lewis's confession, which was now locked in his desk. He thought of the deaths and "accidents" that had followed this young woman like her shadow: the cook, the boy who was killed for not having the pass, the attacks on Margaret, and perhaps many other things that he had not yet discovered. He looked at his old friend with sadness and compassion. He could have said, *You never concerned yourself with either of those girls. You never gave them the least love. You treated them as you would treat your furniture. They were kept polished and shining, but they were never people to you, never your own flesh and blood. You wanted sons, and daughters were nothing to you. You left them alone. You cannot*

*leave people alone. And now you are alone, you
always will be.*

But there was no point, in the name of charity, in
saying one word of this. He looked once again at
Albertine, a wizened, shriveled little thing, with that
dreadful shaking hand and the face in which all
youth and beauty were destroyed. No man would ever
desire her again. He wanted to pity her, but he could
only think that she had destroyed her sister, her lover,
and her father. There was an aura of hate around
her, a terrible cold of the spirit that emanated from
her which chilled his very bones. Then he could not
bear to see her any more. He took hold of the Colonel's arm and led him back to the library, where at
least he could solace himself with wine. Doubtless,
the wine would become more and more of a solace as
the eternal days went by.

And the Captain was thankful to the very depths of
his soul for his own life and own place. He had lost
the girl he wanted, he was unlikely now to marry,
but at least he could be away from this dreadful
house and the curse that lay upon it.

In the village of Adeney Cross, Mrs. Lee was
triumphant. She had, of course, heard the news from
Thomas. It was true that there was no invasion, but
there had been enough disaster to satisfy her greedy
soul. Now the Frenchman and the housekeeper were
both leaving; life could return to normal again. To
celebrate this remarkable occasion, she actually came
into the Loving Sands Inn and demanded a tankard
of ale. This was so astonishing that Mr. Clay for once
fell silent, and all the villagers congregated there to
discuss the scandal fell silent likewise, staring furtively

at this fierce little witch-woman, who stood in the
middle of the floor as if she would take on the whole
world.

And for at least two days afterward, Mrs. Lee was
almost amiable, forgetting to beat her enormous sons
and even—no one quite believed this, but Mrs. Clay
swore it was true—smiling once briefly as she stood
in her cottage doorway to watch the passers-by.

Two days after Christmas, Margaret came to the
front door of the Hall. She had managed to find the
Colonel a new housekeeper, and had said good-bye to
him, though he had entreated her to stay. She saw
how he had aged and was sorry for him, but could not
explain that nothing in the world would make her
stay here a day longer. He made her a present of
money—it would not have entered his head to give
her anything else—which she reluctantly accepted,
and now she was once again on her travels. She took
with her an introductory note to the lady in Elchester
—a note she had discovered left by her bedside.

There was no sign of the Frenchman, which grieved
her to the point of tears, but, ironically, the servants
all seemed sad to see her go, and Thomas, of all
people, presented her with a pound of butter and a
dozen eggs. She was convinced he had stolen these
from the larder, but at least the gift showed good
feeling.

She had, from perhaps a wish to lay a ghost, looked
once more at the Bluebeard Room. The lock had been
forced, and the door stood wide open now, propped
back by a heavy stone. The weapons had all been
removed, and the passageway blocked up so that no
more unhappy prisoners could escape. And as she
stood there, her portmanteau by her side, Margaret

decided deliberately to step once more into the room. And so she did, though she could not force herself to do more than just cross the threshold.

It was only a room—nothing more. She had unlocked the door and entered. She was still alive, she would not die (whatever the romantic poets said), though nothing would ever be the same again. It was not her head she had lost, but her heart.

She came out quickly, then a few minutes later set off down the hill. Captain Ross had offered her a carriage, but she said she would prefer to walk, and he had looked at her oddly but had not persisted.

"Good-bye, Margaret," he said, then, "If you ever change your mind, I shall be here. I am not likely to change mine."

Then she stretched up and kissed him, and to her astonishment he went bright red, muttered something that sounded like the most unseemly of expletives, and almost ran back into his cottage.

She remembered this now. It filled her with no desire to laugh. He was a good man. It was a pity that one did not always love people for being good. And as she thought this, a hand came out to remove her portmanteau from her, and she found the Frenchman at her side.

In that moment she knew, and she saw that he knew also. The next second her features were in order again, but his were not: He was smiling broadly, his eyes danced, there was victory in every line of him.

He said calmly, "May I take your case? I think I had better help you. The hill looks steep, and I can see you are fatigued."

The hill looks steep, and I can see you are fatigued.

The same words, so long ago, so long ago. She said nothing, and they walked down the hill side by side until they came to the sea wall. And there, removing her second-best bonnet, she did something so foolish that she marveled at herself. She threw it over the wall, so that it fell on the Loving Sands. But it was low tide, and the bonnet lay there, not to be devoured for another hour.

She sat down on the wall, her hair blowing in the wind. She said to the Frenchman, who stood beside her, half smiling, his eyes fixed intently on hers, "That is called throwing one's cap over a windmill. Or perhaps I've got it wrong. It sounds a little strange. But it signifies coming to a decision."

"I came to that decision a long time ago," he said, sitting down beside her.

Then she put her hand over his, and he laid his other hand on that, as if they were playing some children's game. He said, "Margaret, you are afraid of ghosts. There are always ghosts." He pointed down at the sands, so innocent now in the morning light. Flora lay beneath them, with her faithless lover at her side, and many others also, swallowed up by the demon that stirred and hummed and dragged its victims down.

She said, "Yes. I am afraid. I used not to be. Now I am, terribly. It matters so much. I said I could not marry you. Now I know that is not true. If you will have me—"

"If I'll have you!"

"But there are the ghosts." And she forced herself to say their names. "Henry. The—the baby. And— forgive me, but it is a ghost too—what we did to each other. You might forgive what I did to you, but can you forgive what you did to me?"

He put his arm around her shoulders. "I think you are a brave girl," he said, "and I believe I love you more than I did at the beginning. Then you were a pretty girl who captivated me—"

"And now I am old and plain!"

"And now you are beautiful." He pulled her gently against him, moving his free hand down her cheek. "It will not be easy. Is anything easy? Captain Ross has promised us a passage on one of the cartel ships. We will get married in Elchester, and then you will come with me. We will go to Provence, which is my home. I doubt the war will be over for a long time, and some of my people may look upon you as the enemy. It is not agreeable. I know that. Will you come with me, all the same? Perhaps what you said is true. It is not possible to forget. But I do not believe that will make any difference to us, for we know each other now, and love each other enough to survive." Then he said again, "It will not always be easy. So tell me, Margaret, that you will come. We will defy Monsieur Bluebeard with his bloodied key and his headless wives. There will be no secrets between us, no hidden rooms. Everything will be as open as the day. *Et alors, mademoiselle?* Let us talk no more of death. It is time we considered life, life together, and left this place which is little better than a graveyard."

She said, "Yes, Philippe. I will come."

He kissed her once, briefly. Then he helped her up from the wall, and, her arm through his, they walked down the road to Elchester.

The Loving Sands lay white and firm and safe. There were two bodies that would reappear in course of time: a girl's and that of a young man with a bullet through his head. Now it was hard to believe in danger, and some of the village children were scrambling across to look for seashells.

But Margaret and the Frenchman were looking at

each other, and did not turn their heads. No ghosts walked after them. Bluebeard's room was open, and Bluebeard's ghost was exorcized. And Captain Ross, who had been watching them from the high prison window, saw them turn the corner and vanish from his view.